Enterprise. Number
all about t

He looked up at Liyan.

Pheromones.

"I'm sorry," he said, and took a step back from the Orion tallith. "I need to speak with my ship."

Pike flipped open the communicator again.

The light on it was flashing red. No signal. What—

"It is I who must apologize, Captain Pike. I had hoped to avoid this scenario. Tactician." The tallith spoke without turning, to an Orion Pike hadn't noticed before, who stood at her shoulder.

"Down!" someone shouted in Pike's ear. Ben's voice; the captain did as he was told and dove to the floor. A phaser beam cut through the air above him; a second later, one of the ceiling support beams crashed to the floor, raising a cloud of dust, cutting them off from the tallith and her guards and most of the others in the room as well.

"Captain!"

He turned and saw Ben holding his weapon. Ross stood next to him. A handful of bodies surrounded the two of them. One of those was Smith's. She wasn't moving. No surprise.

Half her head was missing.

"We have to move, sir," Tuval said. "Now."

... Number One. Pike had forgotten
... all them then. How ...

STAR TREK®

THE CHILDREN OF KINGS

DAVID STERN

Based upon *Star Trek*
created by Gene Roddenberry

POCKET BOOKS

New York   London   Toronto   Sydney

Pocket Books
A Division of Simon & Schuster, Inc.
1230 Avenue of the Americas
New York, NY 10020

This book is a work of fiction. Names, characters, places, and incidents either are products of the author's imagination or are used fictitiously. Any resemblance to actual events or locales or persons, living or dead, is entirely coincidental.

First Pocket Books paperback edition May 2010

POCKET and colophon are registered trademarks of Simon & Schuster, Inc.

For information about special discounts for bulk purchases, please contact Simon & Schuster Special Sales at 1-866-506-1949 or business@simonandschuster.com.

The Simon & Schuster Speakers Bureau can bring authors to your live event. For more information or to book an event, contact the Simon & Schuster Speakers Bureau at 1-866-248-3049 or visit our website at www.simonspeakers.com.

Cover art by Cliff Nielsen; cover design by Alan Dingman

Manufactured in the United States of America

10 9 8 7 6 5 4 3 2 1

ISBN 978-1-4391-5899-9
ISBN 978-1-4391-7319-0 (ebook)

To old dogs, new tricks,
and the Sons (gender-neutral) of the Bird . . . all of us.

Macbeth: Your children shall be kings.
Banquo: You shall be king.

—*Macbeth*
Act I, Scene iii

BOOK I

DEADFALL

ONE

Pike was the last one in. As he entered the briefing room, the others all stood.

"As you were," the captain said, and took a seat at the head of the table. "Thank you for coming. Number One?"

He nodded toward his second-in-command, seated to his right; she leaned forward.

"We've recovered part of the station log," she said. "A small portion—about a minute's worth—from the day of the attack. The images are heavily compressed; artifacts abound, both auditory and visual. The audio, in fact, disappears entirely less than halfway through the recording. But even so—"

"Hang on." Commander Tuval leaned forward. "Part of the station log? Where did that come from?"

A fair question, Pike thought, considering that the base itself—Starbase 18, the Federation's farthest outpost in this sector of the galaxy—was pretty much space junk at this point. A fact Tuval knew better than anyone else in the room. Two days ago, the commander—*Enterprise*'s security chief—had almost died exploring its remains. The skin on the right side of his face was still pink, and he had half-healed burns over most of the right side of his body. His lungs were functioning at sixty percent capacity; according to Dr. Boyce, they'd never reach a hundred percent again. All in all, though, Tuval was lucky.

The other three members of the landing party were dead.

"You can thank our science officer," Pike said, nodding toward Spock, who sat to the captain's right, at the far end of the table. There were seven of them in the room; Chief Engineer Pitcairn, Commander Tuval, and Communications Specialist Garrison on one side of the table, Number One, Boyce, and Spock on the other. "He can explain it to you."

Pike gestured to the Vulcan to go ahead.

"Starfleet's communications infrastructure in this sector is a patchwork affair," Spock said. "You are no doubt aware of this, Commander."

"Of course. The trouble we've had getting through to Starfleet Command . . ."

"This is because some of the subspace amplifiers in this region date back to the early years of exploration; to link these early models with current Starfleet equipment requires the use of multiple communications protocols as well as additional processing modules. It occurred to me that stored within some of those processing modules—"

"You talking about the RECs, Mr. Spock?" That from Chief Engineer Pitcairn.

"The REC-twos, Chief."

"Model twos. Not sure I remember those." Pitcairn frowned—or maybe it was a small smile. On the chief's craggy features, it was hard for Pike to tell the difference.

Three months into his five-year mission with the crew, the captain was still learning their little personality traits. And quirks. And likes and dislikes and how they got along with one another. Which members of which department worked well together and which were like oil and water. In that regard, he'd expected to have some problems with Spock. There were a lot of people who still held a grudge against the Vulcans for the way they'd treated humanity in those early, post–First Contact years. Holding back key technologies, refusing Earthers an equal voice among the quadrant's space-faring races. Most of that seemed to be in the past now, but occasionally, a bit of that xenophobia still popped up. Pike had prepared himself to have to deal with some of that among his crew; he'd suspected he might have a problem with Pitcairn in that regard. Glenn was old-line Starfleet, senior member of the crew, and the longest-serving non-flag officer in the fleet. But the chief and Spock got along like gangbusters.

Would that the rest of his crew mixed half that well.

"The model twos were identical to the original RECs," Spock continued. "Except that they were housed in significantly larger storage frames to allow for a wide range of potential expansion requirements."

Pitcairn was still frowning. "Well . . . they couldn't be completely identical, then, could they? Larger mass, they'd need a larger stabilization unit to make sure they didn't drift off position. Am I right?"

Spock considered the point. "You may be correct, Chief. I only glanced at the construction specifications briefly. I cannot recall the exact increase in mass of the REC-two relative to the original. Perhaps later we can—"

"They might've changed the composition of the beacon, too," Pitcairn said. "They did that a lot, back in those days. Experimented with different materials. I knew a guy who actually worked at Bozeman—"

"Chief. Mr. Spock." Pike leaned forward. Get those

two talking about old Fleet technology, they'd be there for hours. And they didn't have hours. "Let's stay on track."

"Exactly," said Boyce, who looked annoyed. And impatient. An improvement over his mood earlier that morning, at least. "Captain, I would appreciate it if we could hurry things along. Dr. Tambor is still in regen, you know. A critical stage of it, in fact. And I want—"

"I know," Pike interrupted. "You want to be there. We'll wrap this up as quickly as we can."

The doctor nodded, stone-faced, just as angry as he'd been before, when Pike had pulled Tuval out of regen therapy. "He's got another day to go," Boyce had said. "You risk permanently compromising his lung function; you risk all sorts of complications. Why do it? He's not going to be much good in a fight. I won't certify him for any sort of exploratory mission, either." Pike understood his doctor's warnings but didn't feel he had a choice at the moment. He needed Tuval's experience right now; therapy had to wait.

If Conn was alive, it would be a different matter. But Conn was dead, and Tuval's new second was a kid, and he was not going to trust a kid's judgment in these matters.

"To answer your question, Commander," Spock said. "Standard Starfleet protocol automates mirroring of all base logs at Starfleet Archives via subspace transmission. For Starbase Eighteen, this mirroring

takes place via the amplifier designated Echo one-
one-nine, one of the old REC-two amplifiers. It occurred to me that those messages might have needed
processing within the unit before being passed along.
A corollary of that assumption was that portions of
the messages might remain as fragmentary information within—"

"Oh. Automated backup," Tuval interrupted. "Why
didn't you say so?"

Spock frowned. "I believe I just did."

Chief Pitcairn laughed. He was the only one.

"What?" he said. "That's funny."

Maybe it was. But Pike didn't have time for humor
right now.

"All right. Now that we all understand how we got
this information"—the captain looked around the table
and got a series of nods in response—"let's take a look
at it."

Number One leaned forward and waved a hand
over one of the table sensors. The briefing room lights
dimmed. The wall opposite Pike doubled as a monitor screen; it filled now with video static. The speakers hissed an audio version of the same. Then both
cleared, and the screen came to life.

Pike and his officers were looking at the interior of
Starbase 18's flight tower, a circular room with floor-
to-ceiling windows. A man in a Starfleet uniform stood
with his back to them.

"*. . . response yet?*" the man asked. There were two women seated at an instrument console directly in front of him. The one on the left was shaking her head.

"*Nothing, sir. I'm sorry.*"

"*Sensor images continue to fluctuate, Commodore.*" That came from a voice offscreen. "*Considerable ghosting—unable to tell if we're looking at one or two ships here.*"

"*That's a big help.*" The commodore—the man who'd spoken first—turned toward the camera, glaring, angry, giving Pike and the others their first head-on look at him.

Commodore Rafael Higueras. He'd taught self-defense at the Academy in Pike's first year. One of the service's most decorated officers. How—why—he'd ended up in command of a starbase, much less a backwater of a starbase like this one, was a puzzle to Pike. Not one he was going to expend a lot of time or energy trying to solve at this point, however.

"*You ran diagnostics?*" Higueras asked.

"*Yes, sir. Everything checks out fine,*" the offscreen voice said.

"*So tell me what we're looking at,*" Higueras said. "*What type of ship?*"

"*Again, difficult to say. Sensors are having trouble—*"

"*Best guess,*" Higueras snapped.

"*Closest match is a Klingon vessel, sir. Warbird-class.*"

At the briefing-room table, Pitcairn cursed under his breath. Tuval shifted in his seat and swore out loud.

"We have data to go with this audio?" the commander asked.

"No," Spock said. "However . . ."

"Let's watch the vid now, please," Pike said. "Commentary later."

On the screen, Higueras had turned around again and was now standing with his back to the camera, staring out the tower window. Pike couldn't see his face, but he felt as if the man was squinting off into the distance. As if he could see what the instruments couldn't by virtue of sheer willpower.

Give it up, Rafe, Pike urged him silently. *Don't worry about exactly what's out there, just activate your shields. Get a distress signal out. Now. Don't wait. Because if you wait—*

But of course, Higueras did precisely that. Waited. Three full seconds. Same as he had the first time Pike viewed the vid.

The captain had to console himself with the thought that those three seconds would probably, in the end, have made no difference whatsoever. The firepower that had been directed at the starbase . . .

Higueras and his people were doomed any way you looked at it.

"Let's play it safe," the commodore said. *"Activate*

defense systems. Put all ships on yellow alert. And get me—"

The base's comm sounded.

"This is Dr. Corzine. Report, please."

"Speak of the devil." Higueras managed a smile. He leaned over the communications officer and punched a button on the console. "Andreas, we were just about to—"

There was a sudden burst of static, and then the vid went silent, though on the screen, Higueras continued talking in the same easy, relaxed manner.

"We are currently endeavoring to recover audio from this portion of the recording," Spock said. "The odds of doing so, however, are not good."

Higueras suddenly straightened up, a look of alarm on his face.

The console in front of him began flashing a single line of text, white against the black screen:

WEAPONS FIRE DETECTED

Higueras turned and strode directly toward the camera, barking out orders as he came. For a second, his face filled the screen.

Then it went to black. The room lights returned to full-level illumination.

Pitcairn was the first to speak. "Sonofabitch. So it was them after all. Never mind what Kritos said, the damn Klingons . . ." The chief looked up at Pike. "What are we gonna do, Captain?"

"What are we going to do?" Pike glanced toward the porthole at the far end of the room, a two-meter-square window with a view of space and, as luck would have it, 55 Hamilton, the asteroid *Enterprise* was currently orbiting. A geosynchronous orbit a few hundred klicks up kept them in position over a little patch of black that marred the otherwise uniformly gray surface.

Until a few days ago, close-up scans of that little patch would have revealed a rainbow of colors, not just black but the green of hydroponic gardens, the blue of an artificial lake, the golds of rich farmland, the gleaming silver of a half-dozen multistory buildings, which taken together had made up Starbase 18. It had been home to eighty-seven people—civilians, Starfleet personnel, and their families. All of whom were now so much space dust.

"We're going to wait to see what Starfleet has to say, Chief. They have a copy of that recording as well. I expect to hear word from them shortly. In the meantime, I want us prepared for all eventualities. Mr. Garrison."

"Sir?"

"Let's make sure that we don't experience any of those intermittent difficulties contacting Starfleet for the next few days."

"Yes, sir. A suggestion—if we can transit the galactic plane, get the ship above the interference sources—"

Pike shook his head. "We hold position here for the moment, Specialist."

"Aye, sir."

"Mr. Tuval, Chief Pitcairn, you'll make sure the ship and your people are at full combat readiness."

"Sir." Both men nodded.

"Mr. Spock is assembling a report on Klingon weapons developments. You might want to review it with him—sooner rather than later."

"Aye, Captain," Pitcairn said.

"You're talking about the cloaking device?" Tuval asked.

"I'm talking about a lot of things," Pike said. "Cloaking device included."

"And I suppose I get sickbay prepared to be a triage facility," Boyce said.

"We will want to prepare for that possibility," Pike said. "Let's hope it doesn't come to that."

"But if it does," Boyce said quietly, "I could work up some sort of Klingon-specific pathogen, give those murdering bastards a little taste of their own medicine."

At those words, the room fell silent.

"Pun intended, of course," Boyce added.

Pike shook his head. "Not funny, Doctor. Not funny at all."

"And expressly prohibited under Gorengar," Spock added. "Treaty Section Three, Paragraph Four. 'The use of biological/biochemical agents in any deliberate form or fashion shall result in—' "

"He's kidding, Spock," Pitcairn said.

"Gorengar. You think the Klingons are paying attention to Gorengar?" Boyce looked around the table. "Any of you think that? Or—"

"That's enough," Pike snapped, slapping the table with the palm of his hand, so hard that half the people in the room started.

Boyce wasn't one of them.

The doctor glared at him; Pike glared right back.

"Doctor," he said, keeping his voice perfectly steady. "You will prepare sickbay to serve as a potential triage center. You will also choose a secondary triage location and prepare that as well. And you will remember, as I hope you all will remember—"

His eyes went around the room, gazing at each of his officers in turn.

"—that we have proof of nothing yet. We are gathering information. We are not at war, people. Is that understood?"

There were nods all around the table, from everyone, including the doctor. He sat quietly, with his hands steepled on the table in front of him, a smile tugging at the edges of his lips. A totally false smile, Pike knew. Put on, the same way the doctor's anger was really a put-on as well, a cover for what he was really feeling this morning, the same thing he'd been feeling every day for the past week, since they'd first heard the news about Starbase 18. Pain. Heartache. A misery so deep that Pike was willing to forgive him almost anything at this point. The key word there being *almost*.

"Good. Dismissed." Everyone stood then, and started heading for the door.

"No, Doctor," he said to Boyce. "Not you."

TWO

Boyce sat at the table, watching the others leave. Pike waited till they were all gone before turning back to him.

"You want me to apologize?" Boyce said. "Fine. I'm sorry. But you saw that tape. It's the Klingons. The cloaking device. You know it, I know it—"

"We don't know anything for certain at this point. Besides which, an apology wasn't what I was after."

"No?"

"No. What I was going to say . . ."

The captain, still standing, put his hands on the table and leaned forward. "Maybe you should think about taking some time off, Phil."

Boyce shook his head. Time off was the last thing he needed right now. "Thanks for the offer," he said. "But I'm fine."

"I don't think you are," Pike said. "I think you need to give yourself a chance to process what happened. Even if it's just a couple of days—"

"Who's going to run sickbay in the meantime?"

"Yang."

"Yang." Boyce shook his head. "No. He's a competent physician, but . . . no. Maybe when Tambor gets out of regen, I'll take some time."

"How long till then?"

"I'm not sure. I want to err on the side of caution."

"Ballpark?"

"A week . . . ten days."

"I don't know." Pike frowned. "I'm no psychologist—"

"That's right," Boyce snapped. "So let me do my job."

Pike's eyes flashed. The captain was in danger of losing his temper. Boyce wanted him to. He wanted Pike to scream at him so he could scream back. Let the captain know how this pretending that the Klingons hadn't butchered every soul on Starbase 18 was stupid, that what they really ought to be doing was going out and finding the nearest Klingon ship—*Hexar* would certainly do; he didn't find that Captain Kritos anywhere near as engaging as Pike did—and blowing them to Kingdom Come.

Pike, however, got control of himself.

"I don't," the captain said slowly, "want you to interrupt me again. Are we clear on that?"

Boyce forced himself to nod. "Yes. We're clear."

"Yes, sir, is what I want to hear from you."

"Yes," Boyce said. "Sir."

"Thank you."

The two of them glared at each other a moment.

"I have the greatest sympathy for your loss, Doctor," Pike said. "I've been cutting you slack all week because of it. But I cannot allow your attitude to jeopardize our mission."

"It won't," Boyce said. "Speaking of which . . . I'd better get going. Sir. Prepare sickbay."

"Yes," Pike said. "You'd better."

Boyce thought about snapping off a sarcastic salute but decided he'd better get out the door before he made things even worse.

So he did.

Halfway to sickbay, Boyce changed his mind.

He decided to head for the mess instead. For one thing, the coffee there was fresh-brewed, as opposed to the synthesized crap the machine in his office spit out. For another, at this time of day, the mess would be quiet.

And what he needed right this second, more than anything else, was a place to calm down. Gather his thoughts. See if he could get himself together to do as ordered, or . . .

Or what, he didn't know.

He grabbed his coffee and headed for a table farthest from the door.

The Klingons. How could Pike think after viewing that tape that they weren't involved in all this? The captain was either delusional, or he knew more than he was saying—more than he was telling Boyce, anyway. No surprise there; Pike and he had yet to truly bond. The only real friends Boyce had made to date were Tuval and Pitcairn. Ben and Glenn. The closest things he had to contemporaries aboard the ship. Most of the 273-person crew was much younger, like the two junior engineering officers in the corner, the only other people in the room, whom Boyce recognized but couldn't quite put names to yet. He nodded hello to them anyway; they nodded back, sympathy in their expressions.

Boyce was tired of sympathy; hell, he was tired of pretty much everything at this point—the captain, the mission, Starfleet . . .

Maybe this had all been a bad idea, done for the wrong reasons. An attempt to make up for lost time, lost opportunities. Or maybe he'd just had too much to drink last night. Another reason he needed the coffee. He took a long swig of it and looked up.

The mess was crammed in the interior ring of Deck 3, primary hull, the ship's saucer section. Instead of a view of space, the crew got holographs to look at while they ate. Right now, Boyce was staring at one of *Enterprise* in spacedock, under construction. As he stared, it started to change, morphed into a shot of the outdoors, someplace on Earth or one of the colonies. Blue water. Blue sky. Bright yellow sun. Boyce took another sip of coffee and could almost feel it beating down on his skin.

"You fixed me."

Jaya's voice.

Jaya stepping out of the regen chamber on Mobile 7, and looking down at her arms, and then up at him, with wonder in her eyes.

Twelve-year-old Jaya. Skinny little Jaya, stepping forward and throwing her arms around him.

"Dr. Boyce?"

He looked up and saw a young woman standing over him. His heart, for a second, skipped a beat.

The woman had red hair. Pale white skin. But her eyes—

Blue. Not Green.

It wasn't Jaya, of course. How could it be?

It was Hardin, Tuval's new second.

"Sorry for the interruption, sir," she said. "I just wanted to say, I'm sorry for your loss."

Hardin was Australian. She had a thick accent that at times—to him, at least—bordered on unintelligible.

"I appreciate that, Lieutenant Hardin." He managed a smile. "Thank you."

"Yes, sir." Her expression changed, from sympathetic to serious. "And I just want you to know—we'll get those bastards. I promise you that."

"Those bastards . . ."

"The Klingons, sir." Hardin lowered her voice. "Commander Tuval briefed the department on that piece of vid we recovered. From the data buffers."

"I see."

"Yes, sir." A little smile crossed her face. "About time we taught them a lesson, you want my opinion. They've been getting away with things like this for too long. If it's war they want, well, we're ready."

The word gave him pause. War? The Federation and the Empire had been dancing around it for years, a skirmish here, a skirmish there. But it had never escalated much beyond that, except for Gorengar, and after the treaty signed in the wake of that nightmare . . .

He looked into Hardin's eyes, at the smooth, unlined skin on her face and her arms, at the sheen of her hair, and realized just how young she was. Just a kid, really. With a kid's definitive views on right and wrong, a kid's ignorance of shades of gray and the way the world really worked. A kid's certainty about war as the best way to achieve your ends—and a kid's ignorance of what war really meant.

He was about to do his best to convey some of his hard-earned knowledge when a shadow fell across the table.

Hardin's face changed. She straightened up and saluted. "Sir."

The size and shape of the shadow told Boyce who was standing behind him without the need to turn around.

"Ben," he said.

"Doctor."

Tuval came around the front of the table.

"At ease, Lieutenant," the commander said. "I need a word here with Dr. Boyce."

"Yes, sir," she said, and saluted both Tuval and Boyce before backing away.

Tuval took a seat. The little plastiform chair groaned under his weight. Ben was the biggest man—biggest human, anyway—aboard *Enterprise*. Two meters, close to 110 kilos of solid muscle. Built like a tank. Indestructible. Or so he liked to think. Boyce knew better, of course.

No one was indestructible.

"You all right?" the commander asked.

"Me?" Boyce downed the last of his coffee. "I'm fine."

"Captain wasn't too hard on you? Still got a job here?"

Tuval said it with a smile. Boyce knew the man was giving him a chance to unload, to talk about what had happened, not just at the meeting but over the last few days. On the one hand, Boyce appreciated the gesture.

On the other, he just wanted to be left alone.

"Yeah. I've still got a job. Such as it is."

Tuval nodded. "Good. Because I have a bone to pick with you."

"Oh?"

"Uh-huh." The commander pulled something off his belt and slapped it down on the table. A square metal box about the size of a communicator. Boyce recognized it immediately.

"A bronchial shunt."

"Yang gave it to me. Says I have to wear it all the time, or he won't certify me for duty."

"And?"

"And it's ridiculous. I feel fine."

"You need it, Ben. Your lung capacity is down to sixty percent, remember?"

"My sixty percent is better than most people's hundred percent. I got a big mouth, remember?"

"I remember. You sound a little out of breath to me."

"That's because I just came from giving a speech to the department. About the Klingons."

"No." Boyce shook his head. "That's because we had to pull you out of regen early, before the gel finished its job. Which is why you need this thing."

He held up the shunt. The device worked by inserting synthetic microcapillaries through the skin, directly accessing the alveoli in the lungs, measuring the oxygen-transfer rate, pumping in more as necessary, reaching the bronchioles directly. Working at maximum capacity, the shunt contained a single day's supply of oxygen.

"Doc." Tuval's expression grew serious. "You cannot expect my people—much less anybody else—to take me seriously if that thing is stuck to my chest."

"Wear something over it, then. One of the landing-party jackets. A loose-fitting tunic—"

"I tried that. It looks like I'm wearing a power converter under my shirt."

"I don't know what to tell you, Ben. You have a serious injury. On top of which, we're talking about going to war—"

"You're being a nervous Nellie, Doc."

"That's my job," Boyce said.

Tuval glared. Boyce had gotten to know him well enough over the last few months that he knew exactly what was on his mind. The man did not want to show weakness of any kind; the word was just not in his vocabulary.

Boyce sympathized. Under normal conditions, he'd try to find some sort of compromise. But these were not normal conditions.

"Like Yang said, we can't certify you fit for duty without it, Commander. I'm sorry."

"So am I," Tuval said, and ripped the shunt from Boyce's hand.

He got to his feet and slapped it on his chest. A pale blue light emanated from the device's underside.

"Thank you," Boyce said.

Tuval grunted an acknowledgment and then was out the door without another word.

Boyce watched him go. Bronchial shunt or not, the man cut a pretty imposing figure. Boyce doubted anyone would take him less seriously because of the device; Tuval would ignore it entirely from this point onward, Boyce was certain. That was part of what made him a good security officer, Boyce supposed. An ability to adjust to changing conditions. To roll with the punches, as it were.

Boyce envied that capability. He wished, not for the first time, he had more of it himself.

After bawling out Boyce, Pike summoned Number One back to the briefing room. He'd asked her for a readiness profile from all departments even before they'd arrived in the Hamilton system but hadn't had a chance to review it until now. They were finishing up the material when the comm beeped. Pike was closest to the controls; he activated the circuit.

"Briefing room."

"Bridge. Garrison here, sir. I have Admiral Noguchi."

Noguchi. That was quick.

His first officer, who was standing over by the wall monitor, cleared her throat. "I'll wait outside, sir."

"No. It's all right. Stay." He turned his attention back to the comm. "Pipe it down here, Specialist. Scrambled."

"Aye, sir."

Pike activated the room monitor. The screen came up red, filled with first the UFP insignia and then Starfleet's. And then Admiral Noguchi's face.

"Sir," Pike said, straightening in his seat.

"At ease, Chris." Noguchi was in full dress; Pike wasn't surprised. He guessed meetings had been going on all morning.

"I'll get right to the point," Noguchi said. *"We have a divergence of opinion here. Command thinks the recording is proof of Klingon involvement; the Federation Council wants more hard evidence."*

"So my orders . . ."

"For the moment, resume sector patrol. Excalibur *and* Hood *are on their way to you. It'll be another few days before they reach you. We're sending them the long way around, avoiding the border entirely."*

"Sir?"

"We're assembling a fleet," Noguchi said. *"You'll be in command. A temporary field promotion to commodore, effective immediately."*

Pike couldn't keep the surprise—and, he supposed, the dismay—off his face.

This was not how things were supposed to be.

The month after Gorengar, two weeks after Pike had offered up his resignation, the admiral had called Pike into his office and shut the door. He'd offered him a promotion and a command of his own.

Enterprise.

"Not interested," Pike had said, refusing to take a seat.

Noguchi ignored him. "This isn't a warship, Chris. This isn't about guarding supply routes or showing the flag. This is different. A five-year mission. Exploration. You'll be like Magellan. Go beyond where we've been before. Make contact with races we've only read about and find others whose existence we never even dreamed of. No more fighting. No more wars. No more kill-or-be-killed."

"Not what you signed up for," Noguchi—present-day Noguchi, on the viewscreen—said. *"Not what I signed up for, either, believe me. Comes with the job."*

Pike forced himself to nod. "Yes, sir. I understand."

"*Good. You'll receive a coded burst transmission in the next few minutes with new security protocols, which are to govern all future Starfleet communications. In the meantime, you're to resume sector patrol. Stay within three travel hours of your current position.*"

"And Kritos? *Hexar?*" Pike had spoken to Noguchi already that morning, relaying to him the facts he hadn't yet shared with his crew. The reason he thought the situation was shaded grayer than it looked, why the Klingons' guilt was less black-and-white. "Do you want me to try to find them, see if I can get more information on—"

"*We're reaching out through the Vulcans,*" Noguchi said. "*They'll handle any sort of negotiations. If there are going to be negotiations.*"

"Understood, sir."

"*A little bit of reaching out you could do, if the opportunity presents itself . . . the Orions.*"

"You want me to go looking for pirates?"

"*Not at all. Though if you run into any, you might want to remind them that we take protection of our civilian traffic seriously.*"

"Yes, sir."

"*The Orions I'm talking about are members of the Trade Confederacy.*"

"The Trade Confederacy?" That was what passed for a government among the Orions; not much of a government, in Pike's experience. "Aren't they pretty much useless? A formality?"

"They have been in the past, certainly. Over the last few years, though, things have been changing."

"Is that so?"

"Apparently. Their leader seems to be taking a more active hand in things. Someone called the tallith." He pronounced it "taleeth." *"If we actually had a negotiating partner, someone who could help keep the Klingons in check in this part of space . . ."*

"I'll keep my eyes open."

"Good. We'll keep you informed of developments. And Chris, I meant to say, my sympathies on the accident."

"Thank you."

"How's Ben doing?"

Ben meaning Commander Tuval, whom Noguchi had served with.

"Pretty much as you'd expect. Angry at himself for not being more careful. Angrier at the doctor for keeping him in sickbay. Angriest at whoever did it."

"Sounds like Ben. You'll tell him I said hello—and to take it easy. Do what the doctor says."

"I'll tell him. Doubt he'll listen to you any more than he listens to me."

Both men smiled at that.

"Probably not," Noguchi said. *"Good luck, Captain. Noguchi out."*

The wall went to black.

Pike sat back in his chair and let out a long, slow breath. *Hood* and *Excalibur,* on their way. Meaning Captains Vlasidovich and Harrari. Dmitri and Michaela. That ought to be fun.

Not.

"Captain?"

Pike looked up and shook his head. He'd almost forgotten his first officer was still in the room.

"Sorry, Number One. That'll be all."

"Yes, sir," she said, and didn't move.

"There was something else?"

"There is. Some discrepancies I discovered during my analysis of the Starbase Eighteen wreckage."

"Discrepancies?"

"Regarding the pattern of weapons fire. It seems to have been concentrated in two areas: the command tower and a building approximately a klick distant from the base's central core."

A kilometer. The number struck him funny: it didn't make sense. On a starbase, you wanted to keep everything as close as possible. Shorter power lines, shorter distance for the water pumps to push. You did not build structures a klick apart on a starbase unless there was a damn good reason to.

"What exactly was this building?"

"It is—was—new construction. Neither the building nor its purpose is listed in our records. Analysis of remaining structural components suggests a duranium alloy was used for the building's outer skin."

"Duranium. That's heavy-duty stuff."

"Yes, sir. I am checking with Archives regarding the structure's purpose."

"You let me know what you find out. As soon as you find it out."

"Aye, sir. Will that be all?"

"For the moment. Except, let's keep the news about *Excalibur* and *Hood* between us, yes?"

"Yes, sir."

"Thank you, Number One. Dismissed."

"Thank you, sir." She nodded and left the room.

Pike watched her go and shook his head. *Number One.* The words still felt wrong coming out of his mouth. A captain and his first officer were supposed to be joined at the hip, to have a symbiotic, almost telepathic relationship. Three months into their five-year mission, and he still didn't know her given name. She was from one of the Illyrian colonies. The first day they'd met, she'd told Pike her real name was something pretty close to unpronounceable, and she'd preferred "Number One." Insisted on it, in fact. Pike agreed. What choice did he have? He tried to tell himself it wasn't that important, that it was just a name. Number One she wanted to be, Number One she was. Fine. Except . . .

He still couldn't quite get over the feeling that the

name was symbolic of something else. A desire on her part to keep him at arm's length, not to let the bond between them develop into something other than a by-the-book, captain-and-first-officer relationship.

Just another way things were not turning out as planned for him aboard *Enterprise*.

THREE

L ook at the bright side, Ben." Pitcairn smiled. "The power ever goes out, you can lead everybody around the ship. Rudolf the red-nosed red shirt. Or in your case, blue-chested red-shirt."

"Funny." Tuval glared. "Not."

Chief Pitcairn was referring to the shunt Commander Tuval was wearing, which he had attempted to hide underneath a landing-party jacket. Why, Spock could not completely understand. The device had gone unnoticed until a few seconds ago, when the commander had leaned over the science station to discuss one of the weapons Spock had put onscreen, and the jacket had fallen open, revealing the glowing blue device beneath it.

The two men had immediately begun a dialogue about the appearance and utility of the shunt. Spock used the time to begin preparing the next item in his presentation. That was when he noticed a longer-than-usual lag time in the system's response. He quickly traced the delay to unusually high demand on the ship's computing resources coming from the auxiliary science station. One of his subordinates, most likely, he thought, using the prioritized resources available at that station to complete the work. Nothing Spock had expressly forbidden, but common sense should tell them to request permission for such usage, particularly on Alpha Shift.

Yet when he turned in his chair, he saw it wasn't one of his subordinates after all.

It was the ship's first officer. Number One. He hadn't even heard her come onto the bridge. She was leaning over the display now at the aux console, hard at work. As always, he admired her focus. The Vulcan wondered what she was doing. He considered offering his assistance but decided against it, there being little doubt in his mind that she would refuse any help. He had observed in Number One a reluctance to practice the easy camaraderie with the crew that humans seemed to value so highly, the joking repartee that other members of the ship's senior staff—Commander Tuval and Chief Pitcairn foremost among them—excelled at. Such practices were most assuredly not a part of her job description, and many people aboard the ship lacked the same skill set. Spock included himself among that number, though his shortcomings were from design rather than an evolved personality matrix. Captain Pike, though capable of engaging in such repartee, more often than not held himself above it. This was perhaps why Spock already felt more at ease aboard *Enterprise* than he ever had at his previous posting, a research vessel whose commander had been far too emotional, far too outgoing, far too personally involved in his ship's mission, and, frankly, far too cavalier about the parameters of that mission for Spock's taste. Twice, they had broken off long-term research operations to investigate instrumental anomalies the commander found curious. In neither instance had those anomalies amounted to anything. This hunger for the unknown at the expense of procedure was dangerous, in his opinion, though at the moment, Spock felt a bit of it himself.

Because Number One, he now saw, had activated the encryption protocols at her station, so that what she was doing remained private. Spock would have little trouble breaking the encryption protocol, should he so desire, and discovering exactly what the ship's first officer was working on. Of course, he would never engage in such behavior, but—

"What's next, Mr. Spock?" Tuval asked, breaking into his train of thought.

Clearing his mind and the processing resources display from his screen, Spock brought up the material he had assembled a moment earlier.

"The next and final item of my presentation is, of course, the cloaking device." He keyed in a series of commands, and the screen in front of them filled with the image of a machine, a dumbbell-shaped device, a three-dimensional model that began to revolve on its axis. "This image file was provided by—"

"Hang on. Is that a prototype?" Chief Pitcairn asked. "A working prototype?"

"Based on the evidence I have accumulated," Spock said, "I believe so."

"Pretty clear they've moved beyond prototype at this point," Tuval said. "Given what we just saw this morning."

The commander was referring to the recording of the attack on Starbase 18. Spock was not entirely sure he agreed; sensor data from that recording were not consistent with the model of the cloaking device's behavior, at least as he understood it. It was a puzzle still to be sorted out.

"I have used an image-enhancement program to increase the resolution of the file. Note here"—Spock magnified the image—"these markings. Where the device tapers, in the middle."

"Looks like chicken scratch to me," Pitcairn said.

"It's Klingon, isn't it?" Tuval asked.

"It is. A single phrase, which I believe to be the device's identification protocol. Roughly translated, it equates to 'Black Snow Seven,' 'Black Snow' referring to the code name for the cloaking device program, 'Seven' the iteration of this particular model."

An unusually poetic name for a weapon, Spock thought, particularly given the fact that it was a Klingon device. Though there was some confusion about the exact origin of the underlying technology, reference in some of the intercepts to place names that seemed to him more Romulan in origin than Klingon. Regardless, the name was appropriate: Black Snow, falling precipitation, a dark cloud that would not only cover but hide from sight everything that it touched. A cloaking device.

"And this image came from where?" Pitcairn asked.

"Starfleet Intelligence," Spock replied, leaving out the fact that it was highly classified, that he'd only managed to obtain it because he had connections, highly placed ones, within the Archives.

"Starfleet Intelligence." Pitcairn snorted. "There's an oxymoron."

"There are a lot of very smart people in Intelligence," Tuval said.

"Then they're in the wrong place. Skulking around in the shadows—it's not how we do business," Pitcairn said.

"Not how we'd like to do business, ideally. But it's a nasty galaxy out there, Chief. You know that."

"I do. Starfleet stands for something a little different, though. Don't you agree, Mr. Spock?"

The two men glared at each other and then at the science officer.

Spock hesitated. He knew and understood both sides of the argument. He tended to side with Chief Pitcairn's position, having the long, counterproductive example of the Vulcan High Command and its short-sighted actions with regard to the Andorians to draw from, but at this time, he did not particularly wish to advocate either side.

He was saved from having to do so by Lieutenant Garrison.

"Excuse me, sirs," the lieutenant said. "But we're being hailed."

"First officer's on the bridge, Lieutenant," Tuval said, gesturing toward Number One and the auxiliary science station. She was up on her feet even before Garrison—a little red-faced now—had turned to face her.

"Sorry, sir. Hadn't seen you there. We—"

"We're being hailed. I know. Details, please."

Number One took the command chair as she spoke.

"Hail comes from an Orion vessel. Identifies itself as *Karkon's Wing*," Garrison said.

"Pirates?" Tuval had moved across the upper level of the bridge to the weapons station. "What are they, kidding? They're going to take on *Enterprise*?"

"Not pirates," Garrison said. "They claim to be representatives of the Trade Confederacy. They want to talk to our leader." Garrison frowned, translating as he listened. "No. Not leader, exactly. The word they're using is . . . *taleed*. Something like that."

"Tallith," Number One suggested.

"Yes," Garrison nodded. "Their tallith wants to talk to ours."

Tallith. Spock was not familiar with the term.

"I'm sure the feeling's mutual," Number One said. "Please summon the captain to the bridge, Mr. Garrison."

Orions. Pike didn't know a lot about this tallith, but he knew enough about the species to be wary. Pirates and courtesans. Brutes and temptresses. The women with pheromones that had the effect of rendering males of most species "highly suggestible," at least according to the shipboard computer; the males significantly larger, stronger, and more vicious than their human counterparts. *Like us,* Pike thought, *only with animal instincts on overdrive.* As if they had devolved to some more primitive form of creature. Orion civilization itself was a shambles—corrupt government, clan warfare, rumors of genocide. Though if what Noguchi had told him was right, this tallith had begun to turn things around. Well. He'd see soon enough.

The lift door opened.

"Captain on the bridge," said Ensign Colt, who was manning the records station. She blushed as she caught Pike's eye.

Kid had a bad case of hero worship, Pike thought. He recognized the symptoms, having gone through them himself with Commodore Bennett. He'd have to cure her of that later. For now . . .

He stepped down a level, took his chair. "What do we know?"

"Vessel has identified itself as *Karkon's Wing*," Spock said. "*Marauder*-class, with considerable hull and weapon augments."

"A threat to us?"

"No, sir."

"They have weapons, they're a threat," Tuval said.

"Not at this distance, Commander," Spock said. "They are at the edge of our scanning range and holding position. Within the Borderland, Captain."

Pike frowned. The Borderland was a vast swath of territory, portions of which were claimed by (among others) Klingon, Orion, Dorelian, and Huni interests. The area was subject to frequent territorial skirmishes, hijackings, acts of terrorism—it was a dangerous place to travel. Starbase 18 had been located in a little tendril of Federation space that reached inside it, the area Pike and *Enterprise* had been patrolling over the last few weeks. One of the reasons they had had so many encounters with *Hexar* and Captain Kritos.

"All right. Let's see what they want." He gestured to Garrison. "Open the channel."

"Aye, sir."

Pike prepared himself. Given the tallith's achievements, he expected the man would have to be a formidable warrior, first of all. A charismatic leader as well. Experienced. Shrewd. An older man, most likely, a particularly successful merchant, a retired pirate . . . Tuval was right to be on his guard; Pike would have to be, too. Noguchi might want him to feel out the Orions with regard to establishing a closer relationship, but the captain's foremost concern had to remain, as always, the safety of his ship and crew.

The screen came to life. The captain blinked.

The tallith was a woman.

A striking-looking woman at that, with long dark hair, liberally streaked with gray, and dark green skin, wearing what looked like pirate leathers, black with a red and gold insignia stitched on the chest. She sat in a command chair analogous to his own, her expression impassive, impervious. Commanding.

"Greetings. I am Liyan of the Codruta, tallith of the Orion people."

"Christopher Pike, captain of the *Enterprise*."

"Your ship—you and your officers—are well known among my people."

"Your reputation precedes you as well, Tallith. You have accomplished much."

"With much more to do. But I thank you for the compliment." She bowed her head.

Pike supposed he shouldn't have been so surprised, at that. Women were the power behind many of the Orion clans, particularly the traders. The pheromones at work, the females offered themselves up as slaves or courtesans to rich merchants, whom they then began to influence in ways both subtle and obvious. Or tried to, anyway. There were at least as many stories of slave girls reduced to little more than beggars as there were of rich and powerful pirates turned into little more than oversized lapdogs by their women.

This was no slave girl on the viewscreen before him, though. This was a woman used to, and comfortable with, power. Liyan of the Codruta.

Odd that she should have identified herself as being from that clan first and as an Orion second.

"I will come straight to the point, Captain Pike. I request your assistance."

"Assistance."

"Yes."

"Can I ask what type of assistance?"

"I would discuss that when you arrive."

"I don't understand."

"I would like to invite you and your senior officers to come aboard Karkon's Wing *as my guests."*

"I'm sorry," Pike said. "But by terms outlined in the Gorengar treaty, Federation personnel are expressly forbidden from assisting—"

"Gorengar. Of course. I should have been clearer. This is an emergency situation. Exceptions are provided for same in the treaty, are they not?"

"They are. But . . ." Pike scanned the status monitor on the arm of his chair as he spoke. He didn't note any problem with the Orion vessel, its engines, life-support systems . . . "An emergency. May I ask what kind?"

"The crisis is medical in nature."

"We're happy to forward supplies to you."

"Supplies we have, Captain Pike. What we require is expertise. Advanced treatment. Of the kind that only Federation doctors can provide. Let me show you." She gestured toward someone offscreen. A second later, her image disappeared, replaced by what was obviously a sickbay. Diagnostic beds, a variety of old and new, filled with patients, some simply bandaged, others more seriously injured. Dozens, at least. Maybe as many as a hundred.

The sickbay disappeared, and Liyan returned.

"What's happened?" he asked.

"We have been attacked. A series of unprovoked raids on our holdings in this sector, on our ships. This is the most recent. And the deadliest."

"Who's responsible for these attacks?"

"Klingons," the tallith said. *"Two warbirds. The ships appeared from nowhere. Almost like magic. We suspect some new technological advance."*

The bridge around Pike, which had been buzzing with activity, fell silent.

"Very interesting," the captain said. "I think we will take you up on your invitation after all."

FOUR

Every bit of the Borderland was disputed territory, not just the vast interior but the very edges of it, which *Enterprise* and *Karkon's Wing* were both skirting. Those edges were ill defined enough that Pike had the landing party board a shuttle for transport over to the Orion ship, rather than use the materializer. Ben wasn't happy with that decision. He and the captain spent the first few minutes of the shuttle flight arguing about it. Boyce, for his part, didn't have strong feelings on the subject, but he knew a lot of people who did. The evidence, in his opinion, was entirely inconclusive.

In the seat next to him, Lieutenant Hoto droned on. ". . . this database search I have conducted even

this morning has revealed matches between current
Codruta surnames and names of several ruling families
from the days of the Second Empire, indicative of not
just the clan's importance in those times but support-
ive of this tallith's claims to a position of leadership
based upon historical precedent. The name Liyan also
carries with it specific resonances, as the Orion story
cycle most commonly known as the Doerge suggests,
in that . . ."

The doctor tuned her out. The lieutenant—petite,
Asian, female, from sciences—was nice to look at but
excruciating to listen to. Having Spock for a mentor
hadn't helped in that regard. It seemed to Boyce that
she—along with every other member of the Vulcan's
department, for that matter—had now acquired the
habit of peppering her speech with words like "logical," and "fascinating." Which this briefing definitely
wasn't.

He focused on the tricorder again. Or tried to, anyway. His heart wasn't in it. He shut the device down,
checking his medikit. As he did so, his fingers brushed
against something unfamiliar. He reached in and pulled
out a BT shunt. A spare, one he'd brought with him
when Pike had first told him about the mission. Just
in case Tuval had gotten cold feet about wearing his.
The commander—in the seat in front of Boyce, piloting
the ship—hadn't, though. Every so often, when Tuval

shifted position, Boyce caught a glimpse of the little blue light blinking happily away underneath the commander's landing-party jacket.

Pike sat on Tuval's right, nominally at the conn position, but his mind clearly was elsewhere. Boyce's first instinct on boarding the shuttle—before that, in fact, his first instinct on hearing about the Klingon attack on the Orions—was to tell Pike "I told you so," but he'd refrained for some reason, and now he was glad he had. The captain—make that commodore—had a lot on his plate just this second: *Hood* and *Excalibur* on the way, the promotion, war on the horizon. Besides which, the raids the tallith had told them about pretty much proved Boyce's point. The thought of war made him sick, yes, but it made him even sicker to think about the Klingons getting away with what they were doing. Mass murder. They had to be stopped. Here and now.

". . . though some of these references must be acknowledged as inaccurate, otherwise we would have to believe that this is the same Liyan who first assumed clan leadership close to seventy-five years ago, and the woman who contacted us is obviously—"

"Excuse me, Lieutenant." Pike sat up a little straighter in his seat and cleared his throat.

The captain, apparently, was paying attention after all.

"The most relevant question at the moment is whether or not these particular Orions are trustworthy. What kind of reputation this clan, this Liyan, has. Do those databases have anything to say about that?"

Hoto frowned. "That is a difficult question to answer definitively, sir. There exists, within the databases we have access to, anecdotal evidence of piracy, but the incidents seem in my estimation to be related more to skirmishes between the Codruta and other clans. The Singhino, the Caju—"

"The Caju. They're a clan?" Pike frowned. "I thought Caju was more of a generic name for a certain kind of trading interest."

"It is now. The name is originally derived, however, from a single such clan."

Boyce frowned, suddenly remembering something. "What about the Orion syndicate?" He recalled having to deal with pirates from that organization back in the day, who'd intercepted a cargo transport of his at one point. "Where do they fit into all this?"

"The syndicate's influence on current affairs, particularly in this sector of space, is minimal. Their strongholds are concentrated in territories on the other side of the Borderland. Near the Dohelee border."

"That's a long way from here."

"The Orion people have widespread settlements across this part of the galaxy. A cursory reading of the historical evidence suggests that at one time, the Second Empire maintained influence over a considerable area of what is now Federation space."

"Speaking of Federation space," Tuval said. "We're leaving it in five—four—three—two—one. And let me say again, for the record, that I don't think this is a good idea. We are well out of transporter range."

"Noted, Commander," Pike said. "As before."

There were seven of them in the shuttle: the captain, Boyce, Tuval, Hoto, and three red shirts from security. Ross, Smith, and Collins, the latter a grizzled old veteran who had considerable experience as a battlefield med assistant, which was why he was there. Tuval had assigned him to go with Boyce to the Orion sickbay and evaluate the situation. Four security personnel in all. Pike thought that was too many, sent the wrong signals; Tuval thought it was too few. The commander would have brought along a dozen red shirts if he'd had his druthers. And left the captain behind. Along with, no doubt, the shunt. Which reminded him . . .

The doctor pulled the spare out of his medikit and held it out over Tuval's shoulder.

"What's that?" Tuval spoke without turning.

"A spare. In case you want it."

"I don't. But." The man took one hand off the console, though, and took it from him anyway. The shunt was magnetically charged; Tuval slapped it onto the console in front of him, and it stuck there with a resounding *thunk*.

"Be prepared," the Commander said. "That's my motto."

Collins spoke up. "We have docking clearance from *Karkon's Wing*, Captain."

Pike looked forward, and Boyce followed suit.

There, visible through the shuttle's main porthole, was the Orion ship.

"Doesn't look like any *Marauder*-class I've ever seen," Tuval said.

"You can see the silhouette." Collins pointed forward. "Buried under a lot of extraneous stuff, though."

"Weapons enhancements, most likely," Tuval said. "I really don't think this is a good idea, sir."

"I heard you the first time, Ben. And the second." Pike leaned forward, squinting. "Not necessarily sure those are weapons. Looks like some kind of sensor array to me."

What it looked like to Boyce was a hunk of junk. A jury-rigged hunk of junk. He saw exposed conduit leading from one of the forward hull segments to the bow. He was no engineer, but that wasn't standard engineering protocol on any ship he'd ever heard of.

"*Enterprise shuttle, this is* Karkon's Wing. *You are cleared for docking.*"

"Thank you, *Karkon's Wing*," Tuval said. "*Magellan* here. We confirm docking clearance. Initiating procedure now."

The shuttle veered left, coming around the side of the Orion ship, passing a scarred and blackened hull segment on which a few scrawled symbols—Orion letters, Boyce supposed—were barely visible.

"Ready to get your hands dirty, Doctor?" Pike asked.

"Not just yet," Boyce said, and reached into his medikit. "And neither are you."

"What's that mean?"

"It means roll up your sleeve, Captain." Boyce pulled out a hypo. "We wouldn't want you to catch any cooties, would we?"

Pike glared and did as he was told.

Cooties wasn't far from the truth.

The hypos were Starfleet SOP when dealing face-to-face with Orions, pheromone-suppressant drugs designed to curb their responses to the species' females. Pike felt the effect almost instantaneously: a deadening of his sense of smell. A slowing of his reflexes, too, supposedly insignificant, but the captain didn't like it. Tuval liked it even less.

"Doesn't feel right," he said to Boyce, rolling up his sleeve. "Feels like I'm swimming through cotton."

"That'll pass."

"The sensations I am experiencing are quite different," Hoto said. She was looking down at her arms, as if seeing them for the first time. "An acceleration of my metabolism. A disconnection from my surroundings."

"You'll get used to it, too," Boyce said. "Probably even quicker."

The women had gotten hypos as well as the men—a slightly different concoction, the doctor said, because the pheromones affected them in different ways, tended to cause headaches in human females, something to do with the inhibition of certain neural transmitters. So Smith, Ross, and Hoto had gotten stimulants as part of their formula. This was one of the reasons Tuval had wanted women on the security team and why he'd argued for Number One to make the trip rather than the captain. Pike supposed he had a valid point, but there was something slightly insulting, he felt, about sending your second-in-command to treat with the ruler of an entire race. Besides which . . .

He wanted to see this evidence for himself, the sensor readings that Liyan had of the Klingon attacks. If they were as definitive as she'd said—even if they were as definitive as the readings they'd been able to recover from Starbase 18—then Pike would have to admit he was wrong. About a lot of things.

He would also have to prepare himself and the crews of three starships for the very real possibility of war.

Magellan shuddered slightly, then came to rest. Pike stood and moved toward the shuttle hatch.

Tuval stepped in front of him. "Hostile territory. You know the drill," the commander said.

Pike did, having had to perform it several times himself aboard *Lexington.* He stepped back reluctantly. Tuval punched a control on the hatch access panel, and the door slid open. The commander stepped through it, hand resting lightly on his phaser.

"Empty," he called back from the airlock. The others followed him in. Tuval walked toward a second hatch six feet away, at the other end of the airlock. It opened at his approach. A few seconds later, the commander reappeared and gave the all clear.

And Pike, at last, stepped from *Magellan* and onto the deck of the Orion ship.

The first thing he noticed was the temperature, a good ten degrees warmer than *Enterprise,* though the light was dimmer. Next was the gravity, slightly heavier than Earth-normal. The deck gave slightly beneath his feet. The plating seemed thinner than that aboard *Enterprise,* the ceiling lower as well. Maybe two and a half meters high.

"Captain Pike?"

The voice came from his right. Pike turned and

found himself almost face-to-face with one of the largest humanoids he'd ever seen in his life. More than two meters tall, easily. Heavily muscled, deep green skin, long dark hair in a ponytail, dark brown trousers, a dark brown vest to match. His eyes were pinpricks of black, set in a long, angular face.

"I'm Captain Christopher Pike," the captain said, stepping forward.

"I am Gurgis, of the Clan Singhino." The man bowed and stepped to one side. "May I present to you Liyan of the Codruta, tallith of the Orion people."

Behind Gurgis were two other Orion males—not as big as he was but huge nonetheless. Guards, obviously, wearing helmets, sidearms, and ceremonial swords. Maybe not so ceremonial—the edges of the blades caught the light in a way that suggested they were very sharp. And very well taken care of.

The guards stepped to either side, and from between them, a woman stepped forward.

It took Pike a second to recognize Liyan.

She had changed in the interim between first contact and their arrival. She now wore a long gray dress, with a matching robe that trailed behind her. Her hair was pulled back and piled high on her head. She wore something on her head as well, halfway between a crown and a headpiece, gold, encrusted with blood-red jewels.

She was considerably taller than she'd seemed on the monitor, his height, more or less.

She was also, he realized as she stepped forward, one of the most beautiful women he had ever seen in his life.

"Captain. Welcome aboard *Karkon's Wing*. We are honored to have you."

She bowed; Pike did the same.

"On behalf of the United Federation of Planets, thank you. We are honored to be here." He turned and motioned his crew to come forward. "I'd like to introduce you to—"

"Philip Boyce." Another Orion—male, considerably smaller than the others, skin more aqua-colored than green—stepped out from behind Liyan, an excited look on his face. "You are Philip Boyce, are you not?"

"I am." Boyce, an easy-to-read frown on his face— *how does this guy know my name?*—stepped up next to the captain. "And you are—"

The newcomer bowed. "Petri. Medical chief of *Karkon's Wing*."

Pike frowned. "How do you know my doctor?"

The man opened his mouth, but it was Liyan who responded.

"We trade with Argelius, from time to time. Your name—your work—is well known there, Dr. Boyce."

"Indeed. A tremendous legacy, Doctor." Petri pronounced the word strangely—the second part of it, anyway. *Doc-tore.* "Something to be proud of."

"Thank you," Boyce said, not looking happy about the attention at all. Pike understood why. Argelius was not something the doctor would want to be reminded of at this point in time.

"We hope you can be of similar service here, Doctor." Liyan smiled.

Boyce grunted an acknowledgment. Not wanting to give offense, Pike stepped in front of the doctor and answered for him.

"As do we, Tallith. I know the doctor will try his best."

"That is all we can ask." Liyan turned to Petri. "You will escort the doctor to the medical wing, Petri. Show him the injured."

The man bowed. "Of course, Tallith. This way, Doctor."

"We have supplies for you as well," Boyce said. "A half-dozen crates. Aboard the shuttle."

"Excellent." Liyan waved the big man forward. "Gurgis."

He bowed. "I will attend to it, Tallith."

He set off down the corridor, Petri and Boyce following him.

"Mr. Collins?" Tuval prompted. "Weren't you going to . . . ?"

Ben nodded in the direction of Boyce and Petri.

"Yes, sir. On my way." Collins, who had undergone medical training, saluted smartly and started off after the others.

"Captain Pike," Liyan said, "we have prepared a reception in your honor. If you would come this way . . ."

She stood to one side, motioning down the corridor, in the opposite direction from Boyce and Petri.

Pike hesitated. A reception. He'd wanted to get right to business; they didn't exactly have a lot of time to fool around. *Hood* and *Excalibur* were half a day away, the Klingons probably even closer. Boyce had instructions to spend no more than an hour evaluating the medical situation. Pike didn't want to spend any more than an hour, two at the most, aboard this ship. Take a look at that sensor evidence, have Hoto evaluate it and any other data the Orions had. Feel Liyan out on the question of an alliance, the possibility of their two cultures, joined against the Klingons. A reception? There wasn't time, really, and yet . . .

He looked up at Liyan. She was royalty, in effect. Royalty demanded certain ceremony. Noguchi would understand. It made perfect sense.

"Of course," he said, and bowed again. "After you."

She smiled and stepped past him. Pike moved to follow and in that instant caught Gurgis's eye as the man emerged from *Magellan,* carrying one of the supply crates, which had to weigh several hundred pounds on his shoulder.

The man looked at Pike and then past him to the tallith, disappearing down the hall.

He did not look happy at all.

FIVE

It was basic battlefield medicine. As he'd suspected. And since Orion physiology was almost identical to human, Boyce was practically able to work on autopilot. Cauterize here, regenerate there, transfuse . . . after a while, it was easy to forget he was working on living flesh, albeit green. Occasionally, though, he would look up and see a face (if it wasn't a face he was working on), or someone would moan, and he would remember what he was doing and why and who was responsible for his being there. And then the anger would threaten to surface again.

The Klingons, he thought. *Jaya.*

"Dr. Boyce." He looked up. Collins stood there,

concern on his face, gloves on his hands, bloodstains on his tunic. "That's the last of the regen gel."

Boyce nodded. Bad news but not entirely unexpected. They'd been going through the stuff at a very rapid clip, the hour or so they'd been there; there were a lot of burn injuries to deal with. The gel was the one thing they'd brought that the Orions didn't have. Apart from that . . .

Their presence there didn't seem that necessary to him at all. Okay, maybe Petri could use another trained hand or two, but those hands didn't have to be his. Boyce wasn't doing anything a trained nurse couldn't—hell, a half-trained nurse. Collins was as good in these situations as he was. Made him wonder why the Orions had been so glad to see him, so effusive in their greeting.

He finished cauterizing the wound in front of him and straightened. His neck was killing him. He rubbed it and set down the medikit.

"I'm going to take a break," he said out loud, to no one in particular, and headed out of the treatment room into the main hall.

There were perhaps half a dozen Orions milling around. More came and went as he watched, entering and leaving the dozens of treatment rooms in the ship's medical wing. Boyce had lost count of how many he'd been in himself over the last hour or so. Some were huge (two had been the size of cargo bays; it looked to him, in fact, as if they had been cargo bays at one point, two decks high, with walls of rough steel the second level up), some the size of *Enterprise*'s own sickbay, a dozen beds, while others were single-patient rooms. All branched off the central hall that he stood in now.

Petri had given him a thermos of some kind of nutrient drink earlier; Boyce leaned against the wall and downed some of it. Funny little guy, Petri. Nervous little guy. The way he'd jumped when Liyan said boo, the way he'd hurried to obey her every command, reacted to her like a puppet on a—

Boyce stopped drinking, suddenly realizing that they'd all—himself and Pike included—acted exactly the same way when they'd come onboard. Marching here and there, on her orders, without a second thought.

The pheromones. The little cocktail he'd injected them all with . . . He wondered if it had been quite strong enough.

"Dr. Boyce!"

Speak of the devil.

Petri was hurrying toward him, coming out of one of the treatment rooms.

"There you are. Please don't wander off unescorted. The tallith would not want you to come to be injured or exposed to any danger."

"Just taking a break," Boyce said.

"Of course, of course. But you should—"

Someone cried out. A girl. The sound came from behind him.

Boyce turned and saw, down a short stretch of hallway directly opposite the entrance to the wing, three doors. One directly opposite him, closed, with the control pad next to the door blinking red. One to the left and one to the right.

"Who's down there?" Boyce asked. "More patients?"

"No," Petri said quickly. "Or, rather, yes but not victims of the accident. Attack."

The cry came again—from the door on the right.

"Mind if I take a look?" he asked.

"Please, Dr. Boyce." Petri laid a hand on his arm. "Those patients are not your concern."

"When I became a doctor," Boyce said, "I took a vow. A little something called the Hippocratic Oath."

"I am familiar with your oath," Petri said. "But—respectfully—you should focus—"

"Dr. Boyce!"

Collins burst into the hall, concern etched all over his face. He saw Boyce and sighed.

"Doctor, please. Next time, let me know where you're going."

Boyce frowned. Rules. Regulations. He'd joined Starfleet to help out, but this . . . he was a little old for this.

"Where I'm going?" He pointed toward the open door. "Right in there."

And before either of them—Petri or Collins—could say a word, he strode off purposefully down the hall and into the treatment room the cries had been coming from.

It was a single-patient room. Dimly lit. A single diagnostic cot, hooked to a standard analysis screen at the right-hand side of the bed.

Lying on that cot was a girl, an Orion female barely out of her teens. She was dressed in a simple hospital shift. There was a sheen of sweat on her forehead. She was unconscious—at least, that's what he thought, until she opened her eyes and looked at him.

"You are Philip Boyce," she said.

"Yes."

"Dr. Boyce."

"Yes. How do you know my name?"

"Your work on Argelius." She managed a small smile. "It is very well known."

"Apparently so." At least among these Orions, it was. He wondered why.

"What's your name?" he asked, moving around the bed toward the diagnostic screen. He sensed, as much as saw, Petri enter the room, Collins a step behind him.

"Deleen."

"Deleen." He smiled at her and studied the analysis screen quickly. Her temperature was up. Her blood pressure was dangerously high. And if he was reading the screen right, her pain receptors were registering off the scale.

She must be in agony.

"How are you feeling, Deleen?" he asked.

"Dr. Boyce," Petri said. "Please. This is not your place."

Boyce turned and glared at the man. Not his place. He was a doctor. Where else was he supposed to be?

"I'm here to help," he said, turning back to Deleen. "Tell me how you feel."

"Fine," she said quickly. "I'm perfectly fine."

Boyce frowned. What was going on? Why didn't anyone want him to treat the girl?

He looked down at her again and noticed something he hadn't seen before. The veins on her arm were swollen, darkened in color, emerald green against the lime of her skin.

He'd never seen anything like that before.

"Dr. Boyce," Petri said, "I must insist—"

"I'd like to see this patient's history."

"What?"

"Her medical history. Can I access it from this screen, or—"

At that instant, Boyce's eyes fell on a wall of dimly lit machinery behind the cot, on the wall farthest from the door. There, he thought, and took a single step forward.

And stopped dead in his tracks.

There was recessed lighting in the ceiling, a

dim blue cone of illumination that shone down on the wall of machinery. Boyce stared at the piece of equipment directly in front of him for a good three or four seconds before he was able to find his voice again.

"This is a LeKarz sequencer." He ran a hand over the machine; it felt brand-new to him, the metal and glass substrate underneath his palm smooth to the touch. It looked brand-new as well, the surface free of scratches or blemishes or any sort of dings.

"Yes," Petri said.

"You have a LeKarz sequencer."

"We use it to assist in diagnosing certain genetic abnormalities."

Boyce nodded, staring at the machine. Of course they did. That's what the LeKarz was for; it was the most sophisticated genetic-sequencing unit in the galaxy. Incredible machine, incredibly difficult to manufacture. As far as he knew, there were no more than a dozen of them in the galaxy. The Vulcans had been begging for one for years. How in the world the Orions had gotten hold of technology like this, technology Starfleet was notoriously stingy with—

Jaya. Starbase 18.

"We have one." He recalled the last time the two of them had talked, a few weeks earlier, when Boyce had learned that his mission would carry him in her general direction and that there was a possibility *Enterprise* might make a stop at 55-Hamilton.

He had been incredulous then. "A LeKarz."

"Yes."

"Why?" Starbase 18 was a standard Federation outpost, part diplomatic mission, part military base. The medical center was there to treat those personnel assigned to 55-Hamilton. Why would they need—why would they have—a LeKarz sequencer?

"Dr. Boyce?" Collins's voice snapped him out of his reverie. "Is something wrong?"

He stared at the LeKarz.

Yes, he thought to himself, *there is something wrong. Something very, very wrong indeed.*

"No. Everything's fine." He turned, rearranging his features into a smile. "A LeKarz sequencer. Well. Doesn't matter how you got it, I suppose, it's just a godsend that you have it. You're using it diagnostically, I assume, which makes good sense."

"As I said," Petri replied.

"Of course. As you said. You did say that, didn't you?"

He was talking too fast, Boyce realized. Saying too much. Babbling. *Slow down. Calm down. Don't let them see anything's wrong.*

"Mr. Collins?"

"Sir?"

Boyce turned away from the machine and slung

the tricorder around in front of him. "Weren't we supposed to check back in with the captain about now?"

Collins frowned. "About now, yes, sir."

They actually had another fifteen minutes or so by Boyce's count, but Collins, as he had hoped, followed his lead.

"You can handle the check-in, if you would. Tell the captain we're just about wrapping things up here."

"Yes, sir."

"Tell him I'm just looking at a few more patients." He smiled at Petri. "Oh, and tell him they have a LeKarz." He tried to say the word as casually as he could. *LeKarz.* "Tell him to let Mr. Spock know about it, for sure. There were some interesting plant samples from Rhinos V we picked up. He might want to use the machine briefly—that would be all right, if our science officer used the machine, wouldn't it?"

He addressed the latter to Petri, who was eyeing him suspiciously. That didn't matter. Collins had his communicator out. The second Spock heard that word, *LeKarz,* the second he found out the Orions had one, he would know there was something wrong, would know that—

Raised voices came from outside the room. A second later, the door burst open.

Gurgis walked in. His head barely cleared the top of the doorframe.

"What is happening here?" he demanded.

Petri stepped forward. "The doctor was examining Deleen. But I told him—"

Gurgis shook his head. "This is not permitted."

"That's exactly what I said." Petri nodded. "We are leaving now. There is no need—"

"You." Gurgis spoke to Collins, pointing a finger straight at the communicator. "Usage of that device is not permitted. You will put it down immediately."

Collins didn't answer. He didn't put the communicator away, either.

"Put it down," Gurgis said again, and took a step forward.

Collins drew his phaser. "Doctor," he said, "if you would come stand by me—"

Gurgis moved, lunged forward, much faster than Boyce would have thought possible for someone of his size.

Collins fired, phaser set on stun. The beam caught Gurgis mid-leap and slammed into him. A wall of energy, equivalent to the force of a falling piano, struck the Orion in the chest.

It barely slowed him down.

Collins went to fire again, but it was too late.

Gurgis slammed into him, slammed him into the wall, grabbed him by the neck with one hand, and then lifted.

Collins gasped. The Orion smiled and tightened

his grip. Boyce heard something snap. The security guard's eyes rolled back in his head.

Gurgis released his grip, and Collins fell to the floor. So did the communicator.

Boyce, whose own communicator was in his medi-kit, inaccessible, dove for it. He got his hand on it and stood—

And stopped breathing.

Gurgis had his hand around his throat. He lifted Boyce off the ground.

Boyce gasped. Someone screamed.

Petri's face appeared in Boyce's rapidly diminishing field of vision.

"Put him down, you idiot!" the doctor yelled. "The tallith—"

Something hit Petri's face: Gurgis's hand. Boyce saw blood, red blood, just like human blood.

Then he saw nothing.

SIX

His studies in preparatory school had, of course, included some xenobiology, so Spock had on more than one occasion visited Solkar's archives, but paradoxically enough, it was only now, some hundreds of light-years away from his home city of Shi'Kahr, from Vulcan, that he was truly able to appreciate the wealth of information the great explorer had gathered. The Solkar archives were a storehouse of not just physical artifacts but oral histories, data stored in all forms imaginable, history captured at the moment of its creation and brought to Vulcan by Solkar and his successors.

Spock had discovered the initial mention of a "tal-lit" in a series of semimythological narratives collected by Solkar himself, while the explorer was serving what was apparently a fairly painless six months term of captivity at the hands of Orion pirates. These narratives, recited mainly by the leader of his captors, a Captain Ugaro, formed a classic story cycle, akin to that found in pre-Awakening Vulcan mythology, the human tale of the Odyssey, the Klingon cycle of Kahless—a tale of subjugation, exodus, and triumphant return. The "tallit" was a more important figure in this cycle than Spock had initially realized, was in fact one of its major heroes, referred to in multiple sections of the narrative by his given name of K'rgon, rather than his title.

Ugaro's narratives were colorful in the extreme; not only that, the language was reflective of an entirely different technological era. Spock found it fascinating. After reading transcripts of three of the narratives, he decided he wanted to hear the pirate's voice for himself.

He was at his station on the bridge now, doing just that, listening to Ugaro—dead more than a thousand years now—recite the glories of even more distant, more dead times.

"... which K'rgon soon added to his conquests as well. And those systems—those peoples—those warriors—were glad to join him. The Orions of the Second Empire were a force to be reckoned with, sir. The most fearsome warriors ever to grace the quadrant, then or now."

"And yet no trace of this Second Empire exists?" Another voice—calmer, more measured (Solkar's, Spock assumed)—sounded in his ear as well.

"The evidence is out there, sir," Ugaro said. *"I myself have seen relics, on Stannos IV, in a Dunbarri merchant's private museum. Pieces of the Orion fighters, K'rgon's seal still visible on the hulls."*

"Ships from that era?" Solkar asked.

"Most definitely. Two of them, K'ud fighters. Exactly like I told you. Small ships—the wing of K'rgon's attack force. In battle—"

Spock paused the recording, suddenly realizing something.

K'rgon. Karkon. Karkon's Wing.

"Number One," he said.

She turned in her chair. "Mr. Spock."

"I have information to convey to you," Spock began, "which I believe relevant—"

The console behind him chirped.

"We're being hailed, Commander," Garrison said.

"The Orions?"

"No, sir, the *Hexar*."

"Hexar?" Number One frowned, exchanging glances with Spock. "Where did they come from?"

The Vulcan spun back to his console. "One moment." He brought up a sector map, superimposed rough outlines of Borderland, Federation, and Klingon territory on top of it. Added *Enterprise,* a blinking yellow dot, and *Hexar,* a blinking red one.

"Ah," he said.

"Facts, please," Number One prompted.

"Of course." He put the sector map up on the main viewscreen. "If you will direct your attention—"

"Yes," Number One interrupted. "I see."

"See what?" asked Lieutenant Hardin, from the weapons console.

"The Adelson cloud," Spock said.

"The Adelson cloud?" Hardin asked.

"The extremely large nebula. There, in the lower lefthand quadrant of the screen."

"Okay," Hardin said. "I see it. And?"

"*Hexar* was hiding in it."

"Inside the nebula?"

"Precisely, Lieutenant. Or we would have detected their presence sooner."

Number One shook her head. "That's not good. Not good at all."

"I concur," Spock said.

Hardin frowned. "Why is that not good?"

"Favorite Klingon tactic: assemble your fleet inside a nebula," Number One said. "That's what they did at Gorengar, too."

"You think there are more ships hiding in there?"

"Most certainly," Spock said. "The Klingons are no

doubt matching our strategy. Forming an attack force."

Hardin's eyes glinted. She punched a button on the console. "Bridge to torpedo control. Prepare—"

"Belay that," Number One snapped.

"Sir?" Hardin asked.

"We're not at war yet, Lieutenant." The commander gestured to Garrison. "Let's talk first. See what they want."

"The prudent course is to raise shields," Hardin said. "At the least. If we—"

"Do nothing without my express order, Lieutenant." Number One arranged herself in the command chair.

Hardin nodded, tightening her lips, as the sector map vanished from the main viewscreen and the transmission from *Hexar* appeared.

But the figure that came onscreen was not, to Spock's surprise, Kritos.

Instead, a much older Klingon—one of the oldest Spock had ever seen, massive, heavily bearded, wearing Imperial armor of a type and color the Vulcan had previously come across only in historical databases and museum displays—occupied the command chair.

"Federation vessel, I am General K'Zon. You have crossed into the Borderland and are in clear violation of Gorengar. Withdraw immediately, or face the consequences."

Number One's face remained impassive.

"General. I am first officer of the *U.S.S. Enterprise.* Your sensors are in error. By any reading of the sector map, we are in Federation territory."

K'Zon snorted. *"I refer to your shuttlecraft, which our sensors witnessed journey into Klingon territory."*

"The Borderland is neutral territory, General. And the shuttlecraft was responding to a medical emergency. As per terms of Gorengar."

"You have now been warned, Enterprise. *This happens once, and once only. Klingons do not battle with words."* K'Zon snapped his fingers, and the screen went dark.

"Charming." Chief Pitcairn shook his head. "Never thought I'd say this, but I actually miss Kritos."

"Anyone know this K'Zon? Who he is?" Number One asked.

"No," Spock said.

"No," Hardin chimed in.

"Checking records now," Colt said from her station on the far side of the bridge.

"So what happened to Kritos?" Garrison asked.

"I assume that question is rhetorical." Number One rose from the command chair.

"Of course it is," Spock said. "Obviously, he has been replaced. A common enough occurrence in the Empire. And yet the timing invites speculation."

Number One nodded, clasping her hands behind her back as she stared up at the main viewscreen, which now displayed the immediate starfield again. "Indeed."

"The timing . . ." Hardin said. "You mean this close to the attack on Starbase Eighteen?"

"Precisely," Spock said.

"The High Command replaced Kritos, because they wanted us to know they did not approve of the action," Number One said.

"That is one possibility," Spock said. "It assumes *Hexar*'s involvement in the attack."

"Which we have no evidence of."

"Kritos is the senior officer in this sector."

"You mean he was." Number One turned to Colt. "Yeoman?"

"Data on General K'Zon coming through now," Colt replied. "Ranking descendant of one of the Great Houses of the Empire. Significant combat experience, fought the Dourami at Kados V, the Andorians at Pelar, nicknamed . . ." Colt's voice trailed off; she shook her head. "The Butcher of Pelar. The translation's not exact, but—"

"One can infer meaning from the approximation," Number One said. "Thank you, Yeoman."

"Putting someone like K'Zon in command . . . that doesn't seem to me like they're interested in mending fences," Hardin said.

"Unless they wish to negotiate from a position of strength," Spock pointed out.

"Multiple scenarios," Number One said. "Multiple possibilities. In any case, Kritos is gone."

"The captain will want to know," Spock said. Pike and the Klingon had spoken on numerous occasions since *Enterprise* had entered the sector. They had developed, judging from the captain's tone when he spoke of Kritos, a grudging respect for each other.

"The captain will want to know," Number One agreed. "Mr. Garrison?"

The lieutenant nodded. "Opening a channel now."

"A most unusual display, sir. Most unusual." Hoto, seated on the cushions just behind him, leaned forward and whispered in Pike's ear. She needn't have bothered; the noise the dancers were making—the various grunts and exclamations, the slap of the feet on floor, the jangling of the massive ornamental jewelry they wore, both male and female—was loud enough to cover any conversation the two of them might have, short of a full-on screaming match.

And the musicians—five of them, four drumming, one playing an amplified string instrument of some sort—were making more than enough of a racket, even in the quieter passages, to take care of that kind of volume as well.

"Note the males, performing in congruent position with the females. To my knowledge, this lacks precedent within the Orion culture," Hoto continued.

The captain nodded. Frankly, there wasn't really precedent for this kind of dancing anywhere he could think of, except for this bar on Optho III that Loman Stocker had dragged him to once. To his eye, the performance was sex—pantomimed animal copulation—played out in public, at a frenetic, almost desperate pace. Time and time again, each of the dancers changing partners every few seconds, moving faster and faster and faster, wearing, the males in particular, glazed, almost drugged expressions. Which could have been acting as well, Pike supposed, a simulation of the males' instinctual reaction to the female pheromones. He guessed it was supposed to be erotic; it didn't feel that way in the slightest to him. Maybe because of the hypo Boyce had given him earlier. Or maybe because he still hadn't been able to rid himself of the feeling that there was something slightly odd, slightly off, about this entire affair, the dance, the reception itself.

That feeling had started the second Pike entered the reception area and saw the buffet, the musicians, and the line of Orions waiting to greet him. Ship's officers and pirates, merchants and free traders, civilians and courtesans, a dizzying display of color and costume, all of whom seemed—for that brief second before they became aware of his presence—as uncomfortable in the moment as he was.

Actually, he'd felt that sense of unease even earlier. As soon as he and the others—Tuval, Smith, Ross, and Hoto—had begun following Liyan and her guards away from where *Magellan* had docked, deeper into the Orion ship. A sense of unease in his gut, which he initially chalked up to simple geometry, to the fact that the corridors aboard *Enterprise*—those within its primary hull, at least, the saucer section of the ship—were all gentle, flowing curves, whereas those on *Karkon's Wing* were all straight lines. Right angles, sharp turns, sections of corridor branching off the main path at what seemed like random intervals. Some of those branching passages had an entirely different look as well, had clearly been put together using different construction techniques, different construction materials, metals of varying composition and color. As they had walked away from *Magellan* (thirty meters straight ahead, one right turn, fifty meters, up one deck, another thirty meters forward, and through the second entry door on their left), it had become clear to Pike that while the Orion ship's exterior lines mimicked a standard *Marauder*-class vessel, inside the configuration was entirely different. *Karkon's Wing* predated the class entirely, was his guess. How old it was exactly . . .

The music stopped.

The three male dancers collapsed to the floor as one. The three females, who had been hidden behind them, stepped forward now, arranging themselves in single file so that seen from head-on, there seemed to be just one of them. The lead female dancer turned to face Liyan, who was seated on the cushioned platform to Pike's immediate left, and bowed.

The tallith stood and began clapping. The rest of the Orions quickly followed suit. Pike and his crew did the same.

"Magnificent," Hoto said. "Truly amazing. I am privileged to have witnessed such a display."

"Thank you," Liyan said.

"I feel the same," Pike said, though what he felt right at that second was more along the lines of impatience than anything else. "But—"

"You wish to discuss the raids. I understand completely." Liyan gestured toward the other side of the room, where tables of food were being wheeled into place. "Shall we do so while dining?"

She smiled at him. Pike smiled back.

During the dance, the captain had had plenty of opportunity to study the tallith close-up, to see that the smoothness of her skin, the sparkle in her eyes, even the sheen of her hair, came from artfully applied makeup and ornamentation. She was older than she'd seemed initially; the veins on the backs of her wrists, the sag of skin along the tendons in her neck, gave away her years, which Pike put closer toward the upper end of Orion middle age . . . whatever that was.

All that being said, though, there was still something about her . . .

"Better to converse on a full stomach," he replied, and fell into step alongside her. His people fell into place behind him. Tuval, Ross, and Smith at least, Pike saw out of the corner of his eye. He heard Hoto still speaking, her voice fading away—it sounded as if she was talking to one of the dancers—as they crossed the room.

"These raids by the Klingons," Pike said. "How many have there been?"

"That I know of"—Liyan pursed her lips—"a half-dozen."

"And were they preceded by any communication from the Empire?"

"No."

"No demands, no clues to why—"

"Why is obvious," Liyan snapped. "They desire our territory. They desire our resources. To rule and exploit our people."

"There has to be something else," Pike said.

"There is nothing," Liyan said.

She stopped walking, all at once. Pike looked up and saw why. Gurgis stood in front of them, blocking their way.

"I must speak with you, Tallith."

"I am occupied."

"It cannot wait."

"Cannot?" She stared the larger man down.

"Should not, Tallith." Gurgis lowered his gaze. "Should not wait."

She frowned. "Very well. Excuse me a moment, Captain," she said to Pike, and drew the larger man off to one side.

Tuval stepped up alongside him. "Guess we know who wears the pants in this family," he whispered into Pike's ear.

The captain nodded. Indeed they did. It was obvious from the body language of the two as they spoke, the tallith leaning forward to make her point, Gurgis lowering his gaze, avoiding eye contact, submissive.

"Excuse me." Pike turned and found himself face-to-face with an enormously fat, blue-skinned Orion.

"You are the human captain?"

"I am. Christopher Pike."

"I am Kax Chelubi. Of the Caju of the same name." The man bowed low and then lifted his head again. Or *was* it a man? Pike wondered. Chelubi's makeup was so heavily laid on, his (her?) body so shapeless underneath the long flowering cloak, the captain had no idea.

Pike spent the next few minutes listening to a litany of complaints from Chelubi, something to do with Federation tariffs on goods coming from the Klingon Empire through the Borderland. Pike kept trying to explain that he had nothing to do with Federation trade policy; the Orion kept making repeated references to "how well" the captain could do for himself were he to reconsider the tariffs.

It took Pike a good few minutes longer than it should have to realize the merchant was trying to bribe him. He was on the verge of telling Chelubi what exactly to do with those bribes when he felt a hand on his arm.

He looked up and saw Tuval. The commander was frowning. He excused himself from the conversation with Chelubi.

"Ben. Something the matter?"

"I was expecting to hear from Collins by now."

"So contact him."

"I tried." Tuval held up his communicator. "He doesn't answer. Nor does Dr. Boyce."

Which pretty much ruled out mechanical failure; the odds of two communicators breaking down at the same time were pretty infinitesimal. What was going on? Easy enough to find out, Pike knew.

"Let's have Liyan contact sickbay. See if we can get an estimate on how much longer the doctor's going to be." Pike turned and saw that the tallith was still deep in conversation with Gurgis.

"No, sir," Tuval said.

"No, sir?" Pike turned back around. "What's that mean?"

"It means I talk to Liyan. And you get back to *Magellan*. Smith?"

The lieutenant suddenly appeared at his side. Where she'd come from, Pike had no idea.

"Sir?" she asked.

"Get the captain back to the shuttle. Try not to make a scene unless you have to, but—"

"Whoa. Hold on a second, Ben." Pike shook his head. "You're overreacting."

"No, sir. I'm following the manual. Standard landing-party protocol. You know it as well as I do."

Pike hesitated. Tuval was right. In potentially hostile territory, get the commanding officer to safety. Rule number one. Pike had made that call himself, several times, back in the day. But—

His communicator chirped.

Pike smiled. "That's probably Boyce now." The captain reached into his back pocket and flipped the communicator open.

"Pike here."

"*Enterprise. Number One. We have just received a transmission from* Hexar."

She filled him in on the situation.

"Not Kritos?"

"*No, sir.*"

"Damn." Pike frowned. What had happened to Kritos? A thousand possibilities ran through his head, none of them good. Kritos not aboard *Hexar*?

This changed everything, as far as he was concerned.

"I want you to contact Starfleet," Pike said. "Talk to Admiral Noguchi personally. Tell him that Kritos has been replaced."

"*Aye, sir.*"

"In the meantime, hold position. Do nothing to aggravate the situation. We're returning to *Enterprise* at once."

"Captain Pike?"

He looked up and saw Liyan.

"There is a problem?" she asked.

"There is. One second, Number One." Pike lowered the communicator to his side. "Klingons. You should be picking them up on your sensors momentarily."

"Klingons."

"Yes. A battle cruiser. I'm afraid we need to return to *Enterprise* immediately. We—"

"Yes. The battle cruiser." Liyan reached out a hand; her fingertips brushed against the skin on the back of his wrist. Her eyes found his. "We have been tracking the ship for some time now, Captain. I assure you, there's no cause for alarm."

All other conversation in the room faded away. Pike suddenly felt himself the center of attention, felt all eyes in the room on him, on Liyan.

"No cause for alarm," he said.

"No." She smiled. "And there is certainly no need to rush back to your ship before finishing our discussions."

Pike felt the frown on his face soften.

Perhaps he was overreacting just a little. Ben was, too, wasn't he? Maybe overcompensating, being extra careful, because he was wearing the shunt? After all, he'd come there to accomplish a specific task, to talk to Liyan, and that task wasn't accomplished, so—

Something in his hand vibrated. Pike looked down and saw the communicator.

Enterprise. Number One. He'd forgotten all about them. How . . .

He looked up at Liyan.

Pheromones.

"I'm sorry," he said, and took a step back from her. "I need to speak with my ship."

Pike flipped open the communicator again. The light on it was flashing red. No signal. What—

"It is I who must apologize, Captain Pike. I had hoped to avoid this scenario. Tactician." She spoke, without turning, to an Orion Pike hadn't noticed before, who stood at her shoulder.

"Majesty."

"Launch the projector. Immediately."

"Yes, Tallith."

She snapped her fingers, and two of her guards stepped forward.

"Take the humans to the medical level," she said, gesturing to her guards, one of whom reached down to draw his weapon even before she finished speaking. "Treatment Room C. Collect the others there, and wait for further—"

The skin on the guard's arm suddenly blistered and blackened and burned away.

"Down!" someone shouted in Pike's ear, Ben's voice. The captain did as he was told and dove to the floor. A phaser beam cut through the air above him; a second later, one of the ceiling support beams crashed to the floor, raising a cloud of dust, cutting them off from the tallith and her guards and most of the others in the room as well.

"Captain!"

He turned and saw Tuval holding his weapon. Ross stood next to him. A handful of bodies surrounded the two of them. One was Smith's. She wasn't moving. No surprise.

Half her head was missing.

"We have to move, sir," Tuval said. "Now."

Pike drew his own phaser and nodded toward the exit.

"*Magellan*," he said. "Let's go."

SEVEN

"Get him back." Number One stood over the communications console, glaring down at Garrison. "Lieutenant—"

"Trying, sir." He was, indeed, little doubt of that. In a variety of admirably inventive ways, all of which Spock was able to monitor, in real time, through the read-outs at his station. None of those methods, unfortunately, had met with any success.

Captain Pike cut off in mid-conversation. The Orion ship had failed to respond to any of their attempts to hail it. A disturbing situation. Spock could see no reason for their failure to communicate. Data coming in from long-range sensors showed the ship to be functioning normally; he could not conceive of why—

The data on his console changed.

Spock raised an eyebrow. "Long-range sensors indicate the approach of two vessels. Closing rapidly."

"Type and position," Number One said.

Spock opened his mouth to answer, and the two vessels, all at once, became three.

"One moment." He overrode standard processor power distribution, diverting all nonessential system resources to the sensor arrays. The data continued to fluctuate. Instrument error? He checked the maintenance logs, noted the last calibration had occurred early that morning, zero-hundred-ten ship's time. Performed by Crewman Reilly, C Shift. Spock trusted Reilly's work; he had spent long hours training the man. His immediate working hypothesis was that this was not a case of equipment malfunction.

"Mr. Spock?" Number One prompted.

"I am receiving contradictory data from *Enterprise*'s instruments, which I am attempting to resolve. One moment, please."

Interstellar anomalies, random subspace energy fluctuations, even certain types of electrically charged space dust, all of these things and half a hundred others were capable of disrupting the delicate energy patterns *Enterprise*'s sensor arrays used to make their calculations. Spock reset the array, rebooting each of the system's processors in turn—a thirty-second process, at the end of which data began arriving at his station once more. The exact same type of contradictory data. Puzzling. Frustrating.

"Spock?" Number One said again, her voice rising.

"My apologies, Commander. Data are still in flux." Which was an understatement; according to his instruments, the ships were changing physical shape from nano-second to nano-second. Impossible, of course.

And then, all at once, the readings stabilized.

"Two Klingon warbirds," Spock announced. "Moving at five-point-two c, on apparent intercept course." He looked up and met Number One's gaze. "Readings appear similar to those observed on Starbase Eighteen's sensor display."

"Before the attack there." Number One frowned. "Same ships."

Spock nodded. "It appears so."

"Red alert, Lieutenant Hardin," Number One snapped, stepping down to the command chair. "All decks."

"Red alert, aye," Hardin said with a certain degree of satisfaction. She punched a button on the console in front of her, and a klaxon began sounding.

Spock reconfigured his workstation, splitting the display in front of him. He assigned current sensor readouts to the right half of the screen; on the left, he began gathering data from the array's storage buffers.

"They didn't come from Adelson," Number One said, stepping up next to him.

"Correct," Spock said.

"So where did they come from?" Number One asked.

"Uncertain. I am currently attempting to plot possible points of origin." Spock set up the necessary variables within the navigation subprocessor; he began flowing in the data, streaming them from both the ship's memory banks and current sensor input.

"They could have been hiding in the Borderland," Hardin said.

Spock replied without turning. "You are suggesting that the Orions and the Empire have made an alliance?"

"It's possible," Hardin said.

Possible, Spock thought. *But unlikely.* He was about to point out why when the data on his screen changed yet again.

"The Orion vessel is moving," he said. "Accelerating to point-seven-three light speed. The Klingons are changing course to follow."

"On screen," Number One said.

"Switching display," he said, and a second later,

the Orion vessel—a blue dot superimposed on the sector map—and the Klingon vessels—two orange dots so close together that they read as a single image— all headed deeper into the Borderland.

The Orion ship suddenly executed a 180-degree turn. The Klingons again moved to follow.

"We've got to go after them," Hardin said.

Number One ignored her. She turned back to Garrison.

"Nothing from the captain?"

"No, sir. Or the Orion ship."

She glanced over at Spock. "Is it possible the Klingons are jamming the signal?"

"It is possible. We are at the limit of effective sensor range."

"Move us closer, Mr. Tyler. Right up to the line. Do not cross into the Borderland."

"The line's pretty fuzzy there," *Enterprise*'s helmsman said.

"Stretch it as close as you can. Mr. Garrison. See if you can raise either of those Klingon vessels."

"Been trying. No response."

"Energy burst," Spock announced. "Weapons fire from one of the Klingon vessels, directed toward *Karkon's Wing*."

"Commander," Hardin said. "All due respect, we can't just—"

"Lieutenant, I need facts now, not opinions. When I want the latter, I will ask for them. Any damage to the Orion vessel, Mr. Spock?" Number One turned in the command chair.

"Calculating now," Spock said. "One moment."

Data flew across one corner of the screen; as Spock processed them, he heard the turbolift door open. He glanced up and saw Pitcairn stride onto the bridge, muttering to himself as he came.

". . . it was them all along, but does anyone listen to me, no one listens to me . . ."

"Mr. Spock?" Number One prompted.

"Minute directional variation in the Orion ship's course. Possibly due to impact, possibly intentional evasive maneuver."

"Rerouting power outlays," Chief Pitcairn said. "Prioritizing weapons and defense systems."

"Ships are continuing to move deeper into the Borderland," Spock said.

Number One abruptly rose from the command chair and strode toward the front of the bridge, toward the main viewscreen. Thinking. Spock did not envy her position. The landing party, including the captain and two of the ship's senior officers, were trapped aboard an alien vessel, itself now the target of hostilities. All communications lost, *Karkon's Wing* was heading deeper into the Borderland, territory forbidden *Enterprise* by terms of Gorengar.

The commander spun around. *"Hexar,"* she said, looking at Garrison. "Get me *Hexar.* Right now."

"The ship is not registering on our sensors at the moment."

"I am aware of that, Lieutenant. I gave you an order. Hail *Hexar,"* she snapped. "Send this message. We are entering the Borderland in response to an attack on our shuttlecraft. Stand by for further information."

"Aye, sir."

Spock frowned. He understood the rationale behind the transmission. Number One was providing diplomatic cover for their actions, a defense for their violation of Gorengar. Diplomatic of her, too, not to directly accuse the Klingons of being responsible for that attack.

Although it was likely that none of those subtleties would matter in the end. Crossing into the Borderland was tantamount to an act of war.

"If we wait for acknowledgment of the transmission," he began, speaking quietly, "that would provide an additional legal basis for—"

"We can't wait," Number One said. "Not a second longer." She sat back down in the command chair. "Ahead sublight, Mr. Tyler," she said. "Let's go get our people."

"Yes, sir," he said, and *Enterprise* shot forward, across the Borderland.

• • •

The sound of weapons fire from above abruptly ceased. Pike heard a sharp intake of breath from Ross, huddled at his back. He refused to allow himself to react emotionally. Emotion would get him nowhere. Emotion wouldn't change the facts.

Tuval had stopped firing, Tuval was dead.

His job now was to make sure Ben hadn't sacrificed himself in vain.

The captain peered around the edge of the doorframe. Six guards, fifty feet in front of him, guarding the entryway to *Magellan*. Facing the wrong direction—Ben's parting gift to him. The commander had gambled that there would be a second access to the deck they'd come in on, not far from the one they'd originally used. He'd offered to stay behind while the captain and Ross went on ahead.

"I'll hold them here," Tuval had said.

Pike had shaken his head. "We stay together."

"Then we die."

"He's right, Captain." Ross had stepped forward. "It should be me who stays. You two are more important."

"The hell with that." Tuval had glared at her. "Standard emergency protocol. Security commander gives the orders, and my orders are go. Now. While you can."

Pike had heard footsteps down the hall, heading in their direction. Fast.

He had looked at Ben. "Good luck," he'd said.

Which meant good-bye.

"Same to you." Tuval had turned away.

And he and Ross had run. And here they were. Ben was dead, and it was only now, as the captain replayed that scene in his mind, that he realized the entire time they'd been running, from the second they left the wreckage of the reception room behind, Ben had been laboring for breath. Trying to get oxygen into his lungs. Trying, and failing, just as Boyce had warned. That was why he'd stopped at the ladder. It had nothing to do with strategy and everything to do with the fact that Pike had decided to play God with his officer's life, commit his officer to a mission the man wasn't physically capable of carrying out, and now his officer—

"Captain, why are they doing this, sir?

Ross's whispered voice brought him back to the here and now.

"Your guess is as good as mine, Ensign."

He had no idea what Liyan hoped to gain from all of this. Starfleet would hunt her down no matter where she went. Whatever it was she was after, she wouldn't be around long enough to enjoy it.

Unfortunately, the odds were pretty good at the moment that he wouldn't, either.

Pike considered the situation. They had, for the

moment, the element of surprise. What else? Not much. The phaser in his hand, down to about thirty percent power. Ross's phaser, which was probably running even lower. And their communicators still weren't functional. Not a lot to work with. But it would have to do.

A buzzer sounded. Pike peered around the corner again, saw one of the Orions lower his weapon and walk toward the far wall, toward what looked like a comm panel.

Time to go, Pike thought, eyeing the hatchway to *Magellan.*

He turned his head slightly and whispered to Ross. "Stay behind me. Stay low. Phaser on lowest stun setting. Fire only when you have a clear target. Clear?"

"Clear, sir."

"Good." The Orion was at the comm panel, talking. Frowning. Probably getting the news that Pike and Ross were not where they were supposed to be. The other guards hadn't exactly lowered their weapons, but they had relaxed somewhat. Changed their stances, loosened their grips . . .

Pike fired over their heads, a short, high-power burst directed at the thickest of the pipes dangling from the deck plating overhead. The conduit sheared in half and crashed to the floor. Wires sparked; the Orions jumped back, heads whipping around in confusion.

Pike flipped settings on his weapon, chose a target, and fired. The nearest guard crumpled.

One down.

The captain was moving even as the guard fell, diving forward, rolling, just underneath a volley of weapons fire—phased energy beams, at lethal settings. He could literally feel the heat coming off them as he got to his feet again and fired a second time.

Two down.

"They are here!" the Orion at the comm panel screamed. "Reinforcements! They are here, at the shuttle—"

A phaser blast caught him square in the gut; he flew backward through the air and slammed into the wall. Ross's work—good shooting.

Three down.

Pike raised his own weapon again, and fired.

Four.

The phaser flew from his grip. He looked down and saw that his hand was burning. There was smoke rising from his palm. The skin there was black.

"Captain!"

He turned in time to see Ross take a step out into the middle of the corridor.

He was about to say, "Stay low," and then a beam caught her full on, and she froze, an expression of shock on her face.

She vanished.

Pike lunged for the weapon he'd dropped, grabbed it up with his left hand, ignoring the agony from his right. He could feel the dead, charred skin cracking, oozing; it was pain like he hadn't felt in a good long time, since Gorengar. The captain focused, as best he could, on the weapon in his left hand, which he didn't try to fire. He just threw it, right at one of the two remaining guards, the closer one, who was maybe four meters away. The Orion flinched and pulled his head back even as he was pulling the trigger on his own weapon. The movement made him miss; the energy beam flew over Pike's shoulder. The captain charged straight at the man, staying as close to the wall as he could, positioning himself so that the other guard, six meters away, couldn't fire without hitting his own man.

He tried anyway. The beam struck the near guard in the shoulder. He screamed.

Pike reached him, shoved him aside, and opened the access door to *Magellan*.

He burst into the airlock, turning as he entered and sealing the door behind him.

A second later, it began to glow red. The Orion was firing on it with his weapon. Pike gambled that the door would hold long enough for him to launch. He had no alternative.

He punched the inner hatch control, entered the

ship proper, and fired up the propulsion systems. *No time to do a systems check; no time to set a course; just go.*

He sat, cradling his right hand to his chest, and activated impulse thrusters, at the last second remembering to hit the emergency airlock jettison. He heard the sound of metal tearing, and then the shuttle was away, space in the viewport in front of him.

"*Magellan* to *Enteprise. Magellan* to *Enterprise*. It was a trap, the—"

The console squawked. Failure to transmit. The signal, he saw, was being jammed. Wouldn't matter; once he was a little farther out, *Enterprise* would pick him up on its sensors, and—

Something made him turn, then there was movement at the edge of his field of vision.

He looked behind and to his left, where *Karkon's Wing,* a postage-stamp-sized square of silver against the black of space, was visible.

There was something else there, too, a glinting pinprick of light that suddenly grew to the size of a small moon. And then a much larger one. It was silver as well. Metal. A weapon of some sort, a torpedo—

There was a sudden burst of light, and then he slammed forward into the console. The horrific sound of metal tearing, flames, heat, and then cold.

Nothing but cold, and the vast, empty blackness of space.

• • •

They were ten seconds across the demarcation line, ten seconds into the Borderland, neutral territory at best, Klingon space as a worst-case scenario, when *Hexar* reappeared. Accompanied by half a dozen other Klingon vessels—four warbirds and two heavy cruisers. All had emerged from Adelson at virtually the same instant.

"Enterprise." K'Zon glared down at them from the main viewscreen. *"You are now, by your own admission, in violation of Gorengar treaty. Stand down, and prepare to be boarded."*

"Our captain is aboard the Orion ship *Karkon's Wing,* which is currently under attack," Number One said. "We are in the midst of a rescue mission. I am transmitting copies of relevant communications and sensor readings to you now."

She turned toward Spock, who had already, at her command, prepared the data—the last few minutes of readings from the long-range sensors. He shunted it over to Lieutenant Garrison, who attached the relevant communications entries, encoded the entire package, and sent it on in a data burst.

A moment later, on the viewscreen, a Klingon functionary approached K'Zon and whispered something in his ear.

The general's eyes widened. He stood up and shook

a finger at the viewscreen and, by extension, *Enterprise*'s first officer.

"You accuse us of breaking the treaty?" K'Zon's fury was evident. *"Of launching this cowardly attack?"*

"I have presented you with a set of data," Number One said. "An explanation for which I would be very interested in—"

"Do you know who I am?" K'Zon spluttered. *"You speak to the general who won Narendra for the Empire, who fought back the Dourami, who received the chancellor's own thanks a dozen times over, who—"*

"Perhaps," Spock suggested. "These ships now attacking the Orion vessel are privateers. Not of the Empire."

"You are mistaken, Vulcan," K'Zon said, his expression softening not one single iota. *"No Klingon would fight in this manner."*

"I would not have thought so, either," Number One said. "And yet you work to develop a cloaking device that would enable your ships to engage in just such actions."

K'Zon's eyes widened for a second in surprise. Then his expression—Spock wouldn't have thought such a thing possible—grew even fiercer.

"Now you call me a liar," the general said. *"The time for talk is well and truly finished."*

The viewscreen went dark. The sector map reappeared.

"Here they come," Chief Pitcairn said.

"Indeed," Spock said. The Klingon armada. "On intercept course. At current speed and position, we have roughly forty seconds till they are in firing range."

All eyes turned to Number One, who sat motionless in the command chair, studying the viewscreen.

"Chief," she said, "how long till we're in transporter range of the Orion ship?"

Pitcairn shook his head. "Longer than forty seconds."

"How long exactly? A minute? Two? Because if we can hold them off—"

"Commander," Garrison interrupted. "Incoming transmission. From the Orions."

The lieutenant didn't wait for Number One's command; he put the transmission right up on the viewscreen.

It was Liyan. She was someplace other than the bridge, standing in what appeared to Spock to be a banquet room of some kind, but the ceiling had collapsed, at least partially. The air was filled with dust. He glimpsed bodies on the screen behind her.

One of them wore a Starfleet uniform.

"*Enterprise.*" Liyan brushed back hair from her face and coughed. "*Enterprise,* are you there?"

"Right here," Number One said. "Go ahead."

"I have news," Liyan said, and coughed again. "Tragic news."

The transmission finished—and well executed it had been; she was particularly pleased not just with her performance but with the fact that they had turned the human captain's own destructiveness against him, using the damage he'd caused in the banquet hall as backdrop for the announcement of his death—Liyan returned to the bridge of *Karkon's Wing*, well satisfied with the day's work.

"Status," she demanded, taking a seat in her chair.

"Projector returned to Bay One," her tactical officer declared.

"And the Federation shuttle?"

"The wreckage is there as well."

She nodded. Good to have something tangible to return to the Federation; they would deliver the shuttlecraft to *Enterprise*, accompanied by the bodies they had in their possession. Perhaps the story would need to change slightly—perhaps Pike and his crew had been shot down in the act of escaping by the Klingon ship. Of course, an appropriate number of Orion casualties would need to be manufactured as well. A dozen? Perhaps that number was too low. Two dozen? Three? She would consult her engineers. They would run simulations, come up with a believable figure. The exact number did not matter. The point was, the Federation and the Empire would be at each other's throat shortly. No matter that for now, *Enterprise* had retreated back across the border. Soon enough, the two empires would be plunged into battle, all-out war that would preoccupy them for some time to come. A war that would give her the window she needed to operate freely within the Borderland, to bring the other races within its confines to heel, to consolidate power among her own people. To restore the glory of that era, long forgotten, when the Orions were the feared power within this quadrant.

And she—tallith of all clans, rightful descendant and heir to K'rgon's throne—would lead them.

Pride swelled within her; strength coursed through her body. She felt the blood rush through her veins.

She glanced down at her arms and saw the slight darkening of those veins, emerald green against the lime of her skin.

And she was reminded again that all of her plans—everything—depended on *Enterprise*'s doctor living up to his reputation. Speaking of which . . .

"I will be in the medical wing. You will alert me when we are prepared to return the wreckage," she said, standing. "Otherwise, I do not wish to be disturbed."

The officer lowered his head. "Of course, Tallith."

She was halfway to the exit when something occurred to her. "Tactician. A further exception."

"Yes, Tallith."

"If the Klingons and Federation ships begin firing on each other . . ."

"Yes?"

"That I would like to see."

"Of course, Tallith."

They shared a smile, and she left the control room.

BOOK II

DESCENT

EIGHT

Three days after the shuttle's loss—two days after *Excalibur* and *Hood* had come out of warp, twenty-six hours after Captain Vlasidovich had, at Admiral Noguchi's direction, taken command of both *Enterprise* and the nascent UFP fleet now assembling in orbit around 55-Hamilton—Spock was summoned to the briefing room.

He found the new captain and Number One waiting for him. Vlasidovich—a short, stocky man, with a thick head of black, bushy hair, prematurely streaked with gray—sat at the head of the table, a stack of flimsies at his right hand, Number One leaning over his right shoulder.

"Come, come." Vlasidovich spoke without looking up. "I am just reviewing files, Mr. Spock. One moment."

"Of course, sir." Spock clasped his hands behind his back and stood at the far end of the table. Flimsies. Spock had heard of Vlasidovich's preference for studying hard copy whenever possible; he found it puzzling, inefficient.

"We will reroute here and here." Vlasidovich's index finger stabbed at the flimsy in front of him. "More power for the main weapons batteries."

"Yes, sir," said Number One. "I'll bring these to Chief Pitcairn."

"Thank you. I would like this accomplished by ship's dinner. Chief is to tell me if that is a problem, yes?" Vlasidovich smiled, handing her the top flimsy.

Another rumor Spock had heard, now proven to be true. Vlasidovich had a very thick accent.

Enterprise's new commanding officer was from Nova Vestroia, a small colony on the edge of the Alpha Centauri system, one of the first asteroids Starfleet had successfully terraformed. It was settled exclusively by emigrants from what had been part of old Russia. Vlasidovich's grandfather was the leading political figure in Nova Vestroia's history; the list of his accomplishments, of the crises he'd managed to resolve without resorting to violence, was an impressive one. His son, Captain Vlasidovich's father, had been an accomplished politician as well. *Enterprise*'s new commander had a legacy to live up to. Spock hadn't had the time to review Vlasidovich's files in detail, but from what he'd seen, the man was well on his way to doing just that. Youngest captain in the fleet, battlefield promotions on two separate occasions, a commendation from Starfleet intelligence . . .

"If that's all, sir . . ." Number One said.

"Yes, yes, dismissed, Number One." Vlasidovich waved a hand. "Thank you."

"Thank you, Captain." Number One walked past Spock without meeting his eyes.

Over the last two days, since *Magellan*'s destruction, the two of them had not spoken more than half a dozen words. It seemed to Spock that the ship's first officer had gone out of her way to avoid him. They were not close, but still . . .

He found her behavior puzzling for a human.

"So." Vlasidovich stood. "You will forgive me, please, for being unable to speak with you earlier, Mr. Spock? This is how you prefer to be called, yes?"

"Yes." Spock nodded. He had tried, immediately upon Vlasidovich's assumption of command, to meet privately with the captain and had been rebuffed. Other than at the services yesterday—a few, brief, inconsequential words—this was the first chance the two of them had had to speak.

Vlasidovich smiled. "I have been reviewing your file"—he pulled another flimsy off the pile and quickly scanned it—"and noticed an alternative possibility."

"Indeed." The Vulcan raised an eyebrow.

"Yes. Indeed." Vlasidovich smiled again—he did a lot of that, Spock noticed, very different from Captain Pike in that regard—and then spoke, flawlessly, all syllables correctly accented and pronounced, Spock's family name, which included consonant sounds that human beings supposedly were incapable of making with the physical structures contained within their bodies.

Spock couldn't think of a thing to say. He was, quite frankly, astonished.

Vlasidovich laughed, a sound that surprised Spock once more.

Captain Pike, to his recollection, had never laughed.

"As a young man, I have been three years on Vulcan," Vlasidovich said. "Studying at Science Academy, an exchange program, between our peoples."

"Your pronunciation is letter perfect."

"Thank you. Of course, I am showing off. Not all crew will want to call you this name—yes?"

"Not all crew will be capable of calling me by that name."

"To be sure. Perhaps we can discuss Academy further, yes? Tomorrow evening?"

"Tomorrow evening?"

"Dinner I am giving. Senior staff. *Enterprise, Excalibur, Hood.* You will attend, yes?"

A rhetorical question, obviously.

"Of course, sir."

"Excellent." The smile disappeared from Vlasidovich's face. "So. To business. You have been researching Klingon weapon capabilities, I am told."

"That is correct."

"I am awaiting your report."

"I have routed a preliminary draft to you for approval."

"And I appreciate that. But . . ." Vlasidovich gestured to the stack of flimsies. "As you may notice, I have preference for hard copy."

"I will have a member of my department bring you flimsy within the hour."

"Thank you." Vlasidovich sat back down at his chair and turned his attention to the printout next to him. "I look forward to seeing it. In the meantime, I would like a short summary, your own words, of your findings."

Short. The word gave Spock pause. Its meaning was imprecise. To his instructors at Shi'Kahr, short had meant two thousand words. To Admiral Pranang, aboard *Orpheus,* it meant a few hundred words. To

Captain Pike, ten seconds or less. "Compress the information," he had said repeatedly. "Give me the essentials. Don't try to impress me with what you know. With the work you did. Tell me what I need to know. Make my job easier."

Many of *Enterprise*'s human crew felt Pike was unnecessarily brusque at times. Spock did not agree. Brevity was indicative of careful, concise thought—a trait to be admired, in his opinion.

"In brief, the report is largely speculation, Captain," Spock said.

"That is hardly a report, Mr. Spock. Elaborate, please." Vlasidovich spoke without looking up.

So much for brevity.

"The report consists largely of rumor and innuendo, secondhand conversations. There is scant independently verifiable data."

"There is image of cloaking device. This Black Snow. That is primary source, yes?"

"Yes. We have nothing else, however, from what would be considered primary sources. Data from weapons laboratories, experimental procedures, statements by Klingon scientists—"

"Difficult to obtain, primary source material. From within Klingon Empire."

"Undoubtedly."

"Next to impossible, I am told. Klingons are quite—what is word?—paranoid about their weapons.

Quite passionate. Question is, is secondary intelligence reliable?"

"One must consider the source."

"Exactly. And source in this instance is . . ."

"Starfleet Intelligence."

"And . . . your opinion of this secondary intelligence?"

Spock hesitated a second before answering.

Vlasidovich had not stopped reading—his eyes continued to scan the page on the table before him—and yet Spock sensed the captain's attention focused on him at least as much as on the flimsy.

Vlasidovich's service record for the two years immediately following his commendation from Starfleet Intelligence was surprisingly bare; the record of his movements—from border system to galactic hotspot, from isolated outpost to Starfleet Command and back again on multiple occasions—much less so. Those movements suggested to Spock a strong connection to Starfleet intelligence had been forged in the wake of the commendation; the Vulcan suspected, perhaps, that the Captain had spent those two years working for Intelligence. That kind of thing, though, would never show up in an unclassified service record.

Nonetheless, Spock had little doubt as to Vlasidovich's own opinion about the veracity of the information they were now discussing.

The Vulcan cleared his throat and spoke.

"I see no inherent contradiction between intelligence and espionage, sir."

A deliberately neutral response. One that avoided the question more than answered it.

The captain looked up and smiled. "Well, speculation or not, we must take everything in report into account. Particularly cloaking device. Black Snow."

"Yes, sir."

"Could change balance of power between our forces. If it is real."

"Regarding the device's existence—it is, of course, logical to err on the side of caution, sir."

"Agreed. We do not know what Klingons are up to exactly. Luckily for us, they are in same boat, yes? Regarding our own weapon developments?" He moved one stack of flimsy aside and reached for another. "Thank you, Mr. Spock. I will review hard copy of report as soon as I have it. Dismissed."

He turned his attention back to the page. Spock didn't move. It took the captain a good five seconds to realize that.

He looked up again and frowned. "There is more?"

"There is. I would like your permission to examine Captain Pike's logs, sir."

"His personal logs?"

"Yes, sir."

"May I ask why?"

"I have been considering the totality of Captain Pike's actions since the attack on Starbase Eighteen. His words and his deeds. He seemed singularly inclined to the belief that the Klingons were not involved in that attack."

"Ah, I see. You suspect logs may contain reasons for this belief."

"Yes, sir."

Vlasidovich sighed and pushed back his chair from the table. "Mr. Spock. Christopher Pike and I, we are in same class at Academy. He has told you stories, I am sure. Myself, Loman Stocker, Michaela Harrari . . ."

"No, sir."

"This is fact? No stories?" Vlasidovich smiled slightly. "Ah. Of course he has not. Christopher Pike—he was private man. Very private. Never could you tell exactly what he was thinking. Always at Academy, teachers are telling him, speak up, speak up. Explain yourself. But he was man of few words, Captain Pike."

"Yes, sir."

"Few words but well-chosen ones. Chris Pike was brilliant man." Vlasidovich sighed again. "Before we arrive—*Excalibur, Hood*—he has sent message to us. Myself, Michaela, Captain Harrari."

Hood's commanding officer. Spock had yet to meet her or Commander Nolan, Vlasidovich's former first officer, who was now captaining *Excalibur*.

" 'I have reason,' Captain Pike says, 'to believe Klingons not involved in attack on Starbase Eighteen.' So, when I am transferred here, to *Enterprise,* first thing I try to do is examine these logs. The same ones you wish to see." Vlasidovich shook his head. "You will note I say 'try.' "

"Yes, sir."

"I am unable to do so. Records have already been transferred to custody of Starfleet Archives."

"Such transfer is not unusual," Spock said. "You should be able to request copies—"

"I am familiar with procedure, Mr. Spock. Request was made immediately. And denied—just as fast."

"Were you able to ascertain why?"

"I was able to ascertain nothing. No explanation was given." The captain pulled a stack of flimsy toward him, straightening its edges. "Now, please. We both have considerable work to do. Klingon fleet is continuing to gather in Adelson. *Lexington* and *Potemkin* are en route to join us. I need flimsy of weapons report. I need you to consider strategies coordinating ship's processing power with Science Officer Radovitch on *Excalibur . . .*"

Spock understood. He was being dismissed.

"Yes, sir," he said, turned on his heel, and left without another word.

There was indeed, as Vlasidovich put it, considerable work to do. But Spock was Vulcan—in truth, only half Vulcan. Nevertheless, he had the ability to adjust his metabolism so that he could function without sleep for a considerable length of time. Long enough both to accomplish the tasks required of him by his station aboard *Enterprise* and to find out why access to Captain Pike's logs was restricted. What could they contain? Vlasidovich was unable to help him discover that.

Fortuitously enough, though, Spock knew someone who could.

The science officer worked through the rest of his shift. And beyond. Discussed his report on Klingon weapons development at length with Pitcairn and Lieutenant Hardin, who, in lieu of any more senior officer, was now *Enterprise*'s security chief (temporarily, Spock hoped—the young woman displayed an unseemly eagerness for battle, in his opinion). Transmitted a suggested processor-sharing protocol to *Hood* and *Excalibur,* assisted his staff in arranging for suspension of all unnecessary scientific experiments, attended a service for Lieutenant Hoto—the second one in as many nights—and then, and only then, re-

turned to his quarters and had Ensign Janoth, C Shift
communications, open a channel for him to Earth—
San Francisco—at which point Spock activated an
encryption protocol of his own design and waited for
response.

The protocol was based on imagery rather than
a numeric sequence. Images drawn from a shared
heritage—a variant of the Vulcan script, a series of lines
and circles that he had been told by more than one
human resembled musical notation.

This particular sequence of symbols represented
Spock's family name, written as it had been written
thousands of years ago, before the Awakening, before
the time of Surak, who had led his people from the
brink of catastrophic, planet-destroying war onto
the path of peace. There were four symbols missing
from the script now displayed on the monitor in his
quarters.

As Spock watched, those missing symbols began
to appear, one by one, traced onto the screen by the
person at the other end of the scrambled transmission
he had initiated.

There was a faint, barely audible beep, and the symbols disappeared.

A Vulcan female, of late middle age, her hair gone
completely white and pulled back from her face by a
decorative *annahk*—a headband meant to mimic the

ceremonial circlet worn by the priestesses of old—
appeared on the screen.

"Greetings, T'Koss," Spock said.

"Greetings, Spock." She seemed, to his eye, somewhat agitated.

"I have caught you at an inopportune moment, I
fear."

"No. I have been expecting your call."

"Something is amiss?" he said. "Sarek?"

T'Koss was his father's cousin. His source for news
about Sarek, since father and son had disagreed over
Spock's decision to forgo further training at the Vulcan
Science Academy in favor of joining Starfleet. Spock's
one great fear, never voiced, rarely even contemplated,
was that the two of them would not have the chance to
reconcile in this lifetime. That the admiration he felt
for Sarek—the honor and respect for the diplomacy
his father had made his life's work—would go forever
unvoiced.

"On the contrary. Your father is quite well," T'Koss
said. *"He has been named ambassador to Earth."*

Spock nodded. "You will pass on my congratulations, should you have occasion to see him."

*"I am on my way to see him now. The humans are
giving a reception."* Which explained the fact that she
was in civilian garb, rather than a Starfleet uniform. But
not her obvious agitation.

"I will be brief, then," Spock declared. "Starfleet has taken custody of Captain Pike's personal logs, which I believe might contain information critical to resolution of the current crisis."

T'Koss nodded. *"I am aware of this development."*

Spock was not surprised. T'Koss was a senior archivist; there was little that occurred within the facility that she was not aware of.

"Can you assist me in obtaining copies of these logs?"

She shook her head. *"Regretfully, no."*

"May I ask why?"

"They have been encrypted by order of Admiral Noguchi."

Now Spock was taken aback. If Noguchi was involved in this, clearly, the logs contained something of considerable import.

"T'Koss," he said hesitantly. "Under normal circumstances, I would not ask such a thing, but—"

"The logs are encrypted, Spock. As I said. Even if I were to supply you with the raw data—"

"It is likely I could break the encryption."

"Spock." She shook her head and regarded him affectionately.

This was the one drawback to his communications with T'Koss, the Vulcan thought. She tended to treat him sometimes like the little boy he had been when they first met.

"You may not be aware, but recently I received level A7 certification, which—"

"*I am aware,*" she interrupted. "*And I am remiss in not passing on my congratulations. However, Admiral Noguchi has utilized the Daystrom protocol to encrypt Captain Pike's logs.*"

"Daystrom?"

"*Yes.*"

"As in Richard Daystrom."

"*Yes.*"

Spock frowned. In all of Starfleet, he had been the fourteenth person to receive the level A7 certification. Daystrom had been the first. The man was now said to be within reach of the A8 level. He would be the first organic being to achieve such a distinction.

Logic suggested that Spock had little chance of breaking any code Daystrom had designed. At least for this mission.

"Copies of the logs would do me no good, then," he said.

"*That is correct.*"

So he would have to obtain the information he sought in a different manner. One possibility occurred to him immediately: the method he had used to recover the station logs from Starbase 18. It was possible that within *Enterprise*'s own data buffers—

"*Now. In reference to your previous query,*" T'Koss said.

Spock frowned. "My previous query?"

"Regarding Starbase Eighteen?"

"I made no such query."

T'Koss was silent a moment before responding. *"An errant assumption on my part. The request came from* Enterprise. *I had thought you behind it. Forgive me."*

Spock's curiosity was piqued. "What is this query you speak of?"

"It is a trivial matter." She glanced down and tugged at the sleeves of her gown. *"I shall respond through standard channels."*

Spock was about to probe further when T'Koss looked up, and their eyes met for a brief second before she turned away.

What he saw there gave him pause.

It was a myth that Vulcans could not lie, a commonly held misconception. Vulcans could, in fact, lie with the best of them. It was simply that the path of logic they had chosen to follow led them, almost inevitably, to speak the truth, except on the rarest of occasions.

Spock saw instantly that this "trivial matter," as T'Koss had put it, was one of those occasions.

Not so trivial at all, perhaps.

"T'Koss," he began.

"I am sorry, Spock. I must end our conversation. I am expected at the reception." Once more, she avoided eye contact; he understood then that there would be no point in further questioning.

He raised his right hand and formed the Vulcan salute. "Live long and prosper, T'Koss."

She returned the salutation. "Peace and long life." The screen went black.

Puzzling. Disturbing.

He had contacted T'Koss in the hope of solving one mystery, only to encounter a second. A query regarding Starbase 18? Involving what, specifically? And made by whom?

Spock rose from his chair and sought the sanctity of meditation to focus his thoughts.

NINE

B oyce got to his feet.

Someone was coming. Several someones. Footsteps echoed in the hallway outside his cell.

The doctor smoothed back his hair, arranged his
features into what he hoped was a suitably menacing
scowl, and folded his arms across his chest. Collins's
blood still stained his shirt; there were other stains on
his clothes as well. Dirt. Grease. From being dragged
halfway across the ship. And he stank. Good God, he
stank. He needed a shower and fresh clothes.

He needed a weapon.

He needed to take at least one of these people with
him—Gurgis was his top choice—when he died.

The energy curtain—a force field of green light that colored the corridor outside his cell a pale, sickly shade of green—switched off. Its ever-present hum stopped. Boyce heard noises from elsewhere in the ship. The first time in a day, at least. He smelled fresh—relatively fresh, at least—air.

Two Orions stepped into his cell. Males. Big ones.

But not Gurgis. Boyce was disappointed.

He'd woken up in there after Gurgis's attack, after the man had killed Collins. How much time had passed Boyce didn't know exactly. A few days, he guessed; he had no way to record the passage of time—no meals, no visitors, no sensory input of any kind. Just the gun-metal gray walls of the cell, the sickly green of the corridor outside, the hole in the floor that served as his toilet, and the tap that supplied him water.

There had been three interruptions to the monotony.

The first had come a few hours after he'd woken up, when a handful of Orions ran past his cell, panicked looks on their faces. Boyce had screamed at them to stop, to let him out. Anyone running from the powers-that-be on this ship had to be a friend of his, but they hadn't even once glanced in his direction. Part of their haste was understandable—the ship was under attack. The doctor had felt it shake with the impact of weapons fire more than once since he'd awakened, felt the sudden ebb and flow of gravity characteristic of a ship engaged in battle. *Enterprise,* he had thought, and began counting down in his mind the time (minutes, he suspected, not hours) that would pass before he was rescued. Until Captain Pike or Commander Tuval appeared at his cell door, smiling, and let him out.

But the minutes became hours, and the hours days, and he realized that the battle, if it even was with *Enterprise* or some other Federation ship, had not gone the way he'd hoped.

The second interruption had come some time later, after the doctor had woken and fallen asleep twice more. Petri appeared in the corridor, out of breath himself, accompanied by two guards who looked around nervously as he talked.

"My apologies, Dr. Boyce. After the incident—the attack—we moved you here for your own safety. Gurgis. He—his clan—"

"Get me out of here," Boyce said.

"I'm sorry to say it isn't entirely safe yet."

"I don't care."

"I will be back," Petri said. "I will be back."

The man had run off then, before Boyce had a chance to say a word, to ask any of the myriad questions running through his mind, though Petri did indeed, as he had vowed, return later . . . in a manner of speaking.

Gurgis brought him. The third interruption.

Boyce heard the man coming before he saw him, heard heavy, ominous-sounding footsteps over the din of the energy curtain's generator. The giant had appeared in the hall, carrying something in his hand. It was only when he'd turned to face Boyce that the doctor realized what it was.

Petri. Or, rather, the little man's severed head.

Gurgis laughed then and tossed it aside, sent it tumbling down the corridor in one direction, as he turned and walked off in the other.

Boyce had stood there a moment, legs trembling, wondering what sort of madness he had fallen into. There was some kind of infighting going on aboard the ship, obviously. Clan wars, a struggle for power, for dominance, among the Orions themselves. Gurgis on one side and Petri—and the tallith?—on the other.

They really were savages, he thought. Sex-crazed, blood-lusting savages.

Well, if it was blood they wanted . . .

"Back," one of the guards growled, gesturing with his weapon. Boyce had stepped to the front of the cell when the curtain lowered; they obviously didn't want him there.

He glowered and stood his ground.

"Back!" the guard snapped, preparing to raise his weapon again.

Boyce prepared to move.

Part of the training Starfleet had put him through before he'd been allowed into the service. Hand-to-hand combat. Boyce was under no illusions about his ability, particularly given the fact that he hadn't eaten in several days, but still . . .

He had the element of surprise here. The last thing these guards would expect would be for the old guy in front of them to—

The guards stepped aside. Liyan entered the cell.

"What do you want?" he asked her.

"I came to apologize. For your treatment these last few days. It was for your own safety, I assure you."

Boyce grunted. The tallith wore a military uniform; he was half expecting to see Klingon insignia on it. The two—Empire and Confederacy—had made common cause: the attack on Starbase 18 was proof. He wondered if *Enterprise* had found out.

"Order has been restored."

"Wonderful. Where's Captain Pike? And the rest of the landing party?"

"You must be hungry. The guards will take you to more comfortable quarters, and then—"

"Where," he interrupted, drawing the word out so it was two syllables, "is Captain Pike?"

Liyan's eyes flashed. Clearly, she was not used to being interrupted. "Your captain is dead."

"What?"

"Not something I intended, believe me. An accident, more than anything else. It was my hope that I could obtain his—and your—cooperation with the matter at hand."

Boyce, almost without being aware of doing so, sat back on the cot. Captain Pike dead. He felt as if he'd been punched in the stomach.

"Dr. Boyce."

He looked up. Liyan was standing over him.

"I apologize. I sympathize—empathize—with your loss. But time is pressing. And we have much to discuss."

"No, we don't."

"You're wrong about that."

"Really?" He shook his head. "I don't think so."

Liyan motioned to one of the guards behind her. He left the room, returning almost immediately with yet another guard, much smaller, whom he suddenly shoved forward. The smaller guard stumbled and collapsed onto the cell floor, which was when Boyce realized the smaller guard was, in fact, not a guard at all.

It was Lieutenant Hoto.

Boyce fell to his knees and rolled her over.

She was still in her Starfleet uniform—what was left of it, at least. The tunic was burned in several places, torn off at the sleeves. She was barefoot. She stank worse than he did.

Black-and-blue marks all over her face. She'd been beaten. That wasn't the worst of it, though. She was wounded. A phaser burn about four inches long on the upper part of her left arm, a bad one. The flesh was black. The wound was infected, oozing. The skin around it was alternating shades of blue and red.

He looked up at the tallith. For a second, he was too angry to speak. He got control of himself.

"What have you done to her?"

"Nothing. Neither I nor any of those loyal to me would ever perform such atrocities. When the Sing-hino attacked—"

"You killed those people at Starbase Eighteen." He got to his feet again and advanced on her. "What was that, another accident?"

One of the guards stepped forward. "Back, human," he said.

"Doctor, please." Liyan shook her head. "I will ex-plain what occurred at Starbase Eighteen to you when we dine. At present—"

"Dine." He shook his head and gestured toward Lieutenant Hoto. "I'm not dining with you. This woman needs treatment. Now."

The tallith nodded. "Yes. And we need to speak."

"It's like that, is it?"

"It's exactly like that."

He felt his blood begin to boil over again.

"What is it you want?" Boyce asked.

"Just to talk. As I said."

He doubted that. But what kind of choice did he have in the matter?

"Fine. Take us to the treatment center, and then—"

"We can treat the woman," Liyan said, "while you talk to me."

"No." Boyce got to his feet. "I want to see this done right. It won't take long."

"How long?"

"An hour at most, to get her stable."

That was a lie. He had no intention of helping this monster with anything.

"You can have forty-five minutes." She turned to the guard. "Take them to the treatment facility, then bring the doctor to my quarters. Forty-five minutes."

The guard nodded. "Forty-five minutes, Tallith. It shall be as you say."

She left.

Boyce knelt down once more and helped Hoto to her feet.

The treatment took less time than expected. Mostly because he had to amputate Lieutenant Hoto's arm. He had no choice in the matter. The infected tissue had to go, and he had nothing to replace it with. No regen gel.

He left Hoto lying on a screened-off cot in one of the large treatment areas, doped up with enough provoline to keep her unconscious for at least the next couple of hours, and followed the guard, heading up through the ship this time. They moved down a nondescript corridor on the ship's upper deck, up to a nondescript door, and on through. He tried to keep his anger in check the whole time.

That anger, though, began to dissipate the second he saw the food.

Platters of it, bowls of it, laid out on a table the size of the one back in *Enterprise*'s briefing room. His stomach rumbled.

"Dr. Boyce. Please join me."

Liyan was at the table's head; she wore now what she had worn when the *Magellan* landing party had first come aboard: a gray dress, a matching robe, a circlet of gold in her hair. She gestured to the seat nearest her.

Boyce took it, noting the presence of two other women in the room. Younger, beautiful, dressed—barely—in matching outfits. One stood at the tallith's shoulder, a bottle in her hands. As Boyce approached, she poured from that bottle into Liyan's glass and then into his.

The other woman pulled out his chair for him; as he sat, she pushed it back in. Her hair was long and dark. It brushed against the side of his neck, his shoulder.

Boyce wished he could have changed. Bathed.

"This is Vaya," Liyan said, gesturing towards the dark-haired woman as she stepped back from the table. "And Nee'An. They will be serving us tonight."

Boyce nodded hello to both. The dark-haired woman, Vaya, smiled slightly and stared straight into his eyes. She stared long enough that Boyce began to feel uncomfortable. He shifted in his chair.

"I think you'll recognize some of these dishes," Liyan said. "That one there, for instance."

Boyce squinted across the table. "Is that *tadeesh*?"

"It is. Not fresh, I'm afraid—that's not a food that travels well, but . . ."

"I wasn't aware it traveled at all."

Vaya picked up the bowl and brought it to him. The smell brought back memories. His first few years on Argelius, he'd practically lived on this stuff. It couldn't be the real thing, though, a bowl this big; the real thing was a delicacy.

"Please." Liyan gestured. "Go ahead."

Boyce struggled with his conscience for about two seconds. Then he nodded. Vaya filled his plate, and Boyce dug in. It was delicious, better than he remembered.

"More, Doctor?" Vaya asked.

"Please. I haven't had *tadeesh* in—I don't know how many years."

"Seventeen, by my count," Liyan said.

"What?"

"Argelius. That's when you were last there. Isn't it?"

Boyce did the math in his head. "That's right. But how do you know about Argelius?"

"The work you did there—quite remarkable, Doctor. Bringing an entire continent back to life."

"That's an exaggeration."

"Is it?" She sipped her drink. "When you arrived, the area was a radioactive wasteland. Seven years later, there were half a dozen populated settlements."

"It took hundreds of people to do that."

"But you laid the groundwork. You decoded the genomes. You fixed that which had been broken. The DNA of dozens of living creatures. Plants, animals . . . what you did there borders on the miraculous."

"It's science," Boyce said. "Nothing miraculous about it."

"Something you could repeat, then, I take it. Without too much difficulty?"

"What's that mean?"

She smiled. "Eat first, Doctor. Then we can talk. Vaya"—she gestured to the girl who'd brought him the *tadeesh*—"will see to your needs."

The girl stepped forward again and bowed her head. She was not, Boyce noticed, wearing a great deal of clothing.

"I am yours to command, Doctor," she said, and met his eyes.

Boyce was suddenly acutely aware of her presence and his own reaction to it.

Pheromones.

He shoved his plate away.

"Let's just cut to the chase," he said, turning to Liyan. "What is it that you want from me?"

The smile stayed on Liyan's lips, but all trace of amusement vanished from her eyes. "All business now, Doctor, is that it?"

"That's it."

"Very well. Leave us," she said to the two women, who bowed quickly and did just that. "You, too." She spoke to the guard at the door.

"Majesty," he began hesitantly. "I—"

"Leave!" Liyan said, getting to her feet. "Now!"

Boyce slid the knife at his place setting from the table onto his lap.

The man bowed and exited. Leaving the two of them alone. Himself and the woman who'd killed Jaya. And Pike. And close to a hundred other innocent people, give or take.

"Why did you attack Starbase Eighteen?" Boyce asked. "Was it for the LeKarz?"

"In a manner of speaking." She sat back down; Boyce did, too.

"What's that mean?"

"For the LeKarz . . . and for my people."

"Your people. Seems like some of your people are not on the same page as you are."

"The Singhino." She practically spat the word out. "They are trapped in the old ways. The old patterns of thinking. Clan against clan. Whereas I seek something more for our people. *All* of our people. It scares them."

"I don't understand."

"The Singhino—and many of the other clans—are scared. Fearful. They remain apprehensive that my attempts at restoring the glory of our Empire will end in disaster."

Boyce remembered Hoto's briefing on the shuttle; it seemed like a lifetime ago.

"You're talking about the Second Empire," he said.

She smiled. "Exactly. Under K'rgon, the Borderland was ours. I would make it so again."

Boyce understood now. "Which is where the alliance with the Klingons comes in."

"Alliance? With the Klingons?" She looked amused. "What gave you such a ridiculous idea?"

"The attack on Starbase Eighteen, for starters."

"The attack. Ah, of course. The sensor images. The Klingon warbirds."

"That's right."

"They were manufactured."

"I don't understand."

"You will. The Empire and the Orions—we are not allies, Doctor. Quite the contrary, in fact."

Boyce wasn't sure whether to believe her or not. Manufactured sensor images. He'd never heard of such a thing.

Liyan held up her glass, which had only a fingerful of the bright red liquid left in it. "You know what I am drinking?"

"No."

"Firewine."

"Never heard of it."

"It's a Klingon beverage. It's become quite popular among my crew, among many of the Caju. Within the next few years, I expect it to become one of the most heavily traded commodities in this sector." She set the glass down. "The Klingons are deliberately underpricing it now, selling it at a loss to ensure that it spreads. Trade to them is but another method of warfare. Their history is full of such examples, Doctor. Economic expansion, territorial aggrandizement . . . they plan to take over this part of space as well, no doubt. The entire Borderland will be theirs. Unless we stop them."

"We."

"The Federation. And the Orions. Working together."

Boyce almost laughed. There was no *we*. Not after Starbase 18.

"You missed something," he said.

"What?"

"Your little biography of me. You missed something. Someone."

"What do you mean?"

"Jaya," Boyce said. "My daughter."

It was the first time he'd spoken her name out loud since learning of the attack. Somehow, he managed to keep his voice from cracking.

"Your daughter."

"Yes."

"She wasn't mentioned in any of the databases. Or in your personnel record."

"She was from Argelius," Boyce said. "I adopted her there."

"I see. And this is relevant how?"

"She was a doctor," he said, and now his voice did crack, and a picture flashed across his mind, the one he kept in his quarters, the picture of the two of them at her graduation ceremony. "Like father, like daughter," Mark Piper had said when he snapped it. Only now—

"Dr. Jaya Wandruska," said Liyan.

"Yes. Her married name."

"She was assigned to Starbase Eighteen. Of course." Liyan nodded. "That is the reason your work on

Argelius was continually referred to in her files. It makes sense now."

Part of Boyce knew that what Liyan was saying was important, that it was related to the whole reason he was there, the whole reason she'd contacted *Enterprise* in the first place.

Part of him didn't care at all.

"You killed her," he said.

"Unfortunately, I did." The tallith frowned. "This complicates matters."

"Not for me. For me, it makes them a whole lot simpler."

Boyce pulled the knife out from his lap.

Liyan's eyes widened.

He lunged.

TEN

Liyan had seen his clumsy attempts to hide the weapon; she had expected then what was happening now. Idiot. Did he take her for a fool? Did he think she would leave herself unprotected if there was any danger?

Even after Boyce drew the knife, she waited, hoping that he would think better of attacking her. But when he lunged . . .

She moved, too. The serum flowed through her veins, lending her speed, strength. The human's efforts were like a child's. The knife flashed forward, and she seized his wrist.

His eyes widened in surprise. She bent his arm back, and he dropped the weapon. It fell to the floor between them.

She stared at it and felt the blood pounding in her veins, felt the strength circulating in her body. She was tallith; true heir of K'rgon. It was her destiny to rule not just the Orions but the entire galaxy, as K'rgon had in the times of old. That this human dared attack her . . . she had a moment of wanting to pick the weapon up herself, to turn it on Boyce.

Their eyes met. She saw fear within his, fear and surprise. And then his gaze shifted.

"Your arm." He pointed.

Liyan looked down.

Her arm. The veins on it were visibly pulsing, the skin around them darkening.

She felt a tinge of fear. That it was happening this soon, after the last treatment . . .

Time was growing short.

"The girl in the medical wing, Deleen," Boyce said. "The same thing was happening to her."

"Yes."

"What's causing it?" The doctor was frowning. His anger, for the moment, dissipated. He was curious, Liyan saw.

Perfect.

"Come with me," she said. "And I will show you."

What in the hell was going on here?

It wasn't just the fact that Liyan had overpowered him but the way she had done it, the speed with which she moved. Boyce had dealt with other species with accelerated metabolism before, but they were all strictly nonhumanoid. With Liyan, though there must be some sort of enhancement going on here. She must have taken some sort of drug, had some kind of genetic augmentation that enabled Liyan to move the way she had.

Either that, or he was getting old a lot faster than he thought.

"Zai Romeen, Doctor. Have you heard of it?"

Boyce shook his head. "Can't say as I have."

They were walking side-by-side down the corridor, Liyan's guards a few paces behind.

"No reason you should have, I suppose," she said. "It's a single-planet star system on the far edge of the Borderland, several months' travel time from here, even at warp six. We stumbled across it in the wake of our first major clash with the Klingons. Our four marauders, armed to the teeth. Invincible. Or so we thought." Her voice hardened. "The Empire taught us differently. We—this ship, *Karkon's Wing*—were the only one of the four to escape."

"Why are you telling me this?" Boyce asked.

She glanced sideways at him and smiled. "Zai Romeen was where we came out of warp. Not on purpose, mind you. The engines simply stopped working. And there we were, stranded in the middle of nowhere. Without a functional propulsion system, with weapons and shields inoperative. My dream of restoring the Orion people to our former glory—of echoing K'rgon's five-hundred-year reign as tallith—seemed to be over before it started."

"Five-hundred-year reign?" Boyce shook his head. "That sounds more like myth than history."

"Yes, it does." She stopped walking, turned to him, and smiled. "Though I have found—perhaps you have had this experience as well—that at the heart of every myth, there is always the seed of some truth."

They had stopped in front of a hatchway, of a style that looked very familiar to Boyce. It was an airlock, he realized, identical to the one he and the landing party had walked through, coming off *Magellan*.

"Come, Dr. Boyce. Let me show you what we found at Zai Romeen. Or, rather, in orbit around it."

She nodded to one of the guards, who stepped forward and touched a section of wall. It slid aside, revealing a storage locker. The guard pulled out two heavy parkas, handed one to the tallith, the other to Boyce.

She put hers on. Boyce, after a second's hesitation, followed suit.

Liyan preceded him into the airlock. The outer door shut; the inner one opened. Boyce felt a sudden chill.

"The temperature in here is slightly below freezing," she said. "To preserve the samples."

What samples? Boyce was about to ask, but she was already moving, stepping through the airlock, into the docking bay beyond. Boyce followed and, a second later, had the answer to his question.

The docking bay had been converted into a single huge chamber—forty feet wide, twice as long, half again as high. Equipment—Boyce spotted the LeKarz—lay arrayed along the far wall. There were a dozen other people in the room, gathered in groups of two or three around various pieces of machinery.

It was a lab of some sort, he realized.

"Here, Doctor. Come see."

Liyan had moved to the far end of the chamber, to the single largest piece of machinery, a cylindrical object, standing on one end, perhaps four and half meters tall, half a meter in diameter. At first it looked like an unbroken sheet of material, only, as Boyce came closer, he saw that the surface was faceted, built up of smaller, diamond-shaped pieces of metal, perhaps six inches a side. Some of the facets were missing.

"What is this?" he asked.

"A ship."

"A ship?" He walked around the object, stepping over a half-dozen color-coded cables that ran from the cylinder to a diagnostic console six meters away. "Looks awfully small to be a ship."

"It is a single-person craft."

"I don't see a propulsion system."

"I would be surprised if you did. In seventy years of looking, we have yet to find one ourselves."

He turned to face her. "This is what you found at Zai Romeen, I take it."

"That's right. Entirely by accident. It could have lain undiscovered for another ten thousand years, if we hadn't bumped—or, rather, not bumped—right into it."

Boyce frowned. "I don't understand."

"Zai Romeen's single planet is ringed by meteors. This was disguised as one of them."

"Disguised."

"An image projector. There." She gestured toward a sphere, perhaps half a meter in diameter, that lay at the foot of the cylinder—the spaceship. "It's really quite a remarkable piece of equipment."

"Your sensors couldn't tell the difference between a projected image and solid matter?"

"Projector is perhaps the wrong word. The device is capable of creating simulations that can fool even the most sophisticated sensors. Such as those on Starbase Eighteen."

Boyce got it right away. "The attack. This is what you used. To make them think the ships were Klingon . . ."

She didn't answer. She didn't need to.

"It's all very interesting," he said, suddenly angry once more. "All very impressive. Your new technology. But I don't see what it has to do with me."

"New?" Liyan shook her head. "On the contrary. This technology is thousands of years old. From Karkon's time, the Second Empire. Everything you see here"—she swept a hand before her—"is the product of those days. Orion civilization, at its height."

Boyce frowned. He was, admittedly, no historian, though he did know there that had been several—heck, maybe even dozens—highly advanced civilizations in this quadrant, civilizations that had risen to star flight, and fallen back into savagery. But the Orions?

He'd never heard of any sort of technology like this being associated with them before.

"Something else I want to show you, Doctor," she said, and without waiting for a response, she moved past him, heading toward the far corner of the reconfigured shuttlebay, where Boyce saw a group of four scientists huddled together around something. Another diagnostic console, he thought at first. And then, as he drew closer and was able to see past the scientists, he saw the object for what it truly was.

A body.

An Orion, male, of immense size. Bigger than Gurgis, even, with skin a far darker shade of green than on any Orion Boyce had yet seen. Naked and quite obviously dead, laid out on an examining table, part of his chest peeled back, with tubing and sensory instruments of various sizes inserted into it.

The veins on his body stood out like black ropes against his flesh.

"Any progress?" Liyan asked the scientists—three

males, one female—who now stepped a few feet back from the body and regarded the tallith apprehensively.

"Nothing of import, Majesty," the female said.

Boyce took a few steps closer. What Liyan had said earlier about preserving the samples—he understood that now. He could see his breath in front of him, which meant it was below freezing in the shuttle, but . . .

"It's not cold enough in here to keep his body from decaying."

"Under normal circumstances, no," Liyan said. "But these are not normal circumstances."

"I'm getting that," Boyce said.

"You know who this is, Doctor?" She walked around the body, trailing her right hand along the edge of the table as she went. "A rhetorical question, of course," she said before Boyce could respond. "Because you are not Codruta. You are not even Orion. So how could you know the story of K'rgon, or Madragas, or the battle of Akana, where the world killers were subdued. Or the ten sentries, whom K'rgon set to guard the borders of the Empire. But we"—Liyan gestured toward the scientists, who had remained virtually motionless, rooted in place ever since the tallith had approached them—"we who belong to the Confederacy know all those stories. Down to the very names of those ten sentries. Do we not, Zandar?"

The woman nodded. "Yes, Majesty."

"The ten sentries, Zandar," Liyan said. "Can you name them for the doctor here?"

"Yes, Majesty." The woman smiled. A forced smile. In her eyes, Boyce saw sheer, naked terror. "There was Heythum, the first. Boren. Adai and Argost, Marriyan and Munya, Gozen and—"

"Gozen. Thank you, Zandar." She smiled at Boyce. "The ten sentries who guarded the far corners of the Second Empire for the half-millennium K'rgon was tallith—and another five hundred years beyond."

Boyce had heard enough. "Not that I don't appreciate the history lesson, but would you mind telling me what this has to do with me? With why you've brought me here?"

She brushed a hand lightly along the skin of the dead man's upper arm. "This is Gozen," she said.

Boyce frowned. "What?"

"K'rgon's sentry. One of the ten he chose to guard the Empire. This is his body. That"—she gestured toward the ship she had shown Boyce earlier—"his vessel."

"This is Gozen."

"Yes."

"From a thousand years ago."

"That is correct."

Ridiculous, he wanted to say. The body before them couldn't be more than a few days old. Probably a victim of the Singhino attack. He looked over at the scientists. The three males were all still staring at the floor, the female—Zandar—still smiling nervously. Why were they going along with this insanity?

He saw that one of the sensor probes attached to the body ran to a standard chemanalyzer console.

"Mind if I run a little test of my own?" he asked, gesturing toward the device.

"By all means. Help yourself."

Boyce did. He grabbed the probe, ran a standard carbon-dating test, got some clearly erroneous results, recalibrated the machine, and ran the test again.

And got the same clearly erroneous, blatantly impossible results.

"Problem?" Liyan asked.

"There's something wrong with your machine here," Boyce said.

"Why? What is it telling you?"

"That this body is fifteen hundred years old."

Liyan smiled. Boyce frowned. It was a trick. Had to be. He knew a way around it.

He touched the probe to the inside of his own wrist. Sixty-one years. He shook his head.

"The machine is accurate, Doctor," Liyan said.

Boyce spun, lifted the probe from his wrist, and extended it toward her. She held out one arm.

"Go ahead."

He did, touched the probe to her skin, and watched the number change. He'd expected it to go down.

Liyan, by his guess, was at least a decade younger than he was.

But the number went up. And up and up. Seventy. Eighty. Ninety. One hundred. It stopped.

He looked at the tallith and frowned.

And remembered something. Something Lieutenant Hoto had said aboard the courier ship. Something he had paid little attention to then, because it was so clearly wrong. So blatantly impossible. Something about Liyan having assumed leadership of the Codruta seventy-five years earlier.

"No," he said.

"The numbers you see are real, Dr. Boyce."

"You're a hundred years old."

"Give or take a few months."

"How is that possible?"

She reached beneath the jacket she wore and into her cloak and pulled out something. A vial—clear plastic, about the size of the standard hypo, filled with a quarter-inch's worth of black liquid.

"It is possible because of this," she said. "The most important thing we found aboard Gozen's shuttle, Doctor. The germ of truth of which I spoke. The science behind the legend."

I don't understand, Boyce was about to say again, but held his tongue.

Because he did indeed understand. He knew exactly what Liyan was saying.

How could the body on the table be fifteen hundred years old? The woman in front of him going into her second century?

There was only one answer, really. Only one thing that could be in the vial.

He held out his hand. "Can I . . ."

"Have a look? Examine it? Of course. That's why you're here." He took the vial in his hands and swirled the liquid around. It was thicker than water, he judged. Closer to the viscosity of heavy syrup. And the color wasn't black, as he had thought at first, but a deep, dark shade of green.

"There were three of these aboard Gozen's ship," Liyan said. "This is the last."

"The Fountain of Youth," he said.

"More than that, Dr. Boyce. Much more than that."

"What is it exactly you want me to do?" he asked, though he suspected he already knew the answer to that as well.

"What I want you to do." Liyan smiled. "Quite simple. Make me more of this."

ELEVEN

Liyan gave him until the morning to decide; not that Boyce needed the time. She must be delusional, he thought, to suppose that after killing Jaya and Captain Pike—not to mention a hundred or so other people—he'd even consider helping her.

The only thing he had to consider, really, was how he was going to die.

A guard escorted him to the treatment room where he'd left Hoto. To his surprise, she was sitting up in bed, a terminal display in front of her.

"Lieutenant. You're feeling better?"

"Significantly so, Doctor." She smiled.

She looked good to Boyce—better than he'd expected. Not just her physical condition, but mentally ...

she seemed alert. And not depressed—not obviously so, at least, which he might have expected, given what had happened to her. Waking up and finding out she was minus an arm.

"M'Lor has given me access to the ship's medical database," Hoto said. She gestured to an Orion male—aqua-skinned, tall, thin, with a shock of dark bluish-black hair that fell across his forehead—standing nearby. Boyce recognized him as one of Petri's assistants. He'd helped Collins with the regen gel, that first day in the medical wing.

"I am browsing through the immediately available prosthetic implants for my arm," Hoto said. "I am glad you have arrived. Perhaps you can make recommendations."

"Uhhh . . ." Boyce frowned. Browsing through implants? With a smile on her face?

Maybe she wasn't as mentally sound as he'd thought.

"I'll leave you now," M'Lor said.

"We will return for your decision at eight hundred hours tomorrow," the guard added, and then the two left the room.

"Decision?" Hoto asked.

"We'll talk about it in a minute," he said, coming around her bedside to look at the screen. "Now, let me take a closer look at—"

He stopped talking because the computer terminal—

which he had expected to display images of the implants Hoto had been referring to—showed nothing of the kind.

The screen was split into columns, the right-hand column filled with a series of numbers, the lefthand column text. English text.

"These are not prosthetic implants," he said.

"No. That was a ruse."

"So what are you looking at?"

"Output from the ship's mainframe. M'Lor has foolishly interpreted my physical disability as a mental one as well. I have bypassed the rudimentary safeguards put into place by the Orion computer technicians."

"Impressive."

"I have a level five certification from Starfleet."

"Ah." Boyce smiled. Level five. The mention brought to mind an argument he'd witnessed one night in the officers' mess, an argument between Mr. Spock and Chief Pitcairn regarding the relevance of those certification tests. The chief, who hadn't formally been graded in years, dismissed them as singularly unimportant. Spock thought just the opposite, and had gone into mind-numbing detail about why.

"So what are we looking at here?"

Hoto regarded him with suspicion a moment, then continued. "This is control code for some of the ship's systems here, on the left." She pointed to the numbers. "And databases associated with those systems here, on the right." She pointed to the text. "I have learned many things. The control keypads for various cell doors on this floor, for example, can be opened by entering zeph-zeph-gramma—these numbers here." She pointed again.

"Various cell doors. Like that one?" Boyce gestured toward the door M'Lor had just left through.

"I believe so."

"Impressive."

"Thank you, Doctor. Now, the consequences of your decision? To what was M'Lor referring?"

"It's a long story," Boyce said. "I'll give you the short version."

He did. Hoto was frowning when he finished.

"Immortality," she said. "It is a physical impossibility. And yet given the undeniable fact of Liyan's own considerable longevity . . . perhaps . . ."

Boyce sighed. "I don't know what to believe, to tell you the truth. It doesn't really matter anyway."

"Why not?"

"Why not?" He looked at her, a little incredulous. "Because—you heard what I just said, didn't you? What happened to Captain Pike and the landing party?"

"I did hear. But—"

"And the part about the image projector? How they used that to attack Starbase Eighteen?"

"I did hear, sir. However—"

"Eighty-seven people died there, Lieutenant."

"Including your daughter."

"Yes. Including my daughter."

"I regret the loss of life. But it cannot be the sole factor in your determination."

"You ever had kids?"

"I am twenty-three standard years of age."

"That's a no, then."

"That is a no."

"Then you can't possibly know how I feel."

"Mr. Spock would say you must set aside your feelings, sir."

"Not all of us want to be Vulcans when we grow up, Lieutenant."

"Sir." Hoto pulled aside the sheet on her bed with her remaining hand and swung her feet onto the floor. "In gaining access to the Orion mainframe, I have had opportunity to familiarize myself with their historical database as well. I have read news briefs, diplomatic reports, battle summaries, and the like."

"So?"

"Liyan's rule has been beneficial on many levels."

"Beneficial to whom?"

"The Federation, for one."

"Really?"

"Yes. Under the tallith's leadership, pirate attacks in the Borderland and nearby territories have declined nearly two hundred percent."

"What does that mean exactly?"

"In the fifty years prior to her consolidation of power, more than a thousand lives were lost in such attacks. Since then, there have been roughly three hundred fatalities. Most of which came in a single assault orchestrated by the Orion syndicate."

"You're implying she saved seven hundred lives?"

"Approximately. Yes."

"That's faulty reasoning," Boyce said. "You can't count on attacks like that occurring."

"Liyan has instituted policies specifically penalizing clans for them."

Boyce frowned.

"In addition, wars between the clans have almost stopped entirely. There is peace among the Orion peoples for the first time in nearly two hundred years."

"Most of the Orion peoples, anyway," Boyce said, thinking of the Singhino.

"Sir?"

"Never mind. Okay. Her rule has been beneficial on some levels. I'll agree there. That still doesn't mean—"

"There is more," Hoto said. "The Klingons."

Boyce sighed. He'd had a feeling the Klingons would come up again. "What about the Klingons?"

"The presence of a stable, functioning Orion government in the Borderland is a considerable deterrent to further expansion by the Empire in this sector. Which is perhaps the single most important reason—"

He threw up his hands.

"What?" Hoto asked. "Is my reasoning faulty?"

"No. It's her reasoning, too. Which is why I don't necessarily buy it."

"It is a compelling argument. And there is another factor to consider as well. Further reason for you to cooperate with the tallith."

"Go on."

"She will most likely kill both of us if you don't."

Boyce had to laugh. "That I agree with."

"It is no joking matter, Doctor," Hoto said. "If we are dead, there is no one alive to tell the Federation that the Empire was not responsible for the attack on Starbase Eighteen."

"I'm aware of that," Boyce said.

"If you cooperate, there is a chance we can contact *Enterprise*. Tell them that—"

"Contact *Enterprise*?"

"Yes."

"How?"

Hoto walked back over to her bed and touched the terminal.

"Through the Orion mainframe. Given enough time, I believe I will be able to access the ship's communication system. Control it long enough to send out a simple message."

Boyce shook his head. "Which in all likelihood no

one will hear. For all we know, we're completely out of the sector by now."

"You may be correct. I will know for certain shortly." Now she smiled. "I am currently running a subroutine designed to poll the ship's sensors for location data. Within the hour, I expect I will have a fairly accurate picture of our current location, as well as that of the nearest Federation outpost."

"And if we're not near a Federation outpost?"

"I will contact the Klingons."

"And tell them what?"

"The truth." Hoto regarded him impassively. "I sympathize with your dilemma, Doctor. But to prevent an unjust war from occurring, to serve the Federation's larger strategic imperatives—"

"No." He shook his head. "I'm not going to do it."

Hoto sat back down on her bed.

The two of them stared at each other a moment.

Then Hoto shrugged. "Very well. I do not wish to leave my death to the Orions. I have had experience with their savagery already. I believe that within this room, there are chemicals you can use to euthanize—"

"Stop it," Boyce said.

"I will not," Hoto said. "There are consequences to your decisions, Doctor. I am merely laying those out in order to help you reach your determination."

She was right, of course. Boyce knew that. But it didn't matter. He turned away from her. He had to have time to think, space to think, without Hoto staring at him, without the guards or Zandar or M'Lor leaning over him.

But there was, of course, nowhere to go.

He looked at the door and the keypad next to it.

Zeph-zeph-gramma.

He strode quickly toward the door.

"Dr. Boyce!" Hoto called after him. "Where are you going?"

"Somewhere else," he said. He entered the code and stepped out into the hall.

Even as the door closed behind him, Boyce realized he was making a terrible mistake, that there would be guards patrolling the corridor, that they would wonder how he had gotten the exit code, that they would discover Hoto's trespasses and kill both of them no matter his decision.

But he was wrong.

The hall was empty; whatever guards there were, he realized, must be on the main entrance to the medical wing. He was all alone.

Okay, Doctor, he told himself. *Here's that time and space you wanted. Now what?*

He had to face facts. Uncomfortable as they were. Hoto was right, wasn't she? He didn't have a choice here. Helping Liyan was the only course of action that made sense right now, distasteful as it was. Though *distasteful* was nowhere near strong enough a word; *revolting* was closer.

A fountain of youth. A five-hundred-year life span.

Never mind the political, strategic consequences, the whole thing was just wrong. Unnatural.

And didn't that bring back memories.

Your work on Argelius is well known, Doctor.

Boyce leaned back against the wall and sighed.

He was standing, he realized then, in almost exactly the same spot he'd stood that first day, when he'd taken a break from treating the Orion wounded and wound up walking into a nightmare. Collins's death. His imprisonment.

His gaze traveled down the hall again now. To the three doors directly opposite the entrance to the medical wing. The one facing him was still closed, with the control pad next to it blinking red. One to the left and one to the right. The girl Deleen's room.

The lights came on, low intensity, as soon as he walked into the room. She was no longer in there, of course. The LeKarz was gone as well. And there were bloodstains against the far wall—Collins's blood. Otherwise, though, it looked exactly the same. The diagnostic cot, the analysis screen . . .

He looked down at the empty cot and in his mind's eye saw Deleen lying there again.

I'm here to help.

Familiar words; they rang a bell. It took him a few seconds, but then he had it.

Argelius. The Mobile 7 lab. Three years into the assignment that would take up seventeen years of his professional life.

He closed his eyes and remembered.

Boyce was alone in the main research room; the other members of his team were down on the planet's surface. He was staring at the LeKarz data screen, at a three-column list—flora, fauna, native population—of deviations from the planet's underlying genetic code. There were mutations everywhere. Dezzla's syndrome—the immediate cause for concern, the immediate cause for their presence there—was just the tip of the iceberg. A horrible tip, to be sure—a hideous, deforming, ultimately fatal skin condition that had been spreading like wildfire among the population of the southern continent the last ten years—but still, just the tip. The real problem went far deeper than that. The real problem was that the ecosystem, the processes that had evolved over the last billion years of Argelius's life span—no longer worked. Nature itself was broken. And there didn't seem to be any way to fix it.

Boyce leaned back from the LeKarz, rubbed his eyes, and looked out the window.

And almost had a heart attack.

A little face—a thin, pale-skinned, green-eyed face—was staring at him through the lab's main viewport. Which was quite a surprise.

Mobile 7 was thirty feet off the ground.

"Hey!" he yelled. "Hey! Get off there! That's not safe!"

The child—it was only later he found out it was a girl—waved at him. Waved. She was hanging by one hand from the superstructure.

She yelled something back at him. The lab glass wasn't soundproof. What the girl yelled back was a single word: "Food!"

Boyce ended up bringing her into the lab and feeding her.

"Good?" he asked, as she sat at the mess table, shoveling in soup from a bowl as fast as her hands could move.

She nodded and kept eating.

"I'm Philip Boyce, by the way," he said.

The girl was dressed, if you could call it that, in what looked like an old tablecloth, strategically folded over and tied together in several spots. From the way she was attacking the food, Boyce guessed she hadn't eaten in days. Not a big surprise. Planetary civilization on Argelius had broken down a few decades back. On the northern continent, remnants of it—cities, here and there rudimentary government—survived, but here, on the southern continent, things were a lot

more chaotic. More dangerous. One of the reasons
they kept Mobile 7 up off the surface.

She had long, stringy, pale white hair. Boyce put her
age at ten or eleven. On the verge of adolescence and
puberty. Which in her case would be fatal.

She already had the characteristic red spots of
Dezzla's syndrome on the insides of both arms.

"I have more, if you want it," he said. "The soup."

She grunted. Boyce took that as a yes and poured
some into her bowl.

"What's your name?" he asked.

The girl glanced up quickly from the bowl. "Jaya,"
she said.

"Jaya. I'm Dr. Boyce."

"Doctor." She said the word slowly, almost as if
she'd never heard it before.

"That's right." He smiled at her. "I'm here to help."

She smiled, too.

The memory faded.

The empty room came back into focus.

Boyce glanced at the display and was surprised to
see he'd been standing there for almost half an hour.
He was surprised to see something else, too. The
screen appeared to be on standby mode. He waved a
hand over it, and the screen came to life.

It took him a few minutes, but eventually, he was
able to bring up Deleen's information again. The read-

ings he'd been looking at before Collins was killed. He had a little more time now to study them. To go beyond the vitals—temperature, blood pressure, body pH—and look closely at the details. Blood chemistry, for instance. This last set of readings—taken, if memory served, about an hour and a half before he had entered the room—was disturbing. Puzzling. Completely out of whack, if his memory of the basic components of Orion blood material was correct. Levels of certain hormones were way too high, levels of certain immune factors so low as to be almost nonexistent.

Those imbalances could, he realized, account for the discoloration of her veins. Liyan was suffering from the same condition. Did that mean her body chemistry looked the same? That she was suffering from the same imbalances? The fact that the sentry had the same thing—had it much worse, Boyce thought, remembering how swollen and distended her veins had seemed— suggested a connection between the condition and the serum. So the girl was taking the serum? That made no sense. There were only drops left in the last of the three vials they'd found; surely Liyan needed those until more could be made. *If* more could be made. Which, Boyce supposed, was up to him.

Liyan had found the shuttle—the serum—seventy-five years ago. The Orions were a good dozen years behind the Federation technologically, but they were still capable scientists. They must have been trying to duplicate the serum for years, trying pretty hard, in fact; running all sorts of different . . .

Experiments.

A chill ran down his spine.

He looked down at the cot again and back up at the display screen. The numbers flashed through his mind—hormones up, other factors down, blood chemistry completely out of whack. And now he knew why.

The girl had been taking the serum, all right. They'd probably given her dozens of different versions of it, in fact. Trying to find one that worked. Petri had lied. Deleen wasn't a patient.

She was a guinea pig.

TWELVE

Morning found Spock standing inside the open doorway of Shuttlebay 2, looking at Number One, who stood inside the bay, next to the wreck of *Magellan*. She'd been there for a good five minutes, studying it in silence. Spock thought he knew why. Although there would undoubtedly be a memorial of some sort constructed back on Earth—Captain Pike's roots there were long and deep—for now, this chamber, which only yesterday had served as the site for the captain's service, and that of the other members of the landing party who'd perished along with him, was the closest thing Christopher Pike had to a grave.

Enterprise's first officer stretched out a hand and ran it over the gaping hole in the shuttle's fuselage. The sight sparked memories. Spock himself had done the exact same thing when they'd pulled the wreckage in by tractor beam two days earlier. The size of the hole had told him decompression had been instantaneous; everyone inside the shuttlecraft had been sucked out into space within seconds. They'd died within seconds, died in the vast, unforgiving vacuum of space, their bodies never to be recovered. The facts were undeniable, and yet they felt wrong to him somehow, both at the service and now.

Captain Pike dead.

It did not seem logical.

"Mr. Spock." Number One lowered her hand and turned to face him.

"Commander." Spock took a step forward, the sound of his boots on metal echoing throughout the cavernous chamber. "Please forgive the interruption."

"Not at all." She attempted a smile; it looked forced. No surprise. Number One did not smile frequently; the sight of the expression on her face was no more natural, he supposed, than it would be on his. "I was just leaving. I'll let you have some time to pay your respects."

"I have done so already. In point of fact, I came here looking for you."

"Me."

"Yes. I wish to discuss a query you recently sent to the Archives."

Number One's eyes flickered. She hesitated a second before replying.

Spock knew what she was going to say even before she opened her mouth.

"Recently?" She shook her head. "I cannot recall sending any recent queries to Archives."

"This one was transmitted three days ago. Shall I quote the text, to refresh your memory? 'Explanation sought for discrepancy between Starfleet records and evidentiary findings on fifty-five Hamilton.' That was the text of the query. It was accompanied by several image files." Which had taken him several hours to reconstruct, in total. It had taken him several more hours to trace the physical source of the transmission, the location aboard *Enterprise* from which the query had been made. Ironically, once he had that information and the time of transmission in hand, he realized he had actually witnessed the message being sent.

In his mind, he pictured that instant now, Number One hunched over the auxiliary science station, drawing heavily on the ship's processing resources for reasons that at the time he did not then understand.

He was beginning to now.

"Ah." She nodded. "I recall the query. It is not important. A potential line of inquiry, now abandoned."

"May I ask why?"

"No. As I said, it is not important. Particularly given the number and complexity of tasks we have before us, with the arrival of *Potemkin* and—"

"I would still like to know the rationale for your decision."

She looked him in the eye.

She was lying, Spock knew, just as T'Koss had been, yet in Number One's eyes, he saw no sign of agitation, trepidation, insecurity.

She was far more practiced at falsehood.

"I thought I made myself clear, Lieutenant. I abandoned the query. I suggest you do the same."

"I understand. If I could simply examine the responses the Archives may have passed along . . ."

"No."

"Shall I repeat the query myself, then?"

"No," she repeated, her voice taking on added gravity. "Mr. Spock. I am now giving you a direct order. You are hereby forbidden to pursue this line of inquiry. Or to order your subordinates to do so. You are also prohibited from discussing this subject with them or with any other personnel, Starfleet or civilian. Are these orders clear?"

"They are."

"Good."

"I cannot, however, comply with them."

"Orders are by definition not voluntary, Lieutenant.

Disciplinary charges will be filed for failure to obey the ones I have just given you."

"I understand."

"Do you? These are serious charges."

"Against which I shall have to raise a serious defense. Which will not only involve revelation of the query but any and all related research."

Number One stood stock-still, a few feet in front of him, hands clasped behind her back. Impassive. Unperturbed, undisturbed by his threats.

"I will give you a moment to reconsider your refusal, Mr. Spock. And its consequences for your career."

He shook his head. "The time will not be necessary. I am prepared to face any and all consequences."

Anger flashed across her face for a moment and then was gone, replaced by a series of less easily identifiable emotions. Impatience? No, Spock thought. Not exactly.

"Mr. Spock," Number One said. "I do not wish—"

"The query is innocuous enough, on the face of it. I fail to understand the need for secrecy."

"Believe me when I say it is better that way."

"I sense concern in your voice."

"You sense correctly. I would ask you again to abandon this line of inquiry, Lieutenant. For your own sake. Your own safety."

"I cannot," Spock said, in that instant discerning something else of critical importance, a motive of his own, which until this instant he had not been conscious of. "There is something wrong here, Commander. Something to do with the attack on Starbase Eighteen, with the circumstances of Captain Pike's death, with the confrontation between Starfleet and the Klingon Empire . . ."

His voice trailed off, as he found himself suddenly at a loss for words.

"Something wrong." Number One looked at him and sighed. "You are correct. Something is wrong indeed. Terribly wrong."

She turned and walked away.

It took Spock several seconds—and her glancing back and gesturing to him—to realize he was meant to follow.

The Vulcan paused on the threshold of Number One's cabin.

He had never been in the first officer's quarters before. They were considerably more spacious than his, made to seem even more so by the lack of ornamentation and furniture. Within the entire living space, there was but a single couch, a single table. The walls—customized from regulation Starfleet gray to a lighter beige—were bare as well. Spock was surprised. Most humans, particularly the enlisted crew, tended to fill every square inch of cabin space with some sort of personal memento.

But then, as he had come to realize over these few months, Number One was not like most humans.

He entered; the door closed behind him.

Number One had gone directly to the alcove containing her sleeping quarters. She came out now, having removed the landing-party jacket she'd worn to protect her from the cold of the unheated shuttlebay.

"Would you care for tea?" she asked.

"No, thank you."

"I drink it regularly." She went to the materializer and keyed in a series of instructions. "It helps to maintain my focus. My concentration."

"I use meditation for that purpose."

"As do I. Occasionally." She gestured toward a corner of the room, where Spock saw both mat and holographic projectors. And something else: a photographic image, hung on the wall in such a way that it was visible only from certain angles within the room.

He walked toward that image, till he was close enough to pick out details. It was a picture of perhaps two dozen people, most adults, standing in a shallow horseshoe shape around three young people. Two males flanking a single female. All dressed in light green, single-piece jumpsuits, all with similar haircuts. All wearing similarly placid expressions of contentment.

The girl was holding a plaque in her hands. He suddenly recognized her.

"This is you," he said to Number One.

"At my investiture as a citizen of Illyria."

"Your graduation from the Illyrian Cultural Academy."

"Yes." She came closer; the smell of tea came with her. "Eleven standard years ago. I was first in the class. Hence the plaque."

And the name Number One, Spock knew from a casual, curious perusal of her publicly accessible personnel file.

"And this is your family," he said.

"Yes. Those are my brothers, on either side of me," she said. "Hudek is an environmental systems engineer at the Utopia Planetia yards. Leighton is chief minister on Salazar V."

"Impressive accomplishments," Spock said. "Your parents must be proud."

"I suppose they are." Something in her tone of voice caused Spock to turn and study her face. He glimpsed something—sadness? regret?—in her eyes.

Then she turned away from the picture, and the emotion was gone.

"To tell you the truth, Mr. Spock, I'm not entirely surprised that you discovered the query. I had expected, however, that it would take you a little longer to do so."

"The discovery came partially by chance." He told her of T'Koss and his own reasons for seeking information from the Archives.

"Captain Pike's logs." She nodded. "I'd heard they were sequestered."

He had a sudden insight. "The two matters are related—the logs and your query."

"They may be." She sipped at her tea. "I don't know for certain."

She fell silent again, lost in her own thoughts.

"'Explanation sought for discrepancy between Starfleet records and evidentiary findings on Fifty-five Hamilton,'" he repeated. "I am curious—"

"Mr. Spock." *Enterprise*'s first officer looked at him directly. "I ask you one last time. Please. Let the matter lie. For your own sake."

"I am sorry. I cannot."

"Very well." She finished her tea and returned it to the materializer. Then she went back into her sleeping alcove. She came back out, carrying a stack of flimsies about a half-inch thick. Odd. In the three months he had been aboard *Enterprise,* he could not recall seeing a single sheet of flimsy—recycled plastiform—before. And now it seemed to be everywhere.

Captain Vlasidovich's habits, rubbing off on his crew.

That felt, suddenly, wrong to him as well.

"Shall we?" she said, gesturing to the couch. They sat. She set the stack of flimsies on the table in front of them and handed the top sheet to Spock.

It was an image, a photograph, very much like dozens of others he had seen over the last week. Twisted metal, pieces of gray and blue plastiform blocks scattered across the brick-red surface of a planetoid.

"You recognize this?"

"Starbase Eighteen," he said.

"A particular area of Starbase Eighteen."

Spock looked at the image again. It was a portion of the base that had caught his attention earlier, the remnants of a single, relatively large building—perhaps a hundred meters square—set far apart from the command tower and the base's main living and work facilities. An unusually long separation; he had assumed that there was a logical reason for the anomaly and banished the sight from his mind. He had the sudden intuition that perhaps he had been too hasty in doing so.

"Look at the extensive surface scarring, the multiple blast sites," Number One said. "The attackers targeted this building in particular."

"Why? What was it?"

"The same questions I asked, initially. Which proved much more difficult to answer than I'd expected."

"In what sense?"

"We have a map of the base's general layout in the ship's computer. Copies of the original construction blueprints as well. This building is not noted on either."

"A simple explanation. This is a later addition. Our records are out of date."

"*Enterprise*'s databases sync up with Fleet Archives regularly. Maintenance logs have them current as of two months ago."

Spock studied the image again.

"This construction did not take place within the last two months."

"No."

"Then perhaps the maintenance logs are in error."

"The databases are current according to the Archives as well."

Spock frowned. "Then . . . ?"

"They have no record of the building, either." Number One nodded toward the flimsy on the table. "As far as Starfleet Archives are concerned, it doesn't exist."

Spock looked at Number One, at the image, and then frowned.

He rarely dealt in absolutes. The universe was a strange, unknowable place. Scientific theory had yet to account fully for all of its secrets, its myriad inexplicable, implausible phenomena.

This was an instance, though, where absolutes were called for.

The Archives was the single largest repository of data in the known galaxy, custodians of Starfleet mission logs dating back to the original NX-series star-

ships, keepers of the documents that had established
the United Federation of Planets. Every transport
manifest, every personnel transfer, every restraining
bolt, uniform tunic, piece of vinyl, leather, or plastic
that made its way aboard a starbase or a starship or
even a lowly cargo vessel, the Archives had a record of
it. An entire building? There had to be literally thousands of entries related to it—not just blueprints but
material orders, construction logs, progress reports.
The amount of data filed on a project of that size was
simply enormous.

"For the Archives not to have record of this structure's existence is impossible," he said.

"I agree," Number One replied.

Spock understood now T'Koss's agitation. For a
single database to be in error was one thing; for multiple records to be missing—

He sat up straight on the couch.

That was impossible.

"The Archives have been tampered with."

Number One nodded. "That's what I think, too."

"Who would have done this?" Spock asked. "And
why?"

"I've found out a few things." Number One handed
him another sheet of flimsy. A data table, headlined
"Materials composition analysis." "This is a breakdown of the explosive residue Commander Tuval's
landing party sampled at the image site."

Spock studied the data. One piece of information popped out at him right away. "Duranite."

"Yes."

"A duranium alloy. One of the strongest construction materials currently available."

"As well as one of the most expensive."

Spock nodded. Her point was well taken. There were dozens of less expensive duranium alloys of roughly similar strength that could have been used, though now that he was thinking of it, there was something peculiar about duranite . . .

Ah.

"Duranite's secondary constituent," he said, "is kreelite ore."

Number One nodded. "Exactly."

"Kreelite ore is virtually opaque to electromagnetic radiation, impervious to scanning instruments."

"That's right." She took the flimsy back from him. "Whatever was happening in this facility was intended to be kept secret, safe from prying eyes."

"And do you have any thoughts about what that secret might have been?"

Number One slid the remainder of the stack of flimsies across the table.

The top page, Spock saw, contained a single word of text.

"Kronos," he said.

"Kronos." She nodded. "The name repeats several

times in the material I have gathered. It appears to be a clandestine project of some sort."

Kronos. The word had many connotations; one came immediately to mind.

"The Klingon home world."

"Yes."

The look in Number One's eyes made him suddenly ill at ease.

"May I?" He gestured toward the stack of flimsies.

"By all means."

Spock turned the top page of flimsy over and began reading.

THIRTEEN

Boyce had a hard time sleeping that night. He basically didn't. He couldn't stop thinking about Argelius. About Jaya and Mobile 7. About the legacy he'd expected to leave . . . and now never would.

He was sitting up on his cot, hands clasped on his lap, trying to sort things out in his head, when Hoto woke.

"Sir?"

"Lieutenant." He got to his feet. "Good morning."

"Good morning, sir. Are you all right?"

"Fine. A little tired. A little confused."

He expected her to start asking questions then, to quiz him on where he'd gone last night, what he'd done. Hoto had been fast asleep by the time he came back to the treatment room.

Instead, the lieutenant got to her feet and walked across the room. She stopped in front of a storage cabinet and ran her hand across the lockplate. The cabinet popped open. Hoto reached inside and pulled out something in a plastic wrapper.

"Lieutenant?" he called out. "What are you doing?"

She turned back to him and smiled. "Eating, sir. Breakfast." She ripped the wrapper open with her teeth, set it down on a nearby counter, reached inside with her remaining hand, and pulled out what looked like bread of some sort. "As Mr. Spock tells us, an engine, even a finely tuned warp drive, is incapable of running without proper fuel."

"Mr. Spock tells you that?"

"Yes, sir. I believe, however, he is quoting Chief Pitcairn when he does so."

Spock quoting Pitcairn. Boyce could only shake his head.

"Would you care for one?" Hoto nodded toward the cabinet. "They are Orion field rations. According to M'Lor, they supply most basic nutrients required by humans. The taste does leave something to be desired, but—"

"Thanks, but no thanks. Do they have coffee in there?"

"No, sir. M'Lor informs me coffee is not stocked aboard this vessel."

Of course it isn't, Boyce thought. *More good news.*

Hoto brought her "field rations" back to where the cots were. She sat cross-legged on hers, eating, while Boyce told her what he'd done last night after leaving the room. Where he'd gone, what he'd discovered, what he'd concluded.

"I find no flaw in your reasoning, sir. I think the situation most likely is exactly as you posit. They are undoubtedly experimenting on the girl. Which, to me, is a complication but not a determining factor."

"Not a determining factor."

"No, sir. Not in my opinion."

"They're playing God with that girl's life."

"Indeed. For all we know, she is dead already."

"That's a cheery thought."

"We are speaking of but one life, Doctor. Measured against the continued existence of thousands, if not millions. It is ultimately inconsequential."

"Inconsequential? Lieutenant, Starfleet, the Federation, the UFP charter is built on the sanctity of all sentient life."

"Forgive me, sir." Hoto bowed her head. "*Inconsequential* was perhaps a poor choice of words. I—"

The door to the medical wing opened. Two guards entered and took up flanking positions on either side of it.

Liyan strode in.

Boyce glanced at the chronometer on the wall. "You're early."

"A few minutes. Forgive me." She looked at Hoto and then at him. "Have you made up your mind?"

The tallith looked as if she'd had trouble sleeping as well; there were circles under her eyes that her make-up couldn't entirely mask. The veins on her neck seemed more prominent—darker—to him this morning as well. He wondered what those on her arm looked like.

"I'll help you," Boyce said.

"Excellent. We should—"

"On one condition."

"You are hardly in a position to impose conditions."

"The girl."

"Girl?"

"Deleen. The experiments stop."

"What are you talking about?"

"You've been experimenting on her," Boyce said. "Testing out different versions of the serum. I won't be a party to that."

Liyan, to his surprise, actually smiled. "That is your condition?"

"Yes."

"The point is moot. But if that is your condition, I agree, of course."

"Moot." The same little chill he'd felt earlier went down Boyce's spine again. "She's dead."

"On the contrary." Liyan smiled. "She is, all things considered, doing much better. Would you like to see her?"

Boyce glanced over at Hoto. She looked as confused as he was.

"Yes. I would."

"Then follow me."

Boyce, with a last, perplexed look back at Hoto, did as he was told. He followed Liyan and the guards out of the medical wing and up through the ship. It wasn't long before their route started to look familiar to him. They stopped in front of a door he recognized as well.

"Wait a second," Boyce said. "These are your quarters."

"They are." The door opened. "After you, Doctor."

"Why is the girl in your quarters?"

"Where else should she be?" Liyan smiled. "Deleen is my daughter, Dr. Boyce."

He froze in the doorway, utterly flummoxed by the revelation. Liyan, experimenting on her own daughter.

The world around him faded, and the past, for a moment, came rushing back.

Mobile 7 was docked with the *Osler*; Jaya was off somewhere in the larger ship, using/abusing *Osler*'s recreational facilities, she and a half-dozen of the others Boyce and his team had rescued over the last few months. The doctor and his team were in the main lab, Boyce at the head of the conference table.

The fieldwork was done; the experiments had begun. Three weeks in, they'd already reached a turning point.

"Plants are one thing." Neema, at the far end of the table, was shaking her head. "Whether or not the virus is going to work on people—"

"I wish you wouldn't call it a virus." Boyce's tech, a young man named Korby, shook his head. "The connotations—"

"What should I call it?" Neema asked. "It walks like a virus, it replicates like a virus."

"A vaccine," Korby said. "I would prefer you call it a vaccine."

Neema rolled her eyes.

"Outside this lab," Boyce said. "Roger's right, Neema. *Virus* is a bad choice. *Vaccine* is better. Splitting hairs, I know," he said hastily, at the look on her face, "but it's a difference worth stressing. That's not the important thing, though. The important thing is where we are in the testing. Dr. Cadan?"

Boyce spoke now to the only Argelian in their presence, the only Argelian remaining, in fact, on the entire planetary reclamation mission. Cadan was in her late thirties, according to the records. She'd been an assistant health minister in the southern continent's government, before Dezzla's. She'd gotten the disease fairly early on, a milder version, before it mutated. Boyce wasn't sure exactly what it had done to her—something disfiguring. Something that caused her to cover her face with a mask and every square inch of her body with a long-sleeved coverall, so that the only things showing were her hands and, through the mask, her eyes.

Boyce had learned to read those eyes over the last few years. Right now, underneath her mask, he would bet money Cadan was smiling.

"Thank you, Dr. Boyce," Cadan said. "We only just finished running our data through the LeKarz about half an hour ago, so while I can share the results with you, I'm afraid in terms of a visual presentation—"

"Not necessary, Doctor," Boyce said. "The results are what we're interested in."

"Of course. In brief"—she paged through a stack of flimsies in front of her—"the last round of tests confirms the efficacy of the virus. Excuse me, vaccine." She glanced up at Korby. "We worked with three species of animal, widely varying taxonomies, widely varying mutations. We followed these species through two generations and simulated a third and fourth using the LeKarz. The virus eliminated all mutation in a single generation. No significant mutation reappeared in any of the subsequent generations."

"That's great news, Doctor." Boyce smiled. Korby was smiling, too. So were technicians Cauley and Chapel, next to him. And Drs. Finch, Debausset, Melliver, and Staton. Everyone around the table, in fact, was smiling.

Everyone, that is, except Neema.

"No significant mutation." She sat directly across the table from Cadan. She leaned forward now, and spoke directly to the Argelian. "What exactly does that mean?"

"No disabling mutations," Cadan replied. "Nothing disfiguring, nothing that—"

"Could you be a little more specific?"

"Of course." Cadan, Boyce could tell, was no longer smiling. "The erapod, for example. Dezzla had affected the plumage of the males; the feathers were shorter and by and large colorless in the infected groups. Females were choosing mates from uninfected populations or, more often, choosing not to mate at all. Species numbers were down—this is just an estimate—approximately fifty percent over a ten-year period. Injecting infected juveniles with the vaccine and then accelerating their development to sexual maturity, we found the plumage fully restored to species-normal in ninety percent of the individuals."

"And the other ten percent?" Neema asked. "I assume that's where the mutation cropped up."

"That's correct. In the other ten percent, plumage size was nominal, but there were color variations. Monochromatic display."

"And were you able to determine why?"

Cadan sat a little straighter in her chair. "We have begun testing to narrow down the possible causes. I do believe that—"

"So the answer is no. No, you don't know why this new mutation occurs."

The two women glared at each other across the table.

"You are technically correct," Cadan said finally. "We do not, as of yet, know why."

"So three weeks' worth of tests. Mostly positive tests," Neema interjected, swiveling in her chair to face Boyce. "Based on that, you're ready to start treating those kids out there like lab rats?"

Boyce stared at her a moment. Jaya's face flashed before his eyes. So did the faces of those they'd been too late to save. The kids they'd rescued whom he'd watched die, those he'd sedated so they didn't have to spend their last few hours in agonizing pain.

Was he ready to start testing?

"Not the terminology I would have chosen," he said. "Lab rats. But yes. If the alternative is doing nothing, I am ready."

Neema threw up her hands and uttered a series of curse words under her breath.

Boyce did his best to ignore her. "Let's go around the table, get a sense of how everyone feels," he said. "Show of hands."

It wasn't even close. Neema was the only dissenting vote, though Boyce thought he saw Dr. Cadan hesitate before raising her hand as well.

"The ayes have it," he said, getting to his feet. "Let's start preparing the protocol, people."

"And the rats," Neema said. "We ought to start preparing them, too."

Boyce glared. He was about to take Neema to task—for the language, for the sentiment—when he realized that she was right. Insensitive but right. Preparing their lab animals was exactly what they had to do.

He, in fact, already had one particular animal in mind to talk to.

The guard shoved him.

"Hey!" Boyce glared at the Orion, who simply glared back.

"Move," the guard said, and Boyce did.

Through the door and into the room where he and Liyan had eaten dinner the night before. The table was bare of food now. Deleen sat at one end of it. She stood as the tallith—her mother—entered. Stood and bowed her head.

She looked up then and saw him. Her eyes widened. "Dr. Boyce," Deleen said, "I am—surprised to see you."

"The doctor was concerned for your welfare," Liyan said. "Tell him how you are feeling."

"I'm feeling fine." She did indeed look better. Much better. Her skin color was a shade lighter; the veins on her arms were still noticeable but much less pronounced.

He noticed something else about the way she looked as well. There was absolutely no resemblance between the two of them. The tallith was a good bit taller, her features much stronger, more pronounced. Her skin color was different as well, several shades lighter. He would never have suspected the two were related.

"I'm glad to hear it." He looked past her to the tallith. "Your daughter."

"Yes."

"You've been experimenting on your own daughter."

"*Experimenting* is not the word I would have chosen, Doctor," Liyan said.

"What word would you have used?" he asked.

"It is irrelevant at the moment," the tallith snapped. "Now that you have decided to assist us, the experiments, as you refer to them, will no longer be necessary."

"Please." Deleen laid a hand on her mother's arm. "You must not agitate yourself. M'Lor said—"

"I know what M'Lor said. I will not be coddled." She glared at her daughter a moment, and then the glare softened. "But you are right. I will not agitate myself unnecessarily."

"You are laboring under a misunderstanding, Dr. Boyce," Deleen said. "The procedures you refer to, I volunteered for them."

"Why would you do that?"

"The Confederacy must survive. Everything else is secondary."

"Even your life."

"Especially my life."

"Zandar will explain further." Liyan motioned to the guard. "Take Dr. Boyce to the lab. Doctor, you will begin work immediately on replicating the serum. The facility and its personnel will be at your disposal."

The guard stepped up alongside him.

"With your permission," Deleen said. "I will accompany the doctor."

"Of course."

"This way, then."

The guard nodded and fell into step behind them.

They walked in silence for a moment.

Then Deleen cleared her throat. "Dr. Boyce, your daughter."

"What about my daughter?"

"I had not realized that she had been—that she was one of the—"

"One of the what?" Boyce snapped. "One of the people you killed?"

"Yes." Deleen nodded. "I am truly sorry."

Boyce, about to snap again, saw genuine sympathy in her eyes. "Thank you," he said.

"It was a research facility, I understand. Starbase Eighteen."

"Yes."

"What was her function—"

"I really don't want to talk about it," Boyce said.

"Of course. I understand."

A few seconds later, though, he realized he did.

"She was a scientist," he said. "Dr. Jaya Wandruska. She and her partner were both stationed there."

"I see."

They walked on.

"They refused to let us have one, you know," Deleen said.

"What?"

"A LeKarz. The tallith had attempted to trade for one earlier, offered a king's ransom for it. We were refused."

Boyced glared. "That doesn't give you the right to steal it."

"The tallith must not die, Doctor."

"Everything dies," Boyce said.

"Eventually. I suppose so. But not now. Now is a critical moment. If the Confederacy can hold together, we can resist the Empire. If not . . ."

"Don't you think you're being a little bit melodramatic?"

"No." She shook her head. "Did you not hear the fighting these last few days? While you were in your cell?"

The fighting. Boyce remembered the way the ship had shook.

"The other clans are circling, Doctor. They sense the tallith's weakness."

Boyce remembered something else then, what had happened the night before, how Liyan had stopped his attack with ease. "She doesn't seem in imminent danger of dying to me."

"Perhaps not. But neither is she herself any longer. Or, rather, the self she needs to be."

"What's that supposed to mean?" Boyce asked.

Deleen stopped walking and turned to face him. "We are Orions, Doctor. More than any other race in the galaxy, biology determines our destiny."

Boyce was completely lost now. "Biology."

"Yes. A biology we must someday overcome, if we are to regain the glories of our past." She shook her head. "It is a terrible quandary the tallith faces. Terrible things she must do, for the good of our race."

"Like Starbase Eighteen."

"I'm not talking about Starbase Eighteen." Deleen tapped on a segment of the bulkhead next to her, which slid aside to reveal a storage locker. That was when Boyce realized where they were. The lab. The converted shuttlebay.

"You're not talking about Starbase Eighteen," he said.

"No."

"Then what—"

Behind her, the lab door slid open.

Deleen handed him a parka. "You are about to find out."

FOURTEEN

The breadth of material Number One had gathered related to Kronos was impressive. Records of mineral transport from various deep-space mining facilities, images of Starfleet personnel traveling on civilian transports, letters of transit granting cargo freighters permission to pass through hostile territory. She had even gone so far as to purchase limited-time access to the Ferengi Commerce Authority central database, which tracked price, supply, and real-time demand for raw materials such as kreelite ore throughout the Alpha Quadrant.

The FCA also had visual recordings of most of the quadrant's commodity exchanges. It was on one that she had uncovered the name "Kronos." A notation, appearing momentarily on the display screen of a data slate belonging to a merchant who had subsequently purchased forty-six tons of raw kreelite from the Hazzard Mining Confederacy. The notation had been on the screen for but a second before being erased; long enough, though, for the Ferengi to capture it.

Having been through the entire stack of flimsies now—as well as two cups of tea Number One had prepared for him—Spock felt his first, instinctual association was correct. The word referred to the English transliteration of the name for the Klingon home world, Q'nos. There were other possibilities, of course—Kronos as in time, Kronos as in the father of the ancient Earth gods, the grandfather, as it were, of all sentient creatures, Kronos as an English transliteration for the Ferengi *kronner,* a coin of precious metal used in certain sectors of the galaxy where credit was not welcome—but evidence suggested otherwise.

Most convincing of all in that regard were the personnel records Number One had gathered, a large number of whom had direct experience with the Klingon Empire, starting with Commodore Higueras, who had served in the border patrol for years before transferring back to Starfleet Headquarters. His second-in-command, Lieutenant Patrice Njomo, had an impressive record of her own, vis-à-vis the Klingons. She had been part of the team that had attempted to rescue the UFP hostages aboard the Klingon heavy cruiser *Torg,* the ship whose subsequent destruction had led directly to the Gorengar crisis.

Then there was Dr. Tomas Nieldstrom, an expert in the history of the early Empire, who had been a guest lecturer at Starfleet Academy during Spock's time there. There was Dr. Andreas Corzine, whose voice Spock had briefly heard on the salvaged recording from Starbase 18, who twenty years before Gorengar had been part of an exchange program between the most prominent Klingon and human medical academies and who had been, according to Starfleet records, the UFP's most well-regarded specialist in interspecies battlefield medicine.

And then there was the transport of materiel to Starbase 18, the delivery of four Alpha-class power cores to 55-Hamilton, cores that—according to transport manifests—were intended for Building 8. Which Spock assumed referred to the mysterious, unaccounted-for structure on the surface of 55-Hamilton.

What it all added up to he was still not sure.

Spock set the flimsy aside and looked up. Number One had remained standing as he flipped through the flimsies, staring out the ship's porthole, her back to him. She turned around now to face him.

"Finished?"

"Yes."

"So what are they up to?"

"They?"

"The people in charge of this project. The people who tampered with the Archives." She sat down next to him on the couch and straightened the stack of flimsies. "I keep this material in a storage locker in the sleeping alcove, by the way. The combination is 'Kronos.' If anything happens to me . . ."

"You believe you are in danger here? Aboard *Enterprise*?"

"Tampering with the Archives is a court-martial offense, Mr. Spock. I don't think we should be under any illusions about what these people are capable of."

"These people." Spock leaned forward, resting his elbows on the table, steepling his fingers together. "Who exactly are 'these people'?"

She shrugged. "A faction within Starfleet. A cabal of officers, disgruntled politicians . . . no way of knowing for certain."

Spock nodded. There was no shortage of individuals and groups, both within and outside the Starfleet apparatus, who were convinced that Gorengar—the treaty—had been a huge mistake, from both a moral and a tactical perspective.

"Of course, most politicians—most Starfleet officers, too, for that matter—aren't capable of performing stunts like erasing data from the Archives. They need a little help to manage that kind of thing."

"Covert operations," Spock said.

"Exactly."

"Such work is typically the bailiwick of Starfleet Intelligence."

"Yes, it is."

"This complicates matters."

"Yes," she said. "It certainly does."

For one thing, it ruled out contacting T'Koss and informing her of their suspicions, sharing Number One's discoveries, because if Starfleet Intelligence was involved, they would certainly be monitoring communications to and from the Archives.

For another . . .

"I had thought earlier," he said, "that we should share our suspicions with the captain."

She hesitated a second before responding. "I'm not entirely certain that's a good idea."

Spock nodded. "I am forced to agree."

Number One walked over to the table and picked up the stack of flimsies. "I'm going to put this away. Back in a second."

"No matter how we decide to make our suspicions known, whom we decide to tell them to," he said when she returned, "we will need further evidence to back them up."

"Proof of the facility's existence."

"And purpose."

"You have any thoughts on how to go about getting that proof?"

"Commander Tuval's initial site survey lacked specificity," Spock said. "I had intended members of my department to conduct a more thorough search of the area."

"Return to the asteroid's surface? That might be difficult to arrange."

"Perhaps." He thought a moment. "I could generate orders from Starfleet Command, requesting such a survey."

"Generate fake orders?"

"It should be possible," he said. "I do have an A-seven rating."

"So I heard." The trace of a smile flitted across her face and disappeared just as quickly. "If we get caught . . ."

"You are A-six—the next-highest rating aboard the ship."

"Vlasidovich is A-five," Number One pointed out.

"I was not aware of that," Spock said. A5 was expert level as well. Another impressive accomplishment to add to Vlasidovich's list. Still, working together, the two of them—the commander and himself—should be more than capable of keeping their activities hidden from the captain.

The comm sounded, the telltale chime of some-one at her door. Number One looked at Spock, who nodded.

"Enter!" she called out.

Captain Vlasidovich walked into the room.

"As I suspected." The captain put his hands on his hips and glared. "I find the two of you here. Together."

Spock had heard the expression "My heart leaped into my mouth" many times in the years since he had entered Starfleet. Read it, actually, to be more precise, in his review of human literature. He knew what it meant, of course, but he had never understood the phrase's genesis until this very second. He glanced at Number One. Her face revealed nothing. He hoped his was as expressionless.

"You are looking for us," Spock said.

"I have been."

Spock was about to inquire why, when he saw what Vlasidovich was wearing. His dress uniform.

The officers' dinner.

"You are not on bridge, Commander, you are not in lab or your quarters, Mr. Spock, you are seen together in shuttlebay earlier . . . and so I add two plus two and come here."

"I beg your pardon, Captain. The time slipped away from me. I shall return to my cabin and dress for dinner."

"Please do, Mr. Spock. Immediately. I would like for us please to enter as group. *Enterprise* senior officers. Yes?"

"Yes, sir," said Number One.

"Yes, sir," said Spock.

"Good. And in future . . ." Vlasidovich wagged a finger. "Do not think to keep secrets aboard my starship, please. I know everything that is happening here."

FIFTEEN

Biology. The tallith's quandary. Zandar, who seemed to be in charge of the laboratory, did not know what Deleen had been referring to.

"I have been tasked with assisting you in your analysis of the serum. This is my duty, as the tallith has outlined it." She gestured to the LeKarz. "Shall we?"

Boyce shrugged. "Lead on."

He supposed he'd find out what Deleen had been referring to sooner or later.

He followed Zandar over to the machine they'd stolen from Starbase 18.

"I will bring up the relevant information on the primary display," she said, keying in a series of commands.

"The molecular breakdown of the serum, its key components, and their relevant chemical analogues."

Boyce leaned over her shoulder as unobtrusively as he could and watched her work. Right away, he saw that he was going to have to start over at ground zero. Zandar might have been a competent scientist (or not—he really had no way of knowing), but she had a lot to learn when it came to the LeKarz. The machine had come from Starbase 18 in lockdown mode, naturally. The Orions had managed to bypass the password protocols, to get it working, but they hadn't tied in the analysis array to the main memory banks. That left half the machine's functionality—the specialized, high-level databases Starbase 18's personnel had either purchased or programmed in—inoperative, inaccessible for comparative purposes. The analysis they'd done—the work they'd asked the LeKarz to do—was incomplete.

"Is there a problem?" Zandar asked.

He was about to tell her that she was operating the LeKarz, in effect, with blinders on, that she should summon the ship's top computer expert, when he realized that there could be a lot of very sensitive medical information in those databases. A lot of material the Federation might not want the Orions getting their hands on.

"Yes," he said. "I prefer to do my own lab work."

Zandar's expression darkened. "I can assure you, Dr. Boyce, the procedure we followed in analyzing the serum did not deviate in any manner from—"

"Nonetheless," Boyce interrupted, "I'd like to start fresh. With another sample of the serum."

She glared at him a few seconds longer. "As you wish," she said finally, and then pulled a stasis cube from a nearby storage locker.

Boyce inserted it into the machine's input module, then stepped up beside the console.

A LeKarz. It had been a long, long time since he'd used one of these.

He reached for the controls and then realized that Zandar was standing right behind him.

He turned. "If you don't mind, I prefer privacy when I work."

"The tallith said I was to stay apprised of your progress."

"Well, I haven't made any yet, have I?"

Zandar had no answer for that. She bowed, backed off, and left him alone.

Boyce went to work.

The interface came back to him immediately. Kind of like riding a bike. It was almost as easy to override the security lock on Starbase 18's databases. Within minutes, he found himself staring at a screen that displayed the contents of the LeKarz's internal information clusters. Most of the machine's data, he saw, were contained in a node labeled "Kronos."

Familiar-sounding name, and a second later, he realized why. The Klingon home world. He was curious what the connection was. Jaya hadn't mentioned anything to do with Klingons the last time he spoke to her.

His curiosity would have to wait, though. He had work to do.

The deeper he got into that work analyzing the serum, the clearer it became to him why the Orions had been so intent on obtaining the LeKarz. The machine had been created to mimic the behavior of genetic material in situ; the serum was even more sophisticated. And its behavior in isolation, as opposed to its behavior within the serum—and within the Orion bloodstream, for that matter—added another layer of complexity to the analysis. It took him a good hour to sort out the results he understood from those he didn't.

The vial was full of all sorts of stuff he knew for a fact had no effect on the aging process. Different kinds of hormones, chemical substances that in humans had the effect of minimizing the cell damage caused by free radicals, stimulants to speed up the metabolic process. Possibly those things all had different effects on the Orion circulatory system from those on the human. He didn't think so, but he made notes on some of those elements he thought deserving of further study.

That left him with a single, very complicated chemical compound, a polymer—a repeating chain of amino acids—that resembled the DNA molecule more than anything else, though instead of being made up of four basic acids, he saw at a quick glance that this compound contained almost a dozen.

"It took us years to identify the molecule. You do it in a single afternoon."

Boyce turned and saw Zandar standing over his shoulder. "I've had practice," he said.

"Argelius."

"And other places." He was getting tired of everyone reminding him of Argelius. "So what is it?" he asked.

"You are looking, Dr. Boyce, at a molecule we've named gamina."

"A key ingredient in the serum, I assume."

"The key ingredient."

"You've tried to replicate it."

"We have."

"And?"

"Here. You can judge our efforts for yourself. As I know you prefer to do."

Ouch. Well, he deserved that, he supposed.

Zandar produced a second stasis cube, one labeled "Gamina Analogue." Boyce ran it through the LeKarz as well. He took as long with those tests as he had with the original molecule. The results puzzled him. He ran the tests a second time. The data came out just the same.

He stood back from the LeKarz. Zandar was right there, alongside him.

"There's no difference between the two," he said.

She nodded. "Not that we could find."

"They have the same molecular weight, same chemical composition, same atomic structure."

"Yes. But the analogue doesn't work."

"Show me," he said. "Please."

She stared at him a moment, then nodded. "Of course."

She set up a simulation on the LeKarz, a split screen. The original gamina molecule on the left, the gamina analogue on the right. She introduced both into a computer-modeled simulation of the Orion bloodstream. Nothing happened. The gamina molecule—both versions—drifted.

She accelerated the simulation. On the left, the gamina molecule began attaching itself to other chemicals in the bloodstream, bonding with them, transforming them. Boyce estimated that it would take him weeks to figure out exactly what was happening there. At a minimum.

On the right, the gamina analogue was bonding as well. But only with itself. Bonding and forming a compound that decreased in motility and flexibility with each additional molecule that latched on. A molecule that soon became large enough to interfere with the flow of the bloodstream itself.

"This is what's causing the distension of the veins," Boyce realized. "In Liyan and her daughter."

"Yes."

The simulation continued, the transformations on the left screen, the agglomeration of gamina analogue on the right. Blood flow continued to decline; blood pressure, conversely, began to rise. The condition was dangerous, Boyce realized. More than that, potentially fatal.

He remembered the look that had flashed across Liyan's face when she had seen the veins on her arms—not just surprise but fear. He understood why.

M'Lor says you must not excite yourself unnecessarily.

Her blood pressure had to be a point of concern as well. Maybe he was wrong, Boyce thought. Maybe Liyan was sicker than he'd assumed.

"Do you have her medical history?" he asked Zandar. "The tallith."

She hesitated a moment, then nodded. "Yes. I will bring it up on one of the terminals. Come."

She led him across the bay to another terminal where she brought up Liyan's medical history. Complete medical history, starting from when she was a child. There was a lot of data; Zandar left him to browse through them. Hundreds of different screens of information, including recordings and photographs. He was particularly struck by an image of Liyan as a young woman, the tallith at twenty standard years. She looked exactly like her daughter.

He wondered when she'd changed.

The machine's primary screen was movable; he rotated it so that instead of facing him, the screen lay flat before him, like the surface of a desk. He drew a line with his finger and split the display window. Liyan's treatment history on the left, a blank screen on the right. One by one, he dragged the images of Liyan from their associated historical files into the empty space, till he had them arranged one on top of the other, earliest to latest. He closed the treatment-history pane and set the images to play before him in a slide show.

The first one, the young Liyan, as she'd looked seventy years earlier. The next few, much the same. Then one of her in a body cast, roughly, if he was remembering right, at the time of the Klingon attack. The time of their discovery at Zai Romeen. More images flew past. He came to one from sixty-six years ago. Liyan posed in front of a blank wall, wearing a medical gown, a determined look on her face.

He found the associated medical file and read through it. One phrase jumped out at him right away. A notation from the attending physician: "Stardate 1807.1. Treatments begin."

Boyce moved on to the next image. It was, according to the date, two weeks later. Boyce detected no significant difference in her appearance. Except . . .

He scrolled back to the first image and then forward to the second one again. Liyan was dressed the same in both, posed the exact same way, standing in front of the same nondescript wall, in what Boyce thought he recognized now as the medical wing. A plain white wall, the same shade in both pictures.

Her skin color, though, looked different to him, slightly darker in the second. He moved ahead to the next picture and then the next. Two months of treatment. By then, the differences in skin tone were obvious. As were other changes.

In the first two years of treatment, she grew six inches. She gained thirty pounds. But somehow, the weight, the height . . .

She'd been an attractive woman before the treatments began; afterward, even more so. Much more so. Just looking at these pictures, Boyce found her . . . beautiful? Yes. Alluring? Absolutely. More than that, though. Really, it was hard to stop looking at her. She was—what was the word he was looking for?

Intoxicating. That was it. Intoxicating.

Good God. Biology. The tallith's quandary.

He knew now exactly what Deleen had been talking about.

SIXTEEN

On a handful of occasions, Captain Pikc had conducted ship's business during dinner. Those meals were typically in *Enterprise*'s briefing room and consisted of food designed to be eaten quickly, by hand, with a minimum of fuss, a minimum of distraction, so that more important matters could be attended to.

Captain Vlasidovich's idea of a working dinner was entirely different.

For one thing, the meal was in the officers' mess, rather than the briefing room. For another, all attendees were in full dress uniform, rather than the everyday Starfleet outfit. And they were being served in courses—a wide variety of cuisines from cultures and races all across the galaxy as opposed to buffet-

style. There were twenty of them in all, the senior staff
of three *Constitution*-class starships currently orbiting 55-Hamilton. It felt more like a state dinner or a
banquet than a working meal. Spock did not approve.
Initially. And yet . . .

As the evening wore on, he realized that the structure of the meal—the breakdown of the dining experience into courses, with associated interruptions for
presentation of the dishes, serving of the food, clearing of the plates—facilitated shifts of conversational
topics and partners. Spock was seated at the far end
of the long dining table from Captain Vlasidovich,
who, as host, was at the head. On his immediate left,
at the foot of the table, was Captain Harrari of *Hood*
and to his right, *Hood*'s science officer, Lieutenant
Carl Vayentes.

Enterprise was represented by the captain, Number
One, himself, Chief Pitcairn, and Lieutenants Hardin
and Garrison.

For most of the meal, Spock just listened to the others talk. In particular, Captain Harrari, who seemed to
him a formidable intellect. She held forth on a wide
variety of subjects during the meal, discussed warp
technology with Chief Pitcairn, colonial politics with
Captain Nolan, the current state of Starfleet terraform-
ing with Lieutenant Garrison and himself.

When the plates at last had been cleared and dessert
and after-dinner drinks had been served and set out on

the table, Captain Vlasidovich tapped his coffee cup with a spoon, signaling for quiet.

He stood and raised his glass, which was filled with a pale yellow sparkling beverage of some sort. An alcoholic beverage. Spock did not approve of alcohol.

"I wish to propose toast," Vlasidovich said. "To crews of *Excalibur, Hood,* and *Enterprise*. Braver men and women I could not wish to go to battle with."

Shouts of "Hear, hear!" echoed down the table. All raised their glasses and drank. Most of them were drinking alcoholic beverages as well. Spock was drinking water. Number One—who sat far down the table from him, on the opposite side, between Captain Nolan and Lieutenant Commander Radovitch of *Excalibur*— was drinking tea. It had been a long day for the two of them; it was going to be an even longer night.

They had plans.

Upon arriving at his own quarters to change for dinner, Spock had sat down at his workstation, intending to send *Enterprise*'s first officer a message. Encrypted, naturally. He found one waiting for him, from her, as he discovered when he broke the encryption on it, a process that took him close to a minute to complete.

Her thoughts paralleled his. *Enterprise*'s senior officers off-duty for the evening, following the banquet. *Hood* and *Excalibur*'s not on shift, either?

It was the perfect time for the mission they had discussed, a trip to the surface of 55-Hamilton.

He looked across the table now and met Number One's gaze.

Not long now.

"Also." Vlasidovich remained standing, but the broad smile on his face vanished, replaced by a more serious, somber expression. "I wish to salute Captain Christopher Pike."

The conversation around the table died.

"And crew from *Magellan*," Vlasidovich continued. "We serve—we fight if necessary—to make sure their sacrifice was not in vain."

The "Hear, hears" returned, even louder than before.

"I'll second that toast with one of my own." Chief Pitcairn stood now as well. "To Captain Pike, to Ben Tuval. If there are better men in the galaxy, I haven't met them yet."

Pitcairn drained his glass and sat, almost before anyone else could join him.

The chief had been largely silent all evening. Spock would characterize his mood as brooding, verging on anger, even. The captain's death had upset him more than most. Spock knew Pike's first assignment on graduation from the Academy had been aboard the *Olympus*, a light cruiser. The captain and Pitcairn—already chief engineer aboard that vessel—had met there and become, if not friends, then great admirers of each other's capabilities.

"I have a toast as well, Dmitri. If you don't mind." Captain Harrari stood now. She was small, dark-skinned, and slight and spoke with a very clipped, very precise accent. A British accent, she informed Spock when he asked during the meal. She, her siblings, her parents, and her grandparents were long-standing citizens of the British Isles.

"Not at all. Go ahead," Vlasidovich said. "Please, Michaela."

Harrari raised her glass. "To peace," she said.

"To peace," Vlasidovich replied instantly. "With those who want peace."

Harrari smiled. "Whose toast is this, Dmitri? Mine or yours?"

Vlasidovich bowed. "Yours, of course. Forgive me."

"Thank you. To peace, then." Everyone drank, some with noticeably less enthusiasm than others.

Spock could not entirely determine the nature of Harrari's relationship with Vlasidovich. Her views on the threat posed by the Klingon Empire and the wisdom or necessity of any potential war were diametrically opposed to his. And yet the two of them obviously greatly enjoyed each other's company; from what Vlasidovich had hinted at earlier, they had been friends for a long time.

"If the Klingons wanted peace, they wouldn't have appointed K'Zon to head their fleet." That comment came from Captain Nolan, Vlasidovich's former first officer, a lean, intense-looking man, who sat at the far end of the table, at Vlasidovich's right hand.

"Precisely." Vlasidovich nodded. "K'Zon is general at Malboundian. Commander of fleet at Dourami. A great warrior. War hero. That tells us a lot, yes?"

"It tells me the Klingons are running out of officers, if they have to drag a relic like K'Zon out of mothballs to take charge." Harrari's security officer—a Tellarite female named Greekang, who had been, for a Tellarite, at least, uncharacteristically silent during most of the meal—took a sip from her drink as laughter filled the room.

"It could be a negotiating tactic," Harrari said after the laughter died down.

"A bluff." Vlasidovich smiled. "Do you think Klingons this subtle, Mr. Spock?"

"Unlikely. But possible."

"Klingons subtle." Nolan snorted. "Tell that to the people at Starbase Eighteen. Oh, wait. I forgot. You can't. They're all dead."

The room went silent a moment.

"You know . . ." Harrari sipped at her own drink—coffee—and then set her cup back down on the table. "Those sensor readings on that recording of yours, Mr. Spock, there's something a little funny about them."

"If by funny you mean the associated fluctuations . . ."

"I do."

"I agree."

"Is fluctuation in readings not to be expected?" Vlasidovich asked. "If we are dealing with cloaking device?"

"If indeed." Harrari shook her head. "I'm not so certain about that."

"You have other explanation for readings?"

"No. But I have other facts."

"Go on."

"Some chatter we've recently picked up from Kitulba."

"The Klingon weapons facility?" Spock asked.

Harrari nodded. "One and the same. The prototype was being constructed there."

"Black Snow," Spock said.

"Black Snow." Harrari nodded. "Exactly."

"What does this chatter say?" Vlasidovich asked.

"It doesn't say anything explicitly. But reading between the lines, it appears the device has been stolen."

"The cloaking device stolen?" Vlasidovich frowned. "By whom?"

"The prototype is less than two meters tall," Spock pointed out. "A thief could carry it away on a vessel as small as a shuttlecraft."

"Kitulba's at the base of the Phalanx," Harrari added. "Which puts it within striking range of a lot of different races. The Airee, the Romulans, the T'landra . . ."

"Near enough to Federation territory that the Klingons most likely consider us a suspect as well," Number One added.

"I don't buy it," Nolan said. "Who could sneak into a Klingon weapons facility and make off with that kind of technology? Not possible."

Number One cleared her throat and spoke, for the first time all evening that Spock had noticed.

"Starfleet Intelligence," she said. "They have operatives—"

"Starfleet Intelligence." Chief Pitcairn snorted. "Now, there's an oxymoron." The chief took a sip from his drink. It was almost empty. Spock wondered how many the man had had.

"Reminds me of this joke I heard," Pitcairn went on. "This guy applies for a job at Starfleet Headquarters. It's him and these two other people. They take all three—"

Number One leaned forward. "Chief, perhaps now is not the best time to—"

"No, no. This is funny. They give them each a flimsy, a message in an envelope. Sealed, so you can't read what's in it. Then they tell them to take the message to the fourth floor, where they'll get directions on what to do."

Pitcairn drained his glass and continued. He was talking, Spock noticed, much more loudly than usual.

"So these other two head up in a turbolift. The first guy, meanwhile, the second they disappear, he rips the envelope open. You know what the note says?"

Pitcairn looked around the table expectantly.

"Come on. Somebody? Anybody? What does the note say?"

"Congratulations, you're just the kind of person we're looking for. You got the job," Nolan said.

"That's it exactly!" Pitcairn beamed. "Congratulations, you got the job!" He laughed and slapped the table.

Nobody else even smiled.

"What?" Pitcairn said. "It's a joke. Doesn't anyone here like jokes?"

"Chief," Vlasidovich began.

"Chief," Number One said, at virtually the same instant. "Do you think you've maybe had a little too much?"

Pitcairn frowned. "A little too much what?"

Spock stood. "Commander Pitcairn, would you accompany to my quarters?"

"I'm fine," the chief said, waving him off.

"Consider it a personal request," Spock said. "I am feeling a bit under the weather."

Pitcairn frowned.

"In fact, Chief," Vlasidovich said. "Consider Mr. Spock's request an order."

• • •

In the turbolift, Pitcairn kept grumbling. "Not funny. Those guys wouldn't know funny if . . ." The chief shook his head.

"Humor is a difficult concept," Spock said.

"I guess. My dad used to say you meet a man without a sense of humor, turn around and run as fast as you can." Pitcairn turned around, leaned his back against the wall. "Of course, Captain Pike had a terrible sense of humor."

Not having anything relevant to add to that statement, Spock remained silent.

"It's all messed up," Pitcairn said, a sudden, very serious expression on his face. "Everything is all messed up."

"You are talking about Captain Vlasidovich's assumption of command, I assume?"

"Yes. No. I . . ." Pitcairn sighed and leaned his head back against the turbolift wall. "Never mind, Spock. Just never mind."

They rode in silence for a few seconds. Spock could sense, however, that the chief's mood had not altered. If anything, he sensed a growing frustration.

"Something is clearly bothering you, Chief. If you wish to discuss it, now or later, I am available."

"Yeah, sure." Pitcairn barked out a laugh. "Discuss it. Like that would do any good."

Spock frowned. "Chief . . ."

"Look, Spock, I know it's not your idea. Your fault. So don't worry about it."

"I do not know what you are referring to."

"Hey," Pitcairn said, turning to face him. "How long have we known each other, three months? We get along okay, right? You don't have to lie . . ." The chief's voice trailed off. "Wait a minute." He looked Spock dead in the eye. "Is it possible you don't know?"

"Know what?"

Pitcairn yanked the control lever. The turbolift came to a sudden stop, so sudden that Spock almost lost his balance.

Pitcairn put a finger to his lips and then pulled something out of his pocket. A communicator. He pressed a button on the side of it, and a blue light lit up, which was when Spock realized the device had been modified. The standard Starfleet communicator did not have blue lights.

"There," Pitcairn said. "Now we can talk."

"I do not understand."

"Jamming signal." Pitcairn held up the communicator. "Broadwave. High frequency. Although I think I can hear it, too. Maybe I messed up the calibration. Or maybe I had too much vodka. Maybe both."

"Chief . . ."

"It'll read like a power shunt on the main board. A disruption of audio and visual circuits. We got about a minute."

"To do what?"

"To talk about this." He looked at Spock closely. "I figured you had to be in on it. Or that you'd at least spot it right off."

"Chief, will you please tell me what you are talking about?"

"The bug."

"What bug?"

"On the computer system. Well, not a bug, actually, if you want to get technical about it. More like a feedback circuit, so that everything that goes in—every query, every piece of data—gets sent somewhere else. Another terminal. I'm not sure exactly whose, but I can make a couple good guesses."

Spock raised an eyebrow. A surveillance circuit? On the ship's computer?

He was about to speak in absolutes again, to respond with the word *impossible,* because he would have, as the chief said, noted the placement of any such circuit on the system immediately, except . . .

He realized he had not been on the computer system for several hours, since meeting Number One in the shuttlebay. He had been with her, looking at flimsies. He would have had no opportunity to notice any kind of slowdown in the system, any glitches.

"This is disturbing," Spock said.

"You're telling me. Hell, it's more than disturbing. It's—"

The little blue light on the chief's modified communicator began flashing orange.

"Ten seconds," the chief said. "Surveillance on *Enterprise*. Captain Pike is rolling over in his grave right now, I can tell you that."

Something suddenly occurred to Spock. "You're concerned about the captain's legacy, Chief. Captain Pike."

"Yes."

"Then there are some things I wish to discuss with you in private."

"Such as . . ."

The communicator beeped. Pitcairn straightened and started the turbolift up again.

"Maybe I did have too much, after all, Mr. Spock," he said, miming, once more, inebriation. "Maybe you can help me to my quarters."

SEVENTEEN

Boyce worked through lunch; he worked through dinner as well. The doctor kept the tallith's medical file active but also spent a great deal of time studying in a historical database he found after a bit of searching—probably the very database Lieutenant Hoto had referred to earlier. He read about some of those Klingon-Orion conflicts she had mentioned and about some of the relatively recent events in this sector, the ones that did indeed show—as she and the tallith had said—how influential and stabilizing a role Liyan had played in the Borderland over the last half-century.

Now, of course, Boyce knew how.

He yawned. Coffee. He could sure use a cup; he hadn't realized how addicted he'd gotten to the stuff. He missed it. He could practically smell it.

"Dr. Boyce."

He turned and saw Deleen standing behind him. In her hands, she held a steaming mug of brownish-black liquid.

"Would you like coffee?" she asked.

"Coffee." He stared at the mug. He was dreaming, that was it. He had to be dreaming. "Where did you get this?"

She held the mug out, and he took it from her, shaking his head.

"The ship's stores are extensive. It was simply a matter of asking the right people."

"Thank you."

"You're welcome."

Boyce brought the mug to his lips, bracing himself for the worst. It wasn't. Far from it.

"Something the matter?" Deleen asked.

"No," he managed. "Not at all. It's . . . good."

Better than good, in fact; it was the real deal. Not synthesized, not reconstituted. He could tell right off. He hadn't had a cup this good in years. He wondered if there was more.

"I heard you were still working; I thought you could use a stimulant."

"You were right." He smiled and raised the mug. "And this is my stimulant of choice."

She looked over his shoulder and frowned. "Those are my mother's personnel files."

"Yes. I've been spending quite a lot of time looking them over."

"And what have you learned?"

He looked her in the eye and had a feeling she knew exactly what he was about to say. "Gamina's not just an immortality serum, is it?"

"No."

"No. Of course not. It changed her. Outside and in."

He reconfigured the display screen, brought up a chart he'd been looking at. A chart of the Orion circulatory system and associated organs, superimposed on top of a humanoid form.

"My Orion anatomy was a little rusty," he said. "Which was why I needed this." He pointed to the neck area. "These glands here at the clavicle. They're unique to your race."

"Yes."

"Sex glands," Boyce said. "During adolescence, they release a series of chemicals into the bloodstream. Different chemicals for the two sexes. Testosterone analogues in the males, pheromones in the females. The former accelerate growth, the latter sexual attraction. The glands stop functioning after a certain point—child-bearing years in females, late middle age in males. But with gamina . . ."

He cleared the chart and brought up Liyan's file again, the image of her that had struck him so forcefully earlier.

"The glands don't seem to shut off. Production of the chemicals apparently continues," Boyce said. "On and on. Ad infinitum."

He turned to Deleen. "This is what you were talking about before, isn't it? The tallith's quandary? Biology as destiny?"

She nodded. "It is."

Boyce could only shake his head.

Government by seduction. The tallith had been ingesting modified versions of gamina for seventy-five years. That explained her ever-increasing influence within the Confederacy, the way she'd been able to draw the other clans to her side and keep them there.

It explained other things he'd been wondering about as well. Why the little cocktail he'd given the *Magellan* landing party hadn't worked as advertised, perhaps even the speed of her reactions earlier, when he'd tried to attack her. Her speed and her strength.

It explained her desperation now as well.

"We are not proud of it, Dr. Boyce," Deleen said.

"Then change."

"Easier said than done. And impossible at the moment."

"Why?"

"Why?" She studied him a moment, considering. Then a small smile crossed her face. "Come," she said. "I will show you."

Deleen led him downward into the bowels of the ship. It didn't take Boyce long to realize where he was going now, either. The lights grew dimmer; the temperature rose slightly. They were nearing the ship's engineering section, though their destination had nothing to do with warp drive.

They were going back, Boyce realized, to what on *Enterprise* he would have called the brig, the cells where he had been kept his first few days aboard *Karkon's Wing*.

"What's down here?" he asked.

"Not what," Deleen said. "Who."

A second later, she stopped in front of one of those cells, one that looked like—and for all he knew, could have been—the one he had been imprisoned in.

Boyce peered inside it, through the haze of the lime-green energy curtain, and saw Gurgis. The Orion was sitting on his cot, hands in his lap, staring down at the floor.

"Singhino," Deleen said.

He looked up. "Codruta. What do you want?"

"I came to see how you were doing."

"Liar." The man's face was in shadow somehow. Boyce took a step closer and realized that he was wrong, that what he had taken for shadow was in fact a large bruise on one cheek. There were others, too, smaller ones on his face and hands. Some looked as if they were just beginning to heal. Others looked as if they weren't healing at all, as if they were infected.

"You came to taunt me," Gurgis said. "To remind me I live at your whim."

"That's not true," Deleen said.

"Are you injured?" Boyce asked.

Gurgis looked at him. "You are the human. Boyce."

"Yes. You didn't answer my question. Are you—"

"You have chosen poorly, Boyce. The Codruta are destined to fall."

"I haven't chosen anything." Boyce took a step forward, till he was right up against the energy curtain. He could feel its warmth, could hear the hum of the machinery that powered it. "What happened there?"

"The burns?" Gurgis put his hands on his thighs and stood. "Come inside and see."

"That would not be a good idea," Deleen said.

"Why not?" Boyce asked.

"We tried to treat him before. He was not cooperative. To say the least."

"You going to hurt me if I come in there?" Boyce asked, looking right at Gurgis. "That strikes me as pretty counterproductive."

The prisoner screamed and leaped right at him.

Boyce exclaimed in surprise and took a step backward.

Deleen cried out as well. She backpedaled, tripped, and fell to the ground.

Gurgis slammed into the energy curtain. Boyce heard the crackle of electricity, smelled ozone.

Gurgis took a step backward and grunted. Then he looked out through the energy curtain and began to laugh. "Cowards," he said. "Weaklings."

There were fresh bruises on his face, Boyce saw. No. Not bruises. Burns. From where he had run into the energy curtain. The skin on both of his cheeks was singed bright red; it had to be unbelievably painful.

It didn't seem to bother him at all.

"Female." Gurgis glared down at Deleen. "Tell the one who whelped you I am no longer in her thrall. Tell her my people will come for me, and I will make her my dog before she dies."

Deleen sat on the ground, trembling, obviously terrified and trying not to show it.

"It's all right," Boyce said, reaching out his hand and helping her to her feet.

"No. It is not all right at all." She got to her feet and looked over his shoulder at Gurgis, who still stood inches away from the energy curtain, breathing heavily. Breathing, if such a thing were possible, aggressively. Staring daggers at them.

"Now, Dr. Boyce," Deleen said. "Now do you see what I mean?"

He opened his mouth to answer, but the girl had already turned to leave.

EIGHTEEN

Spock stepped up onto the transporter platform.
Number One stepped up alongside him, in a
dark blue evac suit that matched his own, and secured
her helmet.

Chief Pitcairn, still in his dress uniform, stood behind the transporter console, shaking his head.

"You sure about this?" he asked.

"Quite sure," she said. "Mr. Spock?"

"Ready for transport, Commander." He fastened his
helmet and secured the straps on his backpack.

"Because I could definitely rig something up," Pitcairn said. His voice sounded tinny and thin in the evac
suit's audio. "Just on the off chance . . ."

"We made a plan. Let's stick to it." Number One looked over at Spock and then faced forward once more. "Energize."

Pitcairn's hands went to the transporter controls. The chief's modified communicator, propped on top of the operator panel, flashed blue. The chief's hands began to move and then stopped.

He looked back up. "One hour."

"Exactly," Number One said. "We'll be ready for beam-up in one hour."

"Got it," the chief said.

But still, his hands didn't move. Pitcairn's hesitation was understandable. They were breaking protocol here—several times over, in fact. Two of the ship's senior officers beaming into a hostile environment, the chief the only person who knew where they were going . . .

"Secrecy is essential, Chief," Spock said. "You know that."

"I do, I do. It's just that, well, secrecy's one thing. This is hitting me more like stupidity. What if something happens to you? What if something happens to me? You could be stuck—"

"We talked about all this before, Chief," Number One interrupted. And they had—first Spock and Pitcairn, in the chief's quarters, and then the three of them, in the ship's mess, using various electronic countermeasures to maintain their privacy. "Or weren't you listening?"

"I was listening," Pitcairn said.

"I thought you were. And I'm pretty sure you were no longer inebriated. Am I right? You weren't drunk anymore?"

Pitcairn glared. "I wasn't."

"I didn't think so." She matched his glare with one of her own. "So, if you would . . . energize. Please," she said, or started to say. The chief's hands were moving as she started the second word, so that Spock heard the "Pl" just as he was thinking that he hadn't seen the chief this angry in a long while, and the "ease" as the chief's face vanished, and the twisted blackened wreckage of what they were now calling Building 8, the suspected weapons facility, appeared before him.

The images had not done the devastation justice.

Building 8, two stories tall when intact, was now less than half that. The upper level, what was left of it, had collapsed on top of the lower. Support beams and cable dangled before them. Here and there, a splash of color peeked through the gray—painted walls, coded strands of wire, torn fabric.

Beyond those splashes, and the silver and gray of the ruined structure, and the reddish sands of 55-Hamilton, loomed only the blackness of space and the bright white glitter of stars, light-years from where he stood.

One of them seemed particularly bright. More silver than white. *Enterprise,* he realized suddenly.

It seemed a long way off.

"This way," Number One said, and started walking forward.

Spock followed in her wake.

During their initial survey, Commander Tuval's landing party had noted the presence of what seemed to be an intact doorway. On reviewing tapes of that expedition, Spock and Number One immediately identified the doorway as their prime target, their best chance at getting deeper into the building's ruins, finding more evidence of what Building 8 was—and wasn't.

When they arrived at the door's presumed coordinates, however, it was gone. Buried, Spock presumed, underneath a pile of rubble.

"This way." Number One gestured to her left. "Maybe we could find another way inside."

Spock looked over the scene before him. He understood Number One's instinctual reaction. On this side of the building, the outer wall seemed largely intact, at least up to the second level, which meant, presumably, that the lower levels would be walkable. The fact that the door Commander Tuval had discovered was now gone, however, meant the structure might still be unstable. It certainly looked it.

"Given our limited time constraints, that does not seem feasible," Spock said. "I suggest we concentrate our energies on a more detailed analysis of the materials available to us."

"The wreckage? Commander Tuval did that already," Number One responded. "Come on."

She began walking to her left, around the outside of the building. Half walking, half bounding—the gravity on 55-Hamilton was practically nonexistent. Spock followed, careful not to exert too much energy. He felt, instinctually, as if he could leap upward and escape the asteroid's gravitational pull entirely.

Number One stopped walking. "There's something here. Looks like an exhaust vent of some kind."

It did indeed look like a vent; it ran from ground level to a height of two meters and was perhaps half that width. What sort of device required a vent that big? A power generator was Spock's first thought, although, as he remembered the plans for Starbase 18, there was a generator with more than sufficient capacity located in a sublevel of the command center. Could Building 8 have required its own separate power source? Recalling the four Alpha-class power cores delivered to 55-Hamilton, the answer to that question was obvious.

Number One laid a hand on the vent itself, felt around the edges gently, exactly as Spock would have done, taking great care not to exert force on the structure.

"We have to remove the facing."

"How would you suggest we do that?"

"I was going to ask you," she said.

"Not a phaser." They would be unable to focus its energies precisely enough. "Perhaps we could use an engineering tool of some sort."

"Perhaps." She did not sound convinced.

"I will endeavor to find us something." Spock set his pack down on the ground and opened the outer compartment. There were a lot of tools in there. None seemed entirely right. He closed the outer compartment and opened the inner one.

"Chief Pitcairn," Number One said.

Spock looked up. "Excuse me?"

"What we could really use right now is Chief Pitcairn." Number One had her back to him, hands on her hips, staring at the vent. "He'd know exactly what this was, how to get the facing off. Whether or not it was even worth doing that. For all we know, this could dead-end inside a piece of machinery."

"Chief Pitcairn is on *Enterprise*. Unreachable, for the next fifty-one minutes."

"I know." She turned to face him. "I overreacted before, didn't I?"

"I do not know what you are referring to."

"Chief Pitcairn. When he wouldn't beam us down right away. I overreacted. Calling him a drunk."

"You suggested he was still drunk," Spock corrected. "Not that he was a drunk."

"That's a very subtle distinction."

"But an important one." He selected a tool—a micrograppler—and handed it to her.

She studied it a moment, then nodded. "This ought to do."

Number One switched the grappler on. She directed the beam toward the top edge of the vent facing, which began, slowly, to bend.

"It appears to be working," Spock said.

"Yes," she said, and worked on for a moment in silence.

When the top edge of the vent had been entirely loosened, she stepped back for a moment. "Time?" she asked.

"Eleven minutes passed, forty-nine minutes till beam-up."

"Good," she said, and started in on the left side of the vent. At this rate of progress, they would have the vent off in another six minutes, which would give them approximately forty-three minutes inside the structure to examine it.

"I do owe him an apology, though, don't you think?" Number One said abruptly. "The chief?"

Spock frowned. The commander was attempting to engage him in a personal conversation. Unusual.

He and Number One had never been close; on matters of command importance, he had always spoken with Captain Pike directly. Off-duty, he spent time with the chief and members of the science department.

He was not aware, exactly, of whom Number One spent her free time with.

"The intricacies of human interactions are not my area of expertise, Commander," Spock said.

"Yes. Well . . . you may have noticed they're not exactly mine, either." She stepped forward and began to work on the left edge of the vent facing.

"Nonetheless," Spock continued, "I feel safe in saying that whether or not you owe it to him, the chief would most certainly appreciate an apology from you."

"Thank you, Mr. Spock." She smiled at him. "I'll keep that in mind."

Something made him look up then. Movement out of the corner of his eye. The wall above was swaying.

"Commander!" he yelled.

She looked not up but at him. The wall began to fall.

Spock made an instinctual calculation and an instantaneous decision. He leaped forward, pushing off the asteroid's surface with all the strength in his leg muscles, slamming into Number One, wrapping his arms around her, driving her to the ground, which seemed to rumble beneath him as they rolled, over and over and over and then—

Stopped.

Something had landed on his leg, his left leg, the lower portion, halting his momentum. Something massive, something that instantly deadened all feeling in that limb.

He was aware that a cloud of dust had risen, obscuring his vision. At the same instant, he felt a sudden sense of cold.

He turned his head and looked over his shoulder. A support beam lay across his leg. His suit was torn. Vapor, atmosphere, life-giving oxygen was escaping into the vacuum around the asteroid.

He had landed on top of Number One. Her eyes were closed. She wasn't moving. He tried to push himself off her and couldn't. The weight of her body on his arms, the weight of the support beam on his leg . . . he was trapped. He turned and twisted and tried in vain to free himself.

Vulcans were capable of regulating their metabolism to a certain extent. Spock immediately lowered his, though, of course, that would do little good against the cold creeping into his bones, against the vacuum.

He closed his eyes and grimaced, trying to force his leg backward, to push it farther under the beam, to use the object's own mass to help close the tear in his evac suit. No luck.

He closed his eyes and tried again.

• • •

He blinked and opened his eyes.

He was lying on his back, staring up at the stars. Still in his evac suit. Number One stood over him.

"You're all right," she said.

He sat up. "I appear to be."

He glanced down at his suit, where the tear had been.

"I patched it," Number One said. "You should be all right until we transport. In another"—she glanced at her tricorder—"twenty minutes, eleven seconds."

Spock flexed his leg. It was sore where the beam had lain atop it. He sat up and attempted to judge the severity of the injury. "Deep muscle trauma," he said. "Some swelling."

"A sprain."

Spock nodded. "I believe so. There might be a rudimentary first-aid kit in the pack."

Number One checked. There wasn't.

"No matter. Treatment is not imperative. The injury is hardly life-threatening."

"But it could have been." Number One, who had been kneeling down next to the pack, now stood. "A few centimeters one way or the other . . . you could have died."

"Service aboard *Enterprise*—aboard any starship— is by nature hazardous."

"But this hazard was my fault. My responsibility." She shook her head. "This was a stupid idea, beaming down here. Chief Pitcairn was right."

She truly blamed herself, Spock realized. And not just for this. Many of her actions over the last few days, inexplicable at the time, suddenly made sense to him.

"You consider yourself responsible for Captain Pike's death," he said.

"I was in charge. If I'd moved the ship sooner—"

"Crossed into the Borderland? Started a war?"

She was silent a moment. "The chain of events that led to *Magellan* and its occupants being lost . . . they are my responsibility."

"I fail to see how you could have anticipated those occurrences."

"I can see it very clearly." She shook her head again. "Very clearly indeed."

What Spock could see was that there would be no arguing with her on this point. He pushed himself to his feet—easy enough in the lighter gravity. The problem, he realized, would be maintaining his balance.

"You could use a crutch of some sort. We could use the phaser to cut one of those beams." Number One gestured toward the wreckage behind them.

"Perhaps," Spock said. Though what he could really use now was Dr. Boyce—or, rather, the doctor's medikit. A simple hypo would take down the swelling quickly.

Dr. Boyce, however, was not there.

"Mr. Spock?" Number One was staring at him. "Is something the matter?"

"Dr. Boyce," he said.

"What about Dr. Boyce?"

"His daughter."

"Dr. Wandruska."

"Yes. Her personnel record was not among those you accessed."

"No." He could hear the frown in her voice. "I don't remember seeing her record at all, in fact."

Spock tried to recall what he knew about the woman. What Boyce had told him about her. Dr. Jaya Wandruska, Starfleet medical researcher. Rank of lieutenant. A native of Argelius. Spock had seen a picture of her in Boyce's office; she had the typical Argelian physiognomy. Lean, angular build. A triangular, strong-featured face. Ivory skin, reddish hair. A geneticist who had received numerous commendations for her work, related to the spread of nonspecies-specific pathogens throughout the Alpha Quadrant over the last few centuries. She was an expert in such pathogens, diseases capable of crossing the species barrier.

"Mr. Spock?" Number One asked again. "Is something wrong?"

He did not respond for a second. Was something wrong?

He believed the answer was yes.

In his mind, he added Lieutenant Wandruska to the list of personnel Number One had shown him earlier.

Experts in the Klingon Empire, its weaknesses, its strengths, its history.

A specialist in battlefield medicine.

A historian.

A geneticist.

He could see only one reason to assemble such a group. Such a unique conflux of talents.

The possibility was so chilling, so foreign to him, that he almost dared not speak it aloud.

"Biological warfare," he said quietly.

"Say again?" Number One's voice in his ear came as a surprise; he had forgotten the circuit was open.

"Biological warfare." He turned and faced the wreckage. "This would explain the redundant power cores," Spock said. "As well as the—"

There was a sudden humming noise. Electrical interference, of a kind that took Spock a moment to place. The transporter.

One second, he was looking up at the sky, where *Enterprise* was orbiting.

The next he was staring at the ceiling of the transporter room.

Chief Pitcairn was standing at the controls. Captain Vlasidovich was standing next to him, hands clasped behind his back, frowning.

"Space walk. At oh-three-hundred ship's hours. What is purpose of this, may I ask?"

Spock looked to Number One. He saw her struggling for something to say.

Vlasidovich saw it, too. "Never mind," the captain said. "You will tell me later. We will have long discussion. For now, come with me, please. Both of you. I have something I wish you to see."

"Sir?" Spock asked.

"Your prototype, Mr. Spock. Black Snow. It is real. And we have it." The captain smiled. "Remove suits, please. And come this way."

NINETEEN

Ultimately, it didn't change anything, Boyce realized. Whether he was trying to brew up the fountain of youth, a souped-up love potion, or a combination of the two. He could only work so fast. Besides which, the work, ultimately, was only a delaying tactic. He was buying time for Hoto, giving her the opportunity to hack her way deeper into the Orion system, to find a way to contact *Enterprise,* to get a fix on their current location . . . to stop a war.

He didn't tell Deleen that, of course. He didn't tell her much of anything. After they left Gurgis, she went her way, he went his, back to the medical wing, under escort.

It was later than he thought. Hoto was sleeping when he finally arrived. Boyce washed up as best he could, lay down on one of the diagnostic cots, and closed his eyes.

He wondered what progress the lieutenant had made in determining their location, in determing *Enterprise*'s. Were they still in the Borderland, still in reach of a Federation outpost? Or were they going to have to locate a Klingon base and try to get them the information about the Orions and the technology that had been used to frame the Empire? Would the Klingons believe them? In Boyce's experience—

Someone cried out.

Boyce turned in Hoto's direction. It had to be her; there was no one else on the wing. He squinted in the darkness. The day after an amputation, she could still be experiencing considerable pain. He watched her a moment. She didn't move. On the other hand, she could also just be having a nightmare. The day after an amputation, that wouldn't be entirely unexpected, either.

He lay back down.

Hoto cried out again. A muffled cry, as if she had her face buried in the pillow. Boyce sat up and threw the sheet off. He ought to check on her; better safe than sorry. He got out of bed, walked to the light sensor by the door, and ran a hand over it. Low-level illumination filled the room. He walked over to Hoto's cot and activated the diagnostic sensor. Her vitals looked fine. She was sleeping peacefully now, hands—one prosthetic, one her own—folded across her chest. Good.

He turned to go, and she cried out again.

But her mouth didn't move, which was when Boyce realized that the noises he'd been hearing hadn't been coming from her at all.

They were coming from outside, from the main hall of the medical wing.

Boyce slid on his clothes, entered the code Hoto had pirated for him on the door keypad, and stepped quietly out into the hall.

He heard the noises again, right away.

They were coming from the far end of the hall, to his right, from one of the three smaller treatment rooms there. Not Deleen's old room; that was still empty. Not the one on the other side of the hall, either: the noises came from the room directly in front of him. The keypad there was lit up. Boyce took a step closer and pushed at the door. It didn't give.

A loud noise came from inside. Boyce put his ear to the door; he could hear someone bellowing. Screaming, almost. Boyce couldn't quite make out what they were saying. Crying for help?

He reached for the keypad and then, about to enter the pirated code, paused.

Was this any of his business? Was this safe? Should he go get one of the guards? Those questions and about half a dozen others ran through his mind quickly, and then he dismissed them. This was a medical wing. He was a doctor.

He hit the keys. *Zeph zeph gramma.* The door opened. The room lights were on but dimmed. He took a step forward.

There was a bed in front of him; it looked as if there was someone lying in it. He squinted into the darkness but couldn't make out any details.

Then his eyes adjusted to the light, and his pupils widened in surprise.

There was someone on the bed all right.

That someone was a Klingon.

TWENTY

Dr. Yang arrived and gave Spock a hypo that instantly reduced the swelling in his ankle.

"This mysterious building," Vlasidovich said as they set off down the corridor. "Why do you not tell me about it? Why do you go off on this midnight expedition?"

"We thought to determine what the building was before coming to you," Spock lied. He exchanged a glance with Number One. Had they, in fact, done so? Discovered Building 8's purpose? He wasn't certain. Biological warfare ran counter to everything the Federation stood for; the idea that such a project could be conducted under the auspices of Starfleet . . .

"Regardless. This is not customary procedure. We will have to discuss later." Vlasidovich didn't seem

overly concerned. Spock could understand why. Black
Snow? In their possession? In the captain's position,
that would be his priority as well.

"The responsibility for the expedition is mine, sir,"
Number One said. "It was my idea."

She was attempting to shift the blame, and any associated punishment, onto herself. Spock would have
none of it.

"No, sir," he said. "In fact, it was a joint decision to
conduct the survey in this manner. We both—"

"We have Mr. Tyler to thank," Vlasidovich said.
"He was on duty. Noticed unusual sensor readings
about an hour ago. A trail of energized particles,
traveling right alongside ship. Unusual, I said. Suspi-
cious. So I come to bridge, we analyze exhaust, we
note similarity to engine particles emitted by Klingon
ships, which is when I go to find my science officer."
He glanced sideways at Spock. "Proves more difficult
than I am expecting."

"Yes, sir," Spock said. "I apologize."

"As I said, we discuss later." Vlasidovich gestured
down the corridor. "Ah—we are here."

Here was the shuttlebay observatory, the control
center for all bay operations. Vlasidovich preceded
them through the door, into the observatory proper,
a square room six meters a side that jutted out into
the bay proper, a good nine meters above its floor.
Instrument consoles and computer stations dotted the

room's perimeter. A significant portion of the forward wall was transparent aluminum.

Lieutenant Tyler was seated at one of the consoles. Lieutenant Hardin stood by the far wall. Both turned as they entered.

"We have it, sir," Tyler said. "Bringing it in now by tractor beam."

"Thank you, Mr. Tyler," Vlasidovich said, and smiled.

Spock glanced past the captain, through the observatory window, down toward the bay doors. A ship was indeed coming into the bay.

A craft as long as a standard Federation shuttle but half again as wide and significantly more tapered. The outside of the craft was a highly reflective metal of some sort. Its color seemed somehow to shift between a lustrous gold and a duller yet somehow brighter white.

There was writing on the side. Klingon writing. *qIj ped*—Black Snow.

"Interesting-looking ship," Vlasidovich said.

Number One nodded. "Indeed."

"Closing bay doors," Tyler announced. "Pressurizing shuttlebay."

"Good." Vlasidovich nodded. "Lieutenant?" He gestured toward Hardin, who keyed in something on the console in front of her.

A second later, a squad of a half-dozen security personnel fanned out into the room, weapons at the ready.

Vlasidovich leaned over the console himself and spoke directly into it. "Commander of Klingon vessel. You are aboard Federation starship *Enterprise*. Please come out with your hands raised."

Nothing happened.

"Commander of Klingon vessel," Vlasidovich said again. "Please—"

A line appeared in the ship's previously seamless exterior. It ran from the top portion of the hull down underneath the main fuselage.

Part of the hull folded in on itself. A figure rose from the vessel. A Klingon. He looked around, no trace—and Spock thought this strange—of either anxiety or belligerence visible on his face.

"That's Captain Kritos, I think," Number One said. "From the *Hexar*."

"I think you're right," Tyler said. Spock thought so, too.

"Interesting," Vlasidovich said.

It was indeed. Perhaps Vlasidovich had been right, Spock thought. Perhaps Kritos was part of a dissident faction within the Empire. Perhaps that was why he had been dismissed from command. Perhaps he was bringing the Federation Black Snow as evidence of his goodwill. Perhaps . . .

"Sir." Hardin spoke up. "Just occurred to me. Is it possible that this is just a distraction? I mean, given how easily we picked it up, how they're not even putting up a fight . . ."

"You make an interesting point, Lieutenant." Vlasidovich said. "Please show me sensor readout of surrounding space, if you could, on monitor."

"Aye, sir," Hardin replied.

There was a console to the right of the observation window. Hardin reached to begin reconfiguring it to bring up the requested information.

"Something's happening," Tyler said.

Spock's attention—drawn momentarily to Hardin and her efforts to work the standard science-department interface—returned to the Klingon ship below, where a second black line was appearing in the hull, this one toward the rear of the ship.

"Somebody else in there," Tyler announced. "Picking up life signs now."

The hull began to unfold once more.

"Space around us looks clear, sir," Hardin said to Vlasidovich. "No trace of any other Klingon ships in the immediate area. Of course, if they're cloaked . . ."

"Understood, Lieutenant," Vlasidovich said. "Maintain vigilance, please."

"Aye, sir," Hardin said.

Spock nodded as he looked over the incoming telemetry; he saw nothing unusual there, either. Lieutenant Hardin's concern seemed to him unwarranted.

They were several parsecs from the Borderland now, a long distance from practical operating range for an isolated Klingon vessel. Still . . .

He began calibrating the long-range sensors as well, to scan for the presence of particles similar to those emitted by the Klingon shuttle.

"Second figure leaving the vessel," Tyler announced, in a matter-of-fact way. "Captain," he said then, in an entirely different tone of voice.

"Yes?" Vlasidovich replied.

"Captain," Number One said, and then she laughed.

"What?" Vlasidovich repeated, a note of annoyance in his voice.

Spock looked up from the console.

Vlasidovich was staring out the observation-bay window now, a most peculiar expression on his face. "Captain?" he said.

Spock looked out the window as well.

Christopher Pike stepped down from the Klingon shuttle and started walking toward them.

BOOK III

KRONOS

TWENTY-ONE

"You can lower those, I think," Pike said to the three security guards who were staring at him, open-mouthed, their phasers still pointed at Kritos, who was regarding them with an expression halfway between amusement and anger.

"Captain Pike," one of them said. McLaughlin, that was the man's name. The other two were Mears and Staton. It was all coming back to him now—slowly. Very slowly indeed. He felt as if he'd been away forever.

"Captain Pike." He nodded. "That's me." He took a deep breath and allowed himself a small, tight smile. A week inside the cramped confines of Kritos's shuttle, a week smelling his own sweat and worse . . .

He wanted a shower. He wanted food—honest-to-God, human food. If he had to eat *gagh* one more time . . .

The doors to the shuttlebay slid open again, and Number One walked through, followed a heartbeat later by Spock, Lieutenant Tyler, and . . . Dmitri?

Number One was smiling. He'd rarely seen that expression on her. Spock was smiling, too. That Pike had *never* seen before.

"Sir! How . . ." Number One stopped a few meters away, looked at the shuttle, at Kritos, and then back at him. She took another step forward. Pike thought for a second that she was going to hug him.

"Long story," he said.

"I don't doubt it. It's good to see you, sir."

"Good to see you, too," Pike said, looking around the shuttlebay, catching as many eyes as he could. "Good to see everyone. To be back home."

Spock, he saw, was no longer smiling. Dmitri, though . . .

Vlasidovich stepped forward, shaking his head. "Ah. I am surprised, and yet . . . I am not surprised. Christopher Pike cheats death one more time."

"No cheating involved. Just a lot of luck." The two men shook hands.

"And you bring us a prize," Vlasidovich said, gesturing toward the Klingon shuttle. "Black Snow. Tell me how you did this."

"I didn't." He was about to turn and motion Kritos

forward to explain, when, over Dmitri's shoulder, he saw Chief Pitcairn coming toward him.

The man was crying. He stepped past Dmitri, and before Pike could do anything about it, grabbed him in a bear hug and lifted him off the ground. And held him there.

"Chief," Pike said after a few seconds. "You can put me down now."

"Yeah. I could." Pitcairn sniffed.

But he didn't. Not right away, at least.

"Damn it, Captain," the man said. "You keep pulling stunts like this, I'm going to lose the rest of my hair."

"I think you're gonna do that anyway," Pike said.

Pitcairn laughed.

"What do we do with the prisoner, sir?"

Pike turned and saw Ben Tuval's second, Hardin— only, of course, she wasn't second anymore; she was security chief now—standing next to Kritos. She had not lowered her phaser.

Kritos's expression had moved beyond annoyance, was verging on anger now. One thing Pike knew, after having spent the last week with him: you did not want to get him angry.

"I said at ease, Lieutenant." Pike sharpened his tone, speaking directly to Hardin. "He's not our prisoner."

"He's an alien hostile, in a systems-critical area of the ship," Hardin said, and added, "Sir. Regulations clearly state—"

Pike felt his own temper giving way just a little. Then he felt a hand on his shoulder. Not Glenn. Dmitri.

"Lower your weapon, please, Lieutenant. We have on our side numbers—yes? Ten to one, I believe. No. Eleven to one."

Hardin frowned but did as she was told. Obeyed Vlasidovich, not him. It was Pike's turn to frown now. Two captains—strike that, two commodores; Dmitri had the extra insignia bars on his shirt, just as he did—one starship. Pike hadn't thought that would be a problem, but now . . .

Dmitri took two steps forward and stopped directly in front of Kritos.

"I know of you. You are captain of *Hexar*, yes? Kritos?"

"Yes," Kritos growled. "And you are captain of *Excalibur*. Vlasidovich. Yes?"

"Yes."

The two glared at each other.

"You—" Vlasidovich began.

"You—" Kritos said at the same instant.

Pike could see a round of name calling and general bad feeling was about to begin, so he stepped between the two of them.

"I have an idea," he said. "How about we get something to eat?"

• • •

They had a lot to talk about, obviously. Everyone wanted to know how he'd survived, how he'd ended up with Kritos. Pike had to fill them in on that and more, what he knew now about the Orions and what he suspected. He needed Kritos to do the same. Then there was the matter of Starbase 18, what had really been going on there and who was behind the attack. Chief Pitcairn wanted to talk to him, too, in private. He was pretty insistent about it; Pike had a hard time putting him off. He wondered what was up with that; it wasn't like Glenn to try to take advantage of their friendship that way.

The point was, there was an awful lot to discuss, among an awful lot of people, and they might as well eat while they were doing all that talking. The problem was, Kritos didn't want to leave the shuttlebay. Didn't want to let the cloaking device out of his sight. Not even after Pike promised—and had Dmitri promise— that no one would go aboard the little ship to examine it in his absence, much less remove it from the craft.

"You I trust," Kritos said. "These *petaQ* . . ." He glared at Hardin and Vlasidovich. And everyone else in the shuttlebay, for that matter.

Spock stepped forward. "It would be simple enough to bring food to you, sir. From the crew's mess."

"The crew's mess. Good idea." Pike smiled. "How about one of Carpenter's steaks? A big one." He spread his thumb and forefinger an inch apart.

"Steak?" Kritos bared his teeth. "This is a kind of meat?"

"Yes."

"Good. I will have steak, too, then."

Pike ordered his medium rare; Kritos wanted his raw. Yang, who'd shown up to give Pike a quick physical and whose presence reminded the captain of Boyce, of *Magellan* and the crew members he'd lost, tried to talk to the Klingon about the health risks associated with consuming raw animal flesh. Kritos listened with growing annoyance. Pike was about to send Yang away to do something productive when he caught sight of Chief Pitcairn, standing in one corner of the bay and motioning to him frantically. Spock and Number One were standing alongside him.

"Be right back," Pike said to Kritos and Yang. The captain walked hurriedly over to his senior officers. "Well?"

They all started talking at once.

"There's a bug—"

"There's a building—"

"Your logs—"

Pike held up a hand. "One at a time. Number One?"

"I have to go first," Pitcairn said.

"You'll get your turn."

"No. I have to go first."

Pike frowned. He'd known Glenn Pitcairn for fifteen years, had never known him to behave this way.

"One minute, Chief," Pike said, putting a little steel into his voice.

"The ship's computer is bugged," Pitcairn said.

"What?"

"The ship's computer is bugged."

Pike shook his head in disbelief. "That's not possible."

"Nor is it true," Spock said.

Pitcairn turned and glared at the Vulcan. "Now, hold on a minute, Mr. Spock."

Spock shook his head. "Forgive me, Chief. I just had a moment to work with the system and detected no trace of the feedback circuit you mentioned earlier."

"Feedback circuit?" Pike asked.

"Someone was spying on us," Pitcairn said. "On everything happening aboard the ship. That circuit was there, Mr. Spock."

"Perhaps so," Spock replied. "No longer."

The chief looked upset.

Number One nodded sympathetically. "I believe you, Chief," she said.

"Is that what you wanted to tell me?" Pike asked Spock.

"No," Spock said. "I wished to inform you that your logs have been confiscated by Admiral Noguchi."

Pike nodded. "That doesn't surprise me."

"It does not?" Spock looked surprised; so did Number One.

"No." Not given what he'd told Noguchi earlier about Kritos and *Hexar*. And speaking of Kritos . . .

He turned and saw Yang—skin several shades paler than it had been earlier—backing away from the Klingon.

He also saw Dmitri—who had been talking to Hardin and her security team—walking straight toward him.

"I cannot help but overhear," Vlasidovich said, looking just as angry as Kritos had earlier, "that computer aboard *Enterprise* is bugged? Is this true?"

"Yes," Pitcairn said.

"No," Spock said.

"Why was I not informed of this?"

Pike's officers were silent.

A slow, strained smile broke out on Dmitri's face. After four years at Starfleet Academy together, two of them as roommates, Pike had become an expert at reading the wide variety of his friend's smiles. This one was the "I'm so angry I do not trust myself to talk" kind.

"It doesn't sound like something anyone was sure of, Dmitri," Pike said, trying to smooth things over. "Now, Number One, what was it you wanted to tell me?"

"Yes, sir," she said. "You'll recall before you left for the Orion ship, I had drawn your attention to a structure on the surface of Fifty-five-Hamilton—"

"You're talking about Building Eight," Pike said.

Number One blinked. "Yes."

"Kronos," Pike said. "You found out about it."

She looked at him, then over at Spock. "Yes," she said.

"Kronos?" Dmitri frowned. "What is this Kronos?"

"What we were investigating on the planet's surface, Captain," Number One said.

"Another thing you do not tell me about. Is there perhaps more?" Dmitri, Pike could see, was on the verge of blowing up again. That wouldn't do. "Some other bit of information you might see fit to share with your commanding officer, although perhaps you think that since Captain Pike is back—"

"Not for long," Pike interrupted.

Everyone turned to him.

"Sir?" Number One asked.

"I'm not staying. Captain Kritos and I still have work to do." He gestured over his shoulder at Black Snow.

"Work?" Dmitri frowned. "What kind of work?"

"Not work at all. Pleasure." Kritos bared his teeth. "Vengeance."

"You are going back to the Orion ship," Dmitri said.

"Exactly."

"Back to *Karkon's Wing*?" Chief Pitcairn asked. "Why?"

"As I said, there is blood to spill." Kritos glared at Spock. "Green blood."

"I must point out that Orion blood is red, Captain Kritos," Spock said.

Kritos growled.

"You didn't answer my question," Pitcairn said. "Why are you going back to the Orion ship?"

"Because they're the ones who attacked Starbase Eighteen," Pike said.

"The Orions?" Pitcairn looked doubtful. "Sir, are you forgetting that recording from the command tower—Commodore Higueras, the two Klingon warbirds . . ."

Kritos growled again.

"Make as much noise as you want," Pitcairn snapped. "The facts are—"

"Not facts," Pike said.

"Sir?" Pitcairn asked.

"Those sensor readings—they weren't real. They were images created by the Orion vessel."

"Ah." Spock nodded. "That would explain—"

"The Orions created sensor images sophisticated enough to fool our instruments?" Pitcairn asked. "How?"

"I don't know. Which is why we're going back," Pike said.

Kritos cleared his throat. A reminder.

"Sorry. One of the reasons we're going back," Pike clarified.

"And the other?" Dmitri asked.

Pike sensed Kritos tense behind him. "This is private," the Klingon said.

"You're going to have to tell them about it at some point."

The Klingon growled.

At that instant, the shuttlebay doors opened, and Yeoman Colt entered, carrying a tray full of food. Pike saw the steaks—smelled the steaks—and smiled.

"Yeoman," he said, stepping forward out of the crowd. "Over here."

Colt saw him, and her eyes went wide as saucers.

Nobody had told her, Pike realized.

"Captain Pike," she said, and her mouth dropped open.

Then she dropped the tray. Then she fainted.

TWENTY-TWO

They salvaged the steaks. Yang gave Colt a hypo, and she woke up, red-faced and apologetic. She looked at Captain Pike and started to cry. Then she excused herself. Spock left with her, going to get a second round of drinks from the crew's mess. When he got back, Captain Pike and Kritos were sitting on top of one of the ship's cargo containers, plates on their laps, eating with gusto. He brought them their beverages.

"Should we not have a table brought in?" Captain Vlasidovich said. "Ship's services can do easily."

"Not necessary," Pike said. "We're almost finished here."

As if on cue, Kritos set his plate down on the floor and belched loudly.

"Salutations to your chef, Vlasidovich," the Klingon said, standing. "And to the animal who died to provide my food. A good death."

"I will tell the former, to be sure," Vlasidovich said. "The chef is Captain Pike's man."

"Yes. Of course." Kritos nodded. "Will you two duel for command of *Enterprise* now?"

The two captains looked at each other, then both laughed.

"No. That's not how we do things in Starfleet," Pike said.

"Except at Academy." Captain Vlasidovich smiled. "Golding simulation. You remember, Christopher?"

"How could I forget? Loman kicked your ass."

"After he kicked yours."

"No, first Michaela kicked mine." The two men smiled again.

Number One frowned; she looked confused. Spock was confused as well.

"I do not recall any Golding simulation at the Academy," Spock said.

"Before your time." Chief Pitcairn turned to Captain Pike. "Come on, sir. Finish the story. How did you survive?"

"Luck. Plain and simple," Pike said. "The torpedo blew out *Magellan*'s starboard port, took half the pilot's console with it as well. I managed to lower the radiation shield on that side of the shuttle just before the power went. That kept me from getting sucked out into space. And then . . ." He nodded toward Kritos. "He showed up."

"That's quite a coincidence," Number One said, echoing Spock's own thoughts.

"No coincidence at all," Kritos growled.

"You were tracking the Orions," she said.

"Yes."

"Why?"

"Starbase Eighteen," he said. "I knew they were responsible."

"So this is why you stole Black Snow? To follow them?" Captain Vlasidovich asked.

"Yes."

"And while you were following the Orions, you came on Captain Pike," Number One said.

"Yes. Exactly." Kritos bared his teeth—in a smile, Spock realized—and slapped Captain Pike on the back. "Lucky for you, Pike! Lucky for you!"

"Excuse me, sir," Spock said to Captain Pike. "After the torpedo attack, you were able to restore atmospheric integrity within the shuttle?"

"No. I was not."

Spock frowned. "I do not understand, then. In the time before Captain Kritos rescued you, how were you able to—"

"Breathe?" Pike pulled something out from the pouch on his belt; it took Spock a second to recognize it.

"A bronchial shunt."

"Yes. Dr. Boyce had brought along a spare for Ben. Commander Tuval."

The mention of the missing officers abruptly changed the mood in the room.

"The other members of the landing party, sir," Number One began. "Do we know if any—"

"We were in the middle of a—a reception of sorts when everything fell apart. When I lost contact with you." Pike shook his head. "I lost sight of Lieutenant Hoto. I don't know what happened to her. Smith and Ross I saw die with my own eyes. Ben . . ." Pike nodded grimly to himself. "He's gone, too."

"And Collins?" Number One asked. "Dr. Boyce?"

Pike was silent a moment. "That," he said finally, "I'm not sure about."

"You think they might still be alive?" Chief Pitcairn asked.

"Possibly."

"Almost certainly, in my opinion," Spock said.

"And why is that?" Captain Vlasidovich asked.

"Because of Kronos."

"Again with this Kronos." Vlasidovich looked at him and then at Captain Pike. "I believe it is time for me to find out what exactly this word means."

"Yes," Pike said. "I believe it is."

Then the captain, to Spock's puzzlement, looked at Kritos.

The Klingon looked down at the ground. "I do not wish to speak of this," he said.

Pike laid a hand on Kritos's shoulder. "This is private. What you're concerned about, it'll go no further than the five of us."

Spock glanced around the little circle they'd formed—Pike and Vlasidovich, himself, Number One, and Chief Pitcairn.

"I give you my word," said Pike.

"If Christopher Pike gives his word . . ." Vlasidovich shrugged. "You have mine, too."

"And mine," Number One said.

Pitcairn nodded. "Yeah. Same goes for me, I guess."

"I, too, give my word, Captain Kritos," Spock said, "and you may rest assured that Vulcans do not swear such oaths lightly. However, I must add the proviso that should the information you reveal regarding Project Kronos turn out to be information that if allowed to remain secret could potentially cost lives, there is the probability that I would come to you and ask to be released from my oath, so that—"

"Mr. Spock?" Pike interrupted.

"Yes, sir."

"What on earth are you talking about?"

Spock looked at the captain. There was something odd going on here. "Project Kronos, sir," he said.

"Yes," Pike said. "I understand that. But what sort of danger were you referring to?"

Kritos was looking at him now as well, also looking perplexed.

"The danger inherent in any sort of biological-warfare program, sir."

Pike's eyes went wide. "Biological warfare?"

Kritos's eyes went wider. "Biological warfare?"

He cursed so quickly that the translator couldn't keep up. He used words Spock hadn't heard since working as an interpreter during some of the more sensitive sessions of the Gorengar negotiations.

"This conversation is ended," Kritos said, backing away. "Our truce is ended, Pike. You have been lying to me."

"Whoa," Pike said. "Easy. Explain why you think biological warfare is involved, please, Mr. Spock."

Spock—aided by Number One, who had done most of the research involved, after all—did so.

They'd barely gotten started before Captain Pike cut them off, shaking his head. "You jumped to conclusions," he said.

"Kronos is not about biological warfare?" Spock asked.

"Good Lord, no," Pike said.

"Then why all the secrecy?" Number One asked.

"It's a very controversial program," Pike said. "The Empire thought it best to proceed behind closed doors, which I understand entirely." He nodded toward Kritos, who had calmed down visibly once more. "Apparently, the Council felt the same."

"Federation Council?" Captain Vlasidovich asked.

"Yes."

Spock was well and truly confused now. "Sir. Kronos, if it does not refer to biological weaponry designed for battle against the Klingons, then what—"

Pike looked to Kritos once more. "Will you explain?"

"Bah. I am a warrior, not a scientist." The Klingon looked around the circle, as if daring any of them to defy that assertion.

"We understand that," Pike said.

Captain Vlasidovich nodded. "Yes. Your reputation precedes you."

Kritos furrowed his brow. "Vlasidovich of *Excalibur*? Are you mocking me?"

"No, Captain. Not at all."

The Klingon glared a moment longer. "Very well," he said, and stood a little straighter. "Kronos. It is the brainchild of scientists. Doctors and geneticists. Chemists and biologists." He uttered a disparaging term then, one that the computer translated as "lab coats." Close enough, Spock supposed, although the term as he understood it from his service as an interpreter had a considerably "earthier" meaning.

The Klingon language database, Spock reflected, needed updating.

"It is biology, Vulcan. You were right about that. But not warfare. It is about the helix."

"The helix," Spock said. "You refer to DNA. Genetic material."

"Yes. Project Kronos is all about the helix. About the fact that between you and you"—Kritos pointed to Spock and Pike—"and between you and me"—he pointed to Pitcairn and then himself—"the helix is much the same."

"Virtually identical," Spock said. "A fact to which I owe my very existence."

"Meaning what?" Kritos asked.

"Meaning I am half-Vulcan, Captain. The other part of me is human. I am the product of cross-breeding between species, which would not be possible without a remarkable degree of genetic congruence. Am I to understand that Kronos is an attempt to utilize those genetic similarities—"

"Wait a second," Chief Pitcairn said. "You mean Kronos is a breeding experiment?"

"No!" Kritos snapped.

Spock shook his head. "That is not what I was suggesting, Chief."

Pitcairn looked confused. "Then what . . ."

Captain Pike cleared his throat. "As I understand it, Kronos is—was—an attempt to pool our knowledge about the DNA we all share. To use what we've each learned—about diseases, aging, and mutation—to set up a common database, to see if we can't help each other find ways to treat some of the more difficult medical conditions. Do I have it right, Captain?"

Kritos nodded. "Yes. Basically."

"Geez." Pitcairn shook his head. "What's the big deal about that? Why all the secrecy?"

"Chief." Captain Vlasidovich shook his head. "You must remember, there are reactionary forces within the Federation. Those who would prefer not a common agenda but one in which voice of mankind is first. And loudest. To suggest we and our enemies are one and the same—"

"Exactly." Kritos and Vlasidovich stared at each other.

"Well. Now that we know what Kronos was," Number One said, "why did the Orions destroy it?"

"Yeah," Pitcairn chimed in. "And how'd they find out about it in the first place?"

"That's a good question, Chief." Pike smiled. "It'll be at the top of my list when I talk to Liyan. As for why they destroyed it, they didn't. Not entirely, at least."

"Not entirely." Pitcairn shook his head. "What's that mean?"

"They stole it. Parts of it, anyway. Personnel, equipment—"

"Personnel? You mean there are survivors?" Number One said.

Pike glanced over at Kritos, who frowned and looked away.

"Absolutely," Pike said.

Spock waited for him to elaborate, but the captain did not.

Kritos, meanwhile, was still looking down at the ground. Shifting his feet, clearly uncomfortable with the topic being discussed. Very interesting.

"Well, this explains their interest in Dr. Boyce," Pitcairn said. "They needed him to operate that equipment."

"That's what I think," Pike said.

"That's why you think he's still alive." Pitcairn shook his head. "Crazy. Well, what are we waiting for? Let's go get him. Go get what they stole."

Silence greeted the chief's remarks.

"We can't do that, Chief," Pike said.

"Why not? Last time I looked, somebody attacks you, you got every legal and moral right—"

"May I remind you Klingons have armada, Chief Pitcairn," Captain Vlasidovich said. "Waiting within Adelson. The second we cross into Borderland—"

"You can tell 'em why we're going, though." Pitcairn turned to Kritos. "Right?"

Kritos glared at him.

"Not right, Chief," Pike said. "Kritos is persona non grata with the Empire right now."

"Right. I forgot. Black Snow." The chief glanced over his shoulder at the cloaking device.

"Is clear what needs to be done," Vlasidovich said.

"What I am not understanding, Captains, why are you here now? What brings you back to *Enterprise*?"

Pike smiled. "Besides the steak, you mean?"

"Yes." Vlasidovich smiled as well. "And pleasure of my company, of course."

"The Orion vessel," Kritos said.

"What about the Orion vessel?" Vlasidovich said.

"The situation there is difficult."

"Elaborate, please."

"Difficult," Kritos said, a little louder. "Complex. Complicated."

"How so?"

"There's fighting aboard the ship. Two separate incidents we've witnessed while flying alongside," Captain Pike said, stepping between the two of them. "Widespread the first time. Much shorter the second."

"Fighting aboard the ship?" Number One said.

"Picked up some chatter, too. The tallith—Liyan—is apparently not as popular as she would have us believe."

"So you need reinforcements, sir," Number One said.

"Yes."

"And the Klingon vessel is only a two-person craft."

Pike nodded. "Exactly."

"Ah. You need bigger ship," Vlasidovich said.

Kritos looked unhappy.

"Yes. I was thinking *Galileo*," Pike said, gesturing toward the shuttle, which sat at the far end of the bay.

"Oh, I get it," Pitcairn said. "We install the cloaking device on that."

Pike nodded once more.

Kritos, if such a thing was possible, looked even unhappier.

In that instant, Spock saw his problem as well. Stealing the Empire's most closely held technology was one thing. Turning it over to Starfleet engineers was quite another.

The first was theft. The second, treason.

TWENTY-THREE

There wasn't, strictly speaking, water rationing aboard *Enterprise*. The ship had state-of-the-art recycling systems designed to conserve every molecule of H_2O the crew consumed (and excreted). But old habits died hard. Personal habits developed in less eco-friendly planetary environments or inculcated aboard older starships, where every drop was precious. All of which was to say that ship's personnel—when they took old-fashioned liquid, as opposed to sonic, showers—kept them down to about a minute. Half the cabins on Deck 2 didn't even have shower stalls. The original ship's design had envisioned communal bathrooms, which were scrapped halfway through in favor of individual WCs but too late for stalls and plumbing on the starboard side. So showers were a luxury for some, arrangements for which had to be made in advance. Time was very limited there.

When Kritos held firm to his idea of installing the cloaking device on his own—with no one, not even Pike, allowed to assist, much less watch—the captain decided to use the downtime to take a shower. He didn't want to boot Dmitri out of the commanding officer's quarters—not yet, at least—so he arranged to use one of the VIP suites on the officers' deck.

It was only when he walked into the room that he remembered that not only did the suite, despite being on the starboard side of the ship, have a shower all its own . . . it had a bathtub.

"Oh," Pike said.

A bath. When was the last time he'd had a bath? Not in his thirties, he was pretty sure about that. And in his twenties . . . he hadn't gotten in all that many showers, even then.

He looked down. There was grime and *gagh* caked into the hair on his arms. He scratched his head and felt his scalp flake off in his fingernails. He stank like the inside of a Denobulan bloodworm cage.

A bath. It would be decadent. Wasteful. Unnecessary.

He ran the water.

He called ship's stores for a clean uniform and then peeled off the coverall Kritos had lent him. He dropped it onto the floor and put one foot in the tub. Then the other.

Ah. This was going to feel—

The comm sounded. Someone at the door. *Hell.*

"Who is it?"

"Dmitri. I must speak with you."

"Come back in ten minutes."

"Ten minutes? No. I must speak with you now."

Pike sighed and slipped a towel around his waist. "Come," he said, walking toward the door.

It opened, and Dmitri walked in.

Michaela was a step behind him. "Chris," she said.

"Hey," he said, turning to Dmitri. "I thought we talked about this. No one else—"

"What are you doing?" Dmitri asked, looking over his shoulder. "You are taking bath?"

"Yes."

Dmitri shook his head. "Wasteful."

"Decadent," Michaela said. "Turning into a softie in your old age?"

"I'm not that old. And I am not a softie. I just spent a week in a Klingon courier ship. With a Klingon."

"So I understand," she said. "A Klingon, a Klingon courier, and the cloaking device."

"That's right."

"Learn anything interesting?"

"If you're asking about the device . . ."

"I am."

"The answer is no."

"You wouldn't tell me if you had, would you? You probably made a promise to that Klingon. Didn't you?"

"I did."

"Which you would keep even if Admiral Noguchi himself gave orders to the contrary."

"That's a hypothetical." He smiled back at her. "I don't like to deal in hypotheticals."

"I remember."

The two of them stared at each other.

"You look good, by the way," Pike said.

She smiled. "Thank you. You look dirty."

He nodded. "Hence the bath."

Looking at Michaela, Pike was reminded of the conversation he'd had with Admiral Noguchi, right after he'd agreed to take *Enterprise*. The admiral had offered him Michaela as his first officer, thought that the two of them might work very well together. Play to each other's strengths, he had suggested. Pike had thought about it for all of two seconds before demurring. "We were together at the Academy, sir. She was top of the class, I was at the bottom. There might be a little sense of competition there, so . . . no." Noguchi had nodded, and the conversation had moved on.

Of course, competition had nothing to do with it. Well, maybe not nothing, but that was only a tiny part of the reason he hadn't wanted Michaela aboard *Enterprise*. Given their history, her presence would be distracting. A constant reminder of—

"What?" she asked.

Pike became aware that he was staring. "Nothing," he said. Definitely, he was better off with Number One. And speaking of Number One . . .

There were a few things he needed to talk to his first officer about. In private. Word of his survival was going to spread throughout the ship pretty quickly, and people were going to start looking at Dmitri as nothing more than a stand-in. Number One was going to have to put the hammer down, make sure the crew knew that as long as Dmitri sat in the captain's chair, he was the boss. No ifs, ands, or buts.

"So that's what you came here to talk about? The cloaking device?" He looked from Michaela to Dmitri and, all at once, understood the reason for her presence. "I get it. You wanted her here to gang up on me so I would—"

"No, no. Chris, you are being—what is word?— paranoid," Dmitri said.

"Really?"

"Yes, really," Michaela said.

"Okay. So why are you here, then?"

"We wish to discuss the Orions," Dmitri said.

"The Orions?" Pike frowned. "What about the Orions?"

"About an hour ago, I received a rather interesting communiqué from one of them," Michaela said. "An offer of sorts."

"An offer?"

"Of alliance."

"Which Orions are we talking about?" Pike asked. "Not the ones who attacked Starbase Eighteen, obviously."

"Obviously," Dmitri said. "These were—what was name of clan, Michaela?"

"Singhino," she said. "The message was from the clan leader."

Pike recognized the name. Gurgis's clan. They'd been involved in the fighting aboard *Karkon's Wing*; at the heart of it, in fact, if he'd correctly interpreted the chatter he and Kritos had overheard while trailing Liyan's vessel.

"They wished weapons delivery," Dmitri said. "Arms to help overthrow dictatorship, they say. Is this right, Michaela?"

"Yes. Arms to defeat the tallith, in exchange for which they would grant us unfettered access to her technology."

"Her technology."

"Very advanced, they say."

"I don't doubt it. It's probably what they used to simulate the attack on Starbase Eighteen."

"Most assuredly," Dmitri said.

"So where do you think they got this technology from?" Michaela asked.

"I have no idea," Pike said.

"Did Kritos?"

"Not that he let on."

He told them then what he knew, what he had found out, from the Klingon about that technology. They talked then about the possibility—the wisdom—of any kind of alliance with a faction of the Orion Confederacy. The trustworthiness of the Singhino, as opposed to the Codruta. As opposed to the Syndicate, or the pirates, or the Caju. Of course, they couldn't make any decisions without talking to higher-ups, but being prepared to make those kinds of decisions quickly and decisively was what command was all about.

And then the talk wound down, and Pike was looking at Michaela and was suddenly very aware of the fact that he was wearing nothing but a towel.

"I must return to shuttlebay. Check on progress Klingon has made transferring cloaking device to *Galileo*," Dmitri said.

"I'll be along shortly," Pike said.

"After your bath," Dmitri said.

"Yes. After my bath."

"Softie," Michaela said. She glanced over Pike's shoulder at the bath. She looked back up at him.

Pike was about to suggest that she didn't need to rush when the door comm sounded.

"Come," Pike called out, and Yeoman Colt walked into the room, carrying the uniform he'd requested. And a couple of extra towels.

"Captain," she said, smiling. "I brought the uniform and some extra towels, and I thought you might like . . ."

Colt's voice trailed off as she noticed Dmitri and Michaela.

"Captain," she said to Dmitri, snapping to attention. "Sir," she said to Michaela. "I mean, Captain."

"Yeoman," Dmitri said.

"Yeoman?" Michaela looked at Pike and smiled. "Interesting. A female yeoman."

Colt flushed. Pike felt himself flushing, too. He didn't know why. Colt had been the computer's suggestion, not his. He had nothing to be embarrassed about. Nor did she.

"Thank you," he said to Colt. "You can set those things down on the counter over there."

"Yes, sir. Captain." She did as told. "Let me know if there's anything else I can do, sir."

"Absolutely," Pike said. "Dismissed."

"Yes, sir. I just want to say, I'm glad—I mean, it's good to have you back, Captain." She smiled at Pike, then looked at Dmitri, and her eyes widened. "I mean—I enjoyed serving under you, too, as well, Captain, but—"

"You're still serving under Captain Vlasidovich, Yeoman," Pike said.

Colt frowned. "You're giving up *Enterprise,* sir?"

"No, I'm not giving up *Enterprise,*" Pike snapped. "I am returning to the Orion ship, though, and so for the moment—"

"Yes, sir, I understand," she said. "You don't need to explain anything to me."

"Of course I don't," Pike snapped. "I just—" He took a deep breath. This was ridiculous. "Thank you again, Yeoman."

"Yes, sir. Thank you, sir."

Colt backed out the door and was gone.

"A female yeoman," Michaela said.

"It is most unusual," Dmitri said.

"Not really," Pike said. "Captain April—"

Michaela actually snorted. "Don't talk to me about Robert April. Please."

Pike opened his mouth—and shut it. He was not getting into that argument again.

"I am returning to shuttlebay," Dmitri said. "Michaela?"

"Coming. I need to get back to my ship."

"Christopher, I will see you there presently," Dmitri said to Pike, and turned for the door.

"Chris." Michaela nodded and started after him.

"Michaela," Pike said.

She turned at the door and smiled over her shoulder. "Softie," she said, and before Pike could respond, she was gone.

He stood there a moment, towel wrapped around his waist, and sighed.

Michaela Harrari.

It was a small universe. And getting smaller every day.

He turned back to the tub. Slipped the towel off, and dipped a toe again. Ice-cold. He drained a little water out of the tub and filled it again.

He stuck his toe in. Too hot. Added a little more cold. Perfect.

The comm sounded.

"I'm busy," he called over his shoulder. "Come back in ten minutes."

"Yes, sir." It was Number One.

He sighed. "Hold on a second," he said, and slipped his towel back on. He took a step toward the door and stopped himself. *No.* If he wanted to talk ship's business, he should be in uniform. Or the closest he had to it at the moment.

He slid back into the Klingon coverall, shuddering in disgust. *Yech.* He felt as if he'd just put on another layer of dirt. And the odor . . .

"Captain? It's really no problem for me to come back later, so—"

"No, no. One second."

He walked to the door, and it opened. Number One, standing in the hallway, came to immediate attention.

"At ease, Commander. Come on in."

She did. "You're taking a bath."

"I'm about to."

"Forgive me, sir. I expected you would have finished by now."

"Yes. Me, too."

"Sir?"

"Never mind. I'm glad you're here. There are a couple of things I wanted to talk to you about."

He shared with her briefly his concern about Dmitri's effectiveness over the next few days. The importance of her being front-and-center with the crew, visibly stressing the need to obey Captain Vlasidovich's commands to the letter.

"Understood, sir," she said when he had finished.

"Thank you. I appreciate—" He stopped talking because he felt something tickling the hairs on his arm.

He looked down and saw a bug. Disk-shaped, green-and-black-striped, three-legged. It was crawling on his arm. He slapped it away.

It made a little buzzing sound and flew off toward one of the ventilation ducts. He stared after it, frowning. He'd never seen anything like that before. He suddenly realized that of course, he hadn't, it was a Klingon bug, which meant that there were probably more of them inside the coverall. An infestation.

He had a sudden, nearly irrepressible urge to rip the coverall off and dive into the bath.

"Okay, Number One," he said. "That'll be all."

"Yes, sir," she said. It was her cue to leave. She didn't take it.

"Was there something else?" Pike asked.

"Yes, sir. The reason I came?"

Pike almost slapped himself in the forehead. "Right. Of course. Go on." *Quickly, please,* he added to himself.

"Yes, sir. In brief, I have found evidence to corroborate Chief Pitcairn's accusation."

"Chief Pitcairn's accusation?"

"The feedback circuit on the computer system."

Pike instantly snapped to attention. "Someone was bugging the ship."

"Yes, sir. I was able to find evidence of several data streams having been rerouted to a holding buffer within the system. Someone then accessed that buffer—representing terminal input, communications activity—from a remote location."

"Any idea who? No, of course not. You would have told me if you knew."

"Of course." Number One nodded. "What I have been able to determine is that whoever did this was a highly accomplished—"

The comm sounded. Someone at the door. Again. Pike rolled his eyes. Ridiculous. What was this, Starbase 1?

"Hang on a second," he said to Number One. "Come!" he shouted toward the door, which then opened.

Lieutenant Hardin walked in. "Sir!" she said, saluting.

She caught sight of Number One and saluted again. "Sir."

"At ease, Lieutenant," Pike said.

"I'm interrupting," she said.

"Yes," Pike said. *My bath,* he thought. "But you're here, so tell me what it is you need to talk to me about."

"Yes, sir. Assignment aboard *Galileo.*"

"*Galileo?*"

"You'll need a security detail, and I want to be part of it."

"Is that so?"

"Yes, sir."

He nodded, looking Hardin over, trying to remember what he could from her personnel file. Lieutenant Amoreena Hardin. Five years out of the Academy, first two years serving at Starfleet Headquarters, general security, two years aboard the *Katyn,* commendations for bravery, a year serving with the Federation ambassador to Andoria. Or was that Gandor? He couldn't remember. What he did recall was Ben Tuval singing her praises. "Kid's got the right stuff," Ben had said.

Well, Pike would see about that.

He narrowed his eyes. "This isn't about revenge, is it?"

"Yes, sir. Of course it is." The corners of Hardin's mouth turned up, just a little bit, for a quick second. It was a smile—there one moment, gone the next.

Pike had to smile, too.

"That, sir, and a little bit of professional pride. The Orions are pretty satisfied with themselves right now, I bet, thinking they put one over on a Starfleet security team. I'd like to show them what we're capable of."

"Say you were given this assignment, Lieutenant," Number One said, stepping forward. "What would your number one priority be?"

"Protecting the captain."

"At what cost?"

"Excuse me?" Hardin asked.

"At what cost?" Number One said. "What would make you give up on that assignment?"

Hardin looked confused. So did Pike. He didn't quite see what his first officer was driving at.

"What would make me abandon the assignment?" Hardin asked. "Nothing."

"So you'd sacrifice what? The shuttle? Your own life?"

"Yes. Both of them. Absolutely."

"Like Commander Tuval did."

"Yes."

"Like Collins and Smith and Ross did."

"Yes. I didn't—"

"Professional pride," Number One said. "Those members of your detail—the commander of your squad—they had it in spades. And for you to imply anything other than that, for you to imply that what happened was in any way related to their performance as officers, is disrespectful to their memory, Lieutenant. Is that understood?"

"Yes, sir," she said.

"Good."

Pike stepped forward between the two of them. Bad blood there. He wondered why. "I'll consider your request, Lieutenant," he said. "Dismissed."

"Thank you, sirs." She saluted Pike and then Number One, spun smartly on her heel, and left the room.

Pike turned to his first officer. "That was a little harsh, don't you think?"

Number One shook her head. "I don't think so, sir."

"Why not?"

"She hasn't learned her place yet," she said, and told the captain about Hardin's actions on the bridge, when the Klingon fleet had confronted them.

"She's young," Pike said.

"Exactly."

"You don't think she should be on *Galileo*?"

"No, sir."

"So whom would you send? We don't exactly have a lot of options at this point."

"Myself."

"You?"

"Yes, sir."

"You're a little overqualified for a security guard."

"It's not a typical mission, Captain."

"I'll think about it."

"It's critical I be on *Galileo,* sir."

"And why is that?"

She took a deep breath. "Permission to speak freely?"

It was, Pike realized, the first time she'd ever asked him that. "Granted." He nodded. "Go ahead."

"As I see it, the mission has two aspects. Find proof the Orions were behind the attack on Starbase Eighteen, and rescue those hostages Kritos mentioned."

"Your point?"

"The second has to take a backseat to the first."

Pike nodded. "Agreed."

"Sir, you say that, but it's my opinion that you'll try to accomplish both."

He smiled. "Of course I will. Is there something wrong with that?"

"It's my opinion that you'll try too hard to accomplish both."

"What's that mean?"

"You are a very capable commanding officer, sir."

"Thank you."

"Not, however, as capable as you sometimes think."

The smile froze on Pike's face.

"Forgive me, Captain," she said hurriedly. "What I mean to say is that you expect the superhuman of yourself. And there are times when you achieve it."

"Thank you," he said stiffly. "I think."

"The problem is that sometimes you plan on it happening."

"You think that's what I'm doing now? With the *Galileo* mission?"

"It seems like a tall order, sir. Even with the advantage of the cloaking device."

He nodded. Maybe Number One had a point. Maybe—

He flashed, all at once, on an image from the past. A memory. He and Noguchi in the admiral's office, discussing why Michaela Harrari *was* the right choice for *Enterprise*'s first officer.

"She'd be good for you, Chris," Noguchi had said. "For those times you get a little big for your britches. She'll knock you down a peg or two."

Now Pike looked at Number One and had a sudden insight into why, perhaps, when he'd passed on Michaela as his first, Noguchi had recommended her.

"Point taken," he said. "Thank you, Number One."

"So you'll speak to Captain Vlasidovich about me joining the mission?"

"I will think about it," he said, and part of that thinking involved not just the point she'd raised but also the things they'd talked about previously, the need for her presence to hold the crew together and to follow up on the investigation into who had bugged the ship's computer and why.

"Thank you, sir. And, by the way, it is good to have you back."

He dismissed her and turned back to the bath.

The water was cold. He sighed, and reached for the controls to fill it again.

And heard Michaela's voice.

Softie.

He drained the tub and took a quick sonic shower.

Kritos peeked out of the shuttlecraft door.

He looked angry, Spock thought. Frustrated.

Which would account for all the cursing that had been coming from *Galileo* over the last few minutes.

"You," Kritos snarled, pointing.

"Me?" Chief Pitcairn asked.

"No. You." Kritos pointed at Spock, who was standing alongside the chief. Pitcairn and Spock had been keeping watch for almost an hour now, making sure that no one entered the shuttle. This after helping *Hexar*'s former captain carry the main assembly of the cloaking device (which Kritos had bundled up in a tarp Crewman Reilly had brought him from ship's stores) inside the little ship.

"May I be of assistance?" the Vulcan asked, stepping forward.

The Klingon crooked a finger. "Come," he said, and disappeared back inside the shuttlecraft.

Spock exchanged a glance with Chief Pitcairn, then followed.

Inside the entryway, he paused. The interior of the craft was a shambles. There was cable lying everywhere—half of the starboard access panels had been pulled free of the retaining strip along the interior hull wall and now lay strewn about the cabin. The cloaking device itself, he saw, was still hidden underneath the canvas tarp, apparently undisturbed.

"Might I suggest," Spock began, "that—"

"I have a question for you, Vulcan." Kritos moved closer and lowered his voice so that it was not much more than a whisper. "I have heard it said," the Klingon hissed, "that Vulcans cannot lie. Is this true?"

Spock hesitated.

"Well?"

This is an interesting ethical dilemma, Spock thought. Clearly, Kritos had called him into the shuttle because he wished to say something to him in private. Logic suggested that he wished to share a confidence regarding the cloaking device, most likely having to do with retrofitting the device to *Galileo*'s systems. It would be in the best interests of Starfleet, and the Federation, that he answer Kritos's question with a lie, that he tell him that Vulcans were incapable of falsehood, and thus lay a firm basis for gaining the Klingon's trust.

The dictates of Spock's conscience, however, required another response altogether. "It is not true," he said. "Vulcans can indeed lie, though they very rarely do so."

Kritos bared his teeth. A smile. "Ha!" he said, so loudly that Spock started. "I knew that! And now I know something else, Vulcan. You may be half-human, but you can be trusted. So, again, I ask for your word."

"Regarding the cloaking device, I assume."

"Yes. Exactly. You must swear to me that you will not reveal a thing of what you learn here to anyone."

"I cannot do that."

"What?" Kritos growled.

"It is likely that there will come a point in time—not today, not tomorrow, perhaps not even for several years in the future—when sharing what knowledge I have of the cloaking device's operation will save lives."

Kritos turned away from him and slammed his fist into the bulkhead in frustration, cursing out loud as he did so. Calling on a Klingon deity, blaming him—or her, the Vulcan supposed—for the current state of affairs. A deity named Druzen. Spock had never heard the name before. Odd. After receiving his assignment as interpreter for the Gorengar negotiations, he had made it his business to familiarize himself with as much of Klingon history, politics, and culture as possible.

"Everything all right in there?" That was Chief Pitcairn's voice, coming from outside the craft.

"Yes," Spock called back, perhaps prematurely, as

the bulkhead where Captain Kritos had punched it now bore the imprint of the Klingon's fist.

"Leave," Kritos said, turning to face him.

"I would be willing to place a time limit—"

"Leave!" Kritos said a second time, taking a step forward.

Spock nodded. "I will be outside, should you require assistance."

He stepped outside the craft proper and stood in the hatch a moment, looking out over the shuttlebay floor.

"Bet you wish you had that phaser with you, hey?" Chief Pitcairn asked under his breath.

Spock was about to reply when he heard Kritos curse and hit the bulkhead again.

"Druzen?" The chief frowned. "Who's Druzen?"

"I am curious as well," Spock said. "I will try to find out."

He stepped back inside the shuttle. Not that he necessarily expected Kritos to tell him anything, but if he could at least keep the Klingon from doing permanent damage to the ship . . .

"What?" Kritos growled, spinning around.

"Who is Druzen?"

Kritos glared. "That is no concern of yours."

"Perhaps not. I am curious, though. I am relatively familiar with the constellation of Klingon deities—"

"Deity? You think Druzen is a god? Hah!" The

Klingon barked out a laugh. "He would no doubt agree with you!"

Spock frowned. "I am confused."

"Druzen is my father," Kritos growled.

"You were cursing him earlier."

"Yes."

"There is conflict between the two of you."

"Of course. Is that not the way, between fathers and sons?"

Spock nodded. "I see your point."

"There is respect as well, though. And honor. And duty. Always duty." He looked at Spock. "You do not know who he is, do you? Druzen?"

"No."

"No. Of course not. You are not Klingon."

"He is a person of some importance, I gather."

"He is the hero of Dourami. The great war, the battle of Kenj-a-kenj, the planet destroyers, which lasted nearly a dozen years, until the Empire emerged victorious." Kritos regarded him skeptically. "You have heard of Dourami, have you not?"

Spock had. It took him a second, though, to remember where. "Yes," he said. "General K'Zon, in communicating to us—"

"K'Zon!" Kritos glared. "You have spoken with K'Zon?"

"Yes. He has taken command of *Hexar*."

Kritos's eyes widened. "What?" The Klingon shot to his feet. "They have given that old fool *Hexar*?"

"It appears so."

Kritos turned around and hit the bulkhead again.

"Stop, please," Spock said hurriedly. "Eventually, you will break either bone or metal."

"You do not understand," Kritos said. "How could you understand? You are not Klingon. To have a father like Druzen—the honor that must be paid—the duties that are required of a son—"

"My father is of the Vulcan diplomatic service," Spock said. "He has just been named ambassador to Earth."

Kritos regarded him for a moment. "Then perhaps you do understand." The Klingon sighed and sat down. "The burden is, perhaps, heavy for you as well."

"It is," Spock agreed. He was not always conscious of it, of course, but as Sarek's son . . . he had much to live up to.

"To be the son of the hero of Dourami . . ." The Klingon leaned forward and put his elbows on his knees. "It requires service. Sacrifice. I understood that. But this—that they have given K'Zon *Hexar* . . ." Kritos shook his head, and fell silent.

"Excuse me," Spock said. "Are you saying you gave up *Hexar* for your father?"

"Yes."

"I do not understand."

Kritos looked up. "My father was kidnapped. It was incumbent on me to rescue him. When those in power would not undertake the necessary steps . . ." Spock took a second to put the pieces together.

"That's why you stole Black Snow."

"Yes. To hunt down *Karkon's Wing*."

Spock's eyes widened.

"Druzen was at Starbase Eighteen when the Orions attacked. He is part of Project Kronos." The Klingon captain got to his feet. "He is the hostage we must rescue."

Pike returned to the shuttlebay in time to see Spock step off *Galileo*. "All set in there?" the captain asked.

"Yes, sir. The cloaking device is operational."

"Good," Pike said, glad to see that Kritos had decided to accept help after all. From someone qualified. The captain had been afraid he would end up helping to install Black Snow himself. Or trying to, anyway. That would have been a lengthy process.

"Sir?"

He turned and saw Number One coming through the bay doors, followed by Dmitri, Lieutenant Hardin, and two security personnel—Mears and Staton again, he thought, although maybe he was wrong; maybe one of them actually was McLaughlin.

"What's this?" Pike asked, gesturing toward Hardin and her squad.

"My idea," Dmitri said. "You will need much manpower, Christopher. Or womanpower, as case may be."

Pike shook his head. "I don't think—"

"I was trying to tell the captain," Number One said, meaning, no doubt, Dmitri.

Pike heard the shuttle door slide open again and turned just in time to see Kritos jump down to the bay deck, with a smile on his face.

"Ah, Pike. You have taken your shower."

"Yes."

"Good. Then the three of us are ready to go?"

"Almost," Pike replied without thinking. "I just have to . . ." His voice trailed off. "Wait a second," he said to Kritos. "The three of us?"

"I have decided the Vulcan will be our companion." Kritos put his arm around Spock's shoulder.

The science officer stiffened. Pike almost smiled at the expression on Spock's face, but he didn't, because he knew how uncomfortable the Vulcan had to be at that second. Physical contact with a stranger—with anyone, for that matter—was not something Spock enjoyed.

"I am honored," Spock managed.

"I thought we decided that I would choose who was going to make the trip," Pike said.

"Yes. And you said you would consult with me. So, here is my consultation. Your science officer, yes? Does this not show how much I trust you, letting your most experienced computer person view Black Snow?"

Pike frowned. It did at that. But . . .

"Interesting," Dmitri said. "I believe the captain's point is well taken."

"Sir," Number One said, looking distinctly unhappy.

"So. We have brains. Now we will need brawn," Kritos said. "Your strongest warrior."

"I'm security chief." Hardin stepped forward.

Kritos looked her over and shook his head. "No. Not because you are a woman but because you are skinny. Scrawny. Like a twig." He squeezed her upper arm with his hand.

"Skinny," Hardin said. "Absolutely. But." She reared back then, and before Pike or anyone else could get a word out, she clocked Kritos right in the jaw.

The Klingon staggered backward and sat down hard on the shuttle deck.

Hardin stood over him and smiled. "Strong enough for you?" she said.

Kritos got to his feet, rubbing his jaw. "No," he said, and backhanded Hardin across the face. It looked to Pike like a little love tap.

Hardin's turn to fall backward and land on her bottom.

"Strong enough for the Orions, though," Kritos said. "You will do."

He helped Hardin—who, Pike saw, was actually smiling—to her feet. It looked to him as if Ben Tuval might have been right about Hardin.

"Captain." His first officer was standing directly behind him. She did not look happy.

"I'm sorry," was all Pike could think to say. "This isn't exactly how I wanted things to go."

"Then change them," she said.

He shook his head.

"Kritos wants Spock," Pike said. "And I can't take both of you from Captain Vlasidovich. Not considering everything we talked about."

She opened her mouth to protest again, then saw the look on Pike's face and shut it. "Yes, sir."

"Thank you."

Spock and Hardin went off to gather belongings and equipment. Engineering personnel did a final systems check on *Galileo* from the outside, assisted by Kritos inside the craft. It did not go smoothly, until Spock returned and moved things along.

Then they loaded up—possessions, supplies, weapons, a spare fuel pack—and the senior crew gathered around to say good-bye. Pike shook hands with as many people as he could and got another bear hug from Chief Pitcairn, a teary-eyed handshake from Yeoman Colt, and a message on his tricorder from Michaela that he immediately erased. The other three boarded the craft then, and he found himself alone with Dmitri.

"Three days," Vlasidovich said. "I give you three days to find Orion vessel, return with proof of this attack. After that, I am talking to Noguchi."

"Three days," Pike said. "That sounds fair."

Especially considering that it wouldn't take them much more than one of those days to find *Karkon's Wing*. Considering the advantage they had already.

"Not one minute more, mind you." Dmitri wagged a finger. "That is three days until you arrive back here. I will not accept message from space saying you have accomplished mission. I must see you with my own eyes."

"Understood."

"It is killing me, you know." Dmitri leaned forward. "Here we have cloaking device in our hands, and we have to—"

"Don't." Pike shook his head. "I gave my word."

"Yes. You are honorable man, Christopher Pike." He smiled. "Reminds me of story from Nova Vestroia my father used to tell me. A man who—"

"Please. No Nova Vestroia stories right now."

"Very well. Good-bye, Captain. And good luck."

"Same to you. Take care of my ship."

"Your ship?" Dmitri smiled. "We will see about that."

"Ha-ha," Pike said, certain his friend was kidding. Pretty certain, anyway.

He jumped up into the hatch, turned, and gave Dmitri and everybody watching from the observation deck a final salute. Then he stepped into the shuttle.

TWENTY-FOUR

A Klingon."

Hoto eyed him quizzically. "You are certain of this?"

"You think I hallucinated it?"

"You did work an extremely long day, sir."

She was sitting up in her bed, drinking a cup of tea. Boyce was drinking one, too—sipping at it, anyway. After that coffee Deleen had brought him, well, the tea didn't quite measure up.

"He's there. I'll take you to him if you like."

"That won't be necessary." Hoto frowned. "Why would there be a Klingon in an Orion sickbay?"

"Well . . . he was sick, for one thing."

"In what way?"

"I didn't have much of a chance to look over the diagnostic sensors. Can't be sure." He'd had very little time at all, in fact. He didn't want to risk someone coming in on him in a place he wasn't supposed to be. The Klingon had a fever; Boyce assumed that was why he was crying out, and the doctor gave him a fever reducer. It seemed to have done the trick; the Klingon's cries, as far as Boyce could tell, had stopped.

"The real question is where he came from," the doctor added.

"A prisoner of war, perhaps," Hoto suggested.

"Maybe. Though he seemed a little old to be . . ." Boyce's voice trailed off.

"Sir? Is something the matter?"

"Kronos," he said, and explained what he'd found out about the data node on the LeKarz.

"You think the two are connected?"

"It would be an awfully big coincidence if they weren't."

"What would a Klingon be doing on Starbase Eighteen?"

"I don't know." Jaya certainly hadn't said anything about it. In any case, Boyce couldn't see how it was relevant at the moment. "Were you able to find anything out about our position in space, where exactly we are?"

Hoto nodded. "Yes. We are within striking range of Federation territory, a day's travel at warp two."

"Does that mean we can reach someone with a message?"

Hoto frowned. "Yes. It does mean that. However, the ship's communications system has proven more difficult to access than I had expected."

"So we won't be able to get off a message to Starfleet?"

"No. I have, however, conceived an alternative plan."

"I'm listening."

"This is an old ship."

"Yes. I noticed."

"Many technical modifications have been made to it."

"I noticed that, too."

"Of course. The point is, the ship's electrical system routinely operates beyond nominal capacity. The conduits are stressed. I believe I can cause a phase cascade reaction, which will overload them quite easily."

"A phase cascade reaction?"

"Yes."

"What's that?"

"An escalating series of disruptions to the ship's power supply."

"You're going to cut the power."

"More than that." Hoto smiled. "Destroy the ship."

"What?"

"Destroy the ship," she said.

"And what's the point in that?" Boyce asked.

"The destruction would occur in stages. I could set different points of overload to provide cover for our escape. There are shuttles aboard this vessel. We could reach one and—"

"If the ship's blowing up, won't everyone be trying to reach the shuttlecraft?"

Hoto frowned. "There is that to consider. The plan can be modified."

"Wait a second. Yesterday you were telling me I had to help Liyan. Today you want me to kill her?"

"Her death is not the intent of the plan. Our escape is."

"And if she dies, that's all right?"

"The plan can be modified. Clearly, it would be better if she did not perish," Hoto agreed.

"Wonderful," Boyce said. "I'll let her know."

Hoto frowned. "Sarcasm is rarely productive, Doctor. Rest assured, the tallith's survival remains important. However, sensor images I obtained the previous evening from the ship's data banks lead me to believe that it is increasingly unlikely. *Karkon's Wing* is being shadowed by several other vessels, most of which, in the estimation of the tallith's key intelligence personnel, either belong to or are affiliated with the clan Singhino. Those same personnel conclude that the ships are likely planning an assault on this vessel."

"That's not good."

"No, sir."

"When do they think this assault is likely to happen?"

"Several days, in the opinion of most. Sooner, according to others."

"And you? What do you think?"

"I have no context to place the data in," Hoto said. "My opinion would be uninformed. And thus valueless."

Boyce nodded. *Fair enough,* he was about to say, but Hoto wasn't through talking.

"However, I have noted among most of those same intelligence experts that a preponderance of message packets have been sent to several currency traders within this sector."

"They're moving their money around."

"Yes, sir."

"Hedging their bets." Boyce was reminded of rats, deserting a sinking ship.

The clock was well and truly ticking then. For Liyan, the Codruta . . . and himself and Lieutenant Hoto to boot.

"We'd better get to work, then," Boyce said, getting to his feet.

"Agreed. I will continue to search for ways to contact Starfleet. And explore alternatives to the ship's destruction."

Boyce nodded. "Good."

And for his part . . . he would continue to play the game he was playing. Pretending to seek answers to the tallith's seemingly insoluble dilemma. The thing was, Boyce realized as he pressed the comm button to summon the guard that would escort him to the lab, that game—the search for the truth about gamina and the mechanisms by which it worked—was, despite everything, beginning to take on a life of its own.

Put another way, he was curious. Anxious to get to work.

The doctor decided to shortcircuit those impulses the second he reached the lab in the converted shuttlebay. He donned his parka and some thermal gloves and returned to work at the LeKarz.

Rather than continue to study the gamina data, though, Boyce decided to start his day off by breaking through the protocols protecting the Kronos data node. He was no computer expert, but he'd spent enough time working with the machine and was familiar enough with the logic of its internal security systems—having set up such protocols himself back on Argelius—that he believed access to the Kronos data was within his reach. He had no idea what information that node might contain. In retrospect, he realized, Jaya had been unduly secretive about what was happening at Starbase 18, what she was actually doing there. Her field of expertise had been pathogens, nonspecies-specific pathogens. Which in layman's terms meant she dealt with viruses capable of crossing the species barrier, diseases that had the potential to affect all manner of races alike. Possibly, the Klingon down the hall from Hoto been at Starbase 18, had been part of her experiments. He figured it wouldn't take him long—an hour or two at most—to find out whether or not that was true.

It turned out, though, that he was wrong.

After a fruitless morning spent hacking away at the encrypted data, Boyce realized he was in above his head. He cleared the display, stood back from the machine a moment, and considered his next step.

Hoto was fairly deep into the Orion ship's computer system; she ought to be able to access any communications related to the Klingon on the medical wing. He'd leave the Klingon to her as well. For the moment.

He left the LeKarz and returned to one of the Orion computer terminals, to his study of gamina and the efforts that had already been made at duplicating the serum. They were considerable. From the moment the serum, and its effects, had been discovered, Zandar and her predecessors had been hard at work trying to uncover its secrets. Their efforts had been inventive, exhaustive, and, ultimately, futile.

They had tried replicating gamina under differing gravitational and atmospheric conditions. They had tried substituting laboratory-produced analogues for naturally occurring substances, and vice versa. They had even tried—Boyce shuddered in revulsion—duplicating the serum in situ, within the bodies of what the experiment summaries referred to as "volunteers." Two people, who'd died immediately and painfully during the replication process.

There had, in fact, been several other "volunteers" involved, fourteen in all. Half of those, Boyce learned, had died from complications related to gamina, heart attacks in some, as a result of higher blood pressure, dementia in others, as a result of decreased blood flow to the brain. Poor circulation had resulted in gangrenous limbs; inadequate nutrition transport within the body had resulted in multiple organ failure. There were pictures—some of them as gruesome as any laboratory experiments Boyce had ever seen—accompanying the records.

The other half, as far as he could tell from the data, were still alive. Not unaffected by the laboratory-created gamina, what the files referred to as gamina-B. All suffered from blood-related diseases, certain factors that, after the serum's introduction, remained too high, others that stayed too low and had to be artificially replicated.

He suddenly realized something.

Zandar was across the bay, with the same scientists she'd been working with the other day. Boyce caught her eye and motioned her over.

"Can I be of assistance?"

"Yes. Deleen. Her records aren't in here." He nodded to the screen.

"No." Zandar nodded. "They are in the medical lab at the moment."

"Can I see them?"

"Of course."

Boyce stepped aside, and Zandar punched a series of commands into the terminal. The records filled the screen.

Boyce glanced at the top page and frowned. "These are the most recent tests?"

"Yes."

"They're five days old."

"She is scheduled for follow-up shortly."

Boyce nodded. "I'd like to test her now. If you don't mind."

"Of course not," Zandar said.

He found Deleen in the tallith's quarters, which turned out to be an entire suite of rooms. She was in a darkened chamber toward the back of that suite, sitting in front of a long, low table a work surface. Scattered across the table were several small, diamond-shaped pieces of metal, maybe six inches a side. They looked, for some reason, familiar to him.

Deleen was holding another of those little pieces of metal in one hand. In the other, she held what looked to Boyce like a scanner of some sort, an electronic device that emitted a thin blue beam, which she was slowly running across the surface of the metal piece.

She looked up as Boyce and his escort entered.

"Doctor." She nodded at the guard, who nodded back and left. "I'm surprised to see you." She set the scanner and the fragment of metal down on the table; as she did so, the light caught the metal, reflecting off it like some kind of mirror.

It came to him then why the fragments looked so familiar.

"Those are from the ship," he said. "The sentry's vessel."

"That's correct."

"What are you doing with them?"

"Trying to extract the data embedded within them. It's not an easy process."

"Data? I thought they were pieces of the ship's hull."

"They are. They served a dual purpose, apparently."

"That's a neat trick."

"Indeed. The Orions of K'rgon's time . . ." She shook her head. "There is so much they knew. So much they were capable of. So much that has been lost. Here."

She handed him the little scanning device. The top screen was full of data that, for a second, looked like gibberish to him.

"Ah. My mistake. Allow me."

She leaned closer and pressed a button on the side of the device. The data on the screen blurred, disappeared, then popped back into focus.

Now, however, it was in English.

"Thank you."

Boyce scanned screen after screen of data, all different kinds: mathematical equations, molecular diagrams, historical summaries, paintings, literature, poetry . . .

"It's a lot to take in," he said.

"That's because it's not organized." She set the device down on the table. "But the way it's all stored, we can access the information, but we can't quite figure out how it's indexed. Every fragment has hundreds of bits of data like this. How it all ties together . . ." She shook her head.

"Why are you looking at all this?" Boyce asked. "I didn't know you were a scientist."

"I'm not. But the tallith's scientists, they are involved in other things. She frowned. "As you should be. The tallith needs that serum, Doctor."

"And I need a sample of your blood."

"For what purpose?"

"To see the effect gamina-B is having on it."

"Of course," she said, and rolled up the sleeve of her garment.

He took a hypo from his medikit and extracted the necessary quantity of blood. She rolled her sleeve back up; he put the vial into his medikit and stood.

"I'll get back to work now," he said.

She nodded. "As will I. Trying to figure out the reason for the discontinuity in this storage system."

Boyce looked down at her and smiled. In that instant, she had sounded like Hoto. The way she focused her attention on the little scanning device, in fact, even reminded him of Hoto. Biology as destiny? He was about to tell her that she should consider herself as proof of what nonsense that was when a chime sounded.

"Excuse me," Deleen said, and rolled her chair across the little room to a comm screen set into the wall. She pressed a button next to that screen, and it came to life, filling with Liyan's image. She looked angry.

"Daughter. Dr. Boyce is with you?"

"He is."

Liyan nodded. "Bring him to the command center. Immediately."

The screen went dark.

TWENTY-FIVE

The command center—what Boyce would have called the bridge on *Enterprise*—was positioned at the very top of the vessel.

The tallith rose from her chair as they entered. "You were not in the lab. Why?"

Boyce explained. Liyan seemed not at all mollified.

"Gamina-B's effects do not concern me, Doctor. I want the serum duplicated. That is where you are to concentrate your efforts." She glared at him. "Is that clear?"

Boyce glared right back.

"In the first place," he said, "finding out why the gamina-B your scientists produced didn't work is critical to avoid repeating their mistakes. In the second place, you can't dictate how research—"

"Bring me Lieutenant Hoto," Liyan snapped.

"Yes, Majesty." One of the Orions seated nearby stood and walked toward the turbolift.

"What?" Boyce said.

"You must learn to listen, Doctor. Listen and obey."

"What do you intend to do?"

"You shall see. When your lieutenant arrives here."

Boyce looked into her eyes. What he saw there frightened him.

Something else he saw made an impression as well. The veins on her neck, standing out like cords against her skin.

"I was trying to obey," he said. "Using my best judgment—"

"Your judgment does not matter!" she shouted.

Boyce—startled—took a step back.

"My judgment is supreme. I will utilize your knowledge, your expertise, as I see fit." She took one step and then another toward him. "Do you understand?"

Boyce looked at Liyan and then quickly, over at her daughter. Deleen looked as shocked as he felt. Boyce saw in that split-second that her eyes, as she looked at her mother, were filled with something as well. Concern.

"Yes. I understand," he said, trying to put all the fear he felt—much of it genuine; who knew what the tallith would do to Lieutenant Hoto; she seemed completely out of control—into his expression.

The tallith's eyes remained fastened on Boyce a moment longer. Then she nodded. "My need for the serum is urgent. You will return to work at once. But first . . ." She sat down in her chair. "Before you return to the lab, I have another task for you."

"Another task."

"You have seen Gurgis."

The change of subject caught him by surprise. "Yes."

"He appeared healthy to you."

"Some burns. Some bruises. I didn't really get—"

Deleen touched his arm. Boyce realized it was a signal.

"But yes," he finished. "Overall, he seemed healthy to me."

The tallith smiled. "Good. That is the information I wish you to convey."

"To whom?"

"The Singhino. Their warlord, their commander, wishes to speak with Gurgis. They desire assurances that he is still alive. I have given those assurances, but they will not take my word. I believe, however, they will take yours. Specialist." She gestured to one of her officers. "We are ready."

The man she spoke to bowed and keyed in a series of instructions on his console.

There was a viewscreen at the front of the command center, similar to but smaller than the one aboard *Enterprise*. It filled, suddenly, with a burst of static.

The static cleared.

An Orion male—head shaved, wearing pirate leathers, looking to Boyce to be at least Gurgis's size, if not larger (scale being hard to judge from only the head and shoulders the doctor could see)—glared down at them.

"You try my patience, Codruta. Where is he?"

"I am tallith," Liyan said. "You will address me as such."

"Tallith, then. Titles matter little to the Singhino. What matters is Gurgis. Where is he?"

"Indisposed, as I said."

"And I said I wanted proof of this."

"I bring you proof. A Federation doctor who has seen him."

She gestured at Boyce to step forward.

"Who are you?" the Orion rumbled.

"Philip Boyce. Lieutenant commander, Starfleet."

"You are the tallith's new toy?"

"I'm nobody's toy," Boyce snapped—though, of course, here and now, that's exactly what he was.

"Yet there you are on Karkon's Wing. *With the Codruta scum."* The Orion shook his head. *"You have chosen your allies poorly, Doctor. Their days are numbered."*

"Your words mark you as a rebel. A traitor to the alliance your commander willingly made," Liyan said. "Gurgis has not released you from those obligations."

"You bewitched him, Codruta. Those vows mean nothing."

"Gurgis will have your head."

"Gurgis is not here. And I am in charge of the Singhino."

Liyan glared. "You are a fool."

Boyce wasn't sure if he should jump in or not—if Liyan wanted him to speak up, to certify that Gurgis was not only fine physically but in full possession of his mental faculties. Probably, the doctor inferred, for the first time in quite a while.

Tell the one who whelped you I am no longer in her thrall.

Boyce could see why the tallith was desperate for gamina—a gamina that would work.

Before he could speak, though, the Singhino on-screen before them leaned forward.

"We are through with talk, Codruta," he said. The screen went dark.

Liyan remained standing, glaring at the screen.

"They are moving out of sensor range once more, Majesty," one of her officers said.

"No doubt rejoining the remainder of their ships. Preparing for another attack." Those words came from an older male, one Boyce hadn't noticed before, a male dressed in a simple gray coverall, who rose now from a seat behind the tallith's command chair.

"Fools. Ready the image projector," Liyan said. "We will bring them to heel once more."

She was smiling. She was, Boyce noticed, the only one.

The older male spoke again. "Majesty, may I remind you, the journey to the Federation starbase has taken us far from our own lines of support. We remain several days' journey away from such territories at maximum warp. Given the tactical situation, would it not be prudent—"

Liyan spun around. "You are questioning my orders, Gorlea?"

The older man shook his head. "No, Majesty. Of course not. But—"

"I am tallith!" she roared, and slapped the armrest of her chair with an open hand. "They will be brought to heel. All who disobey will be brought to heel. Do you understand? All of you?"

She looked around the command center and was met for a second by stony, absolute silence.

"I understand," Gorlea said, and bowed his head.

The others followed suit.

"Human." Liyan turned her gaze on him then. "You will return to the lab. You will sleep there if necessary. You will find a way to duplicate this serum!"

Boyce nodded and bowed his head as well. He didn't dare ask *Or what?*

All he wanted to do was get off the command center—and away from the tallith—as soon as possible.

Judging from the looks on the faces around him, the others felt much the same way.

He made a quick stop at the medical wing first, intending to fill Hoto in on what had just happened, what he'd witnessed, not just the Singhino's apparent determination to attack the Codruta but Liyan's behavior. The door to the room he and the lieutenant had been sharing was open. Hoto was standing across the chamber, looking at a computer terminal, deep in thought. She hadn't even, Boyce realized, heard him come in.

He started toward her. "Lieutenant."

She looked up, surprise on her face. "Dr. Boyce."

Her voice came from behind him. Boyce stopped in his tracks. He was staring, the doctor realized, at Hoto's reflection, her image in a mirror at the far end of the treatment room. He should have realized that instantly; the sleeve of her missing arm, pinned next to her tunic, was on the wrong side.

Mirror image. The phrase, for some reason, struck a chord in his mind. It lingered there for a second and then vanished.

"Why are you here?"

He turned to face Hoto, who sounded not just surprised to see him but affronted.

"Is everything all right, Lieutenant?"

"Is everything . . ." She took a deep breath. "Yes, sir. You surprised me. I was not expecting anyone."

"I don't doubt it." He understood her reaction even more when he came around to see what she was looking at on the terminal.

A blueprint of the ship. A cross-section of the entire Orion vessel—the label *Karkon's Wing* on the top of the screen—with thin, multicolored lines running in every direction on the diagram.

"What's this?"

"The ship's power grid. I have been studying it for some time. I have determined that an initial overload of the processors here and here"—she pointed—"will trigger a sequence of events that will give us time to reach the nearest shuttlecraft."

"You're really going to destroy the ship."

"No," she said. "My intent is simply to cripple the vessel, in particular its weapons and sensor systems, thus allowing us to escape in the shuttlecraft."

"They'll be a sitting target."

"Sir?"

"Karkon's Wing." He filled her in on what had just occurred, Liyan's outburst, the Singhinos' apparent determination to attack.

She was frowning by the time he finished. Her hands raced over the controls; the power grid vanished, replaced by a map of space.

Hoto studied it and shook her head. "There are no vessels in sensor range at the moment."

"No. The ship moved away as soon as they finished talking. But according to one of Liyan's officers, there are several nearby, within striking range."

"We will have to act immediately, in the next few hours."

"I don't see how that's possible. For one thing, I'm going to be in the lab. And you'll be here. For another . . ." He nodded toward the door. "The guards. There's at least one with me all the time, and I know there are two at the entrance to the medical wing."

"I will handle the guards," Hoto said, in a very matter-of-fact way. "You must use your time in the lab productively."

"Excuse me?"

"Proof. We must secure proof of the image projector's existence. Proof that the Orions were behind the attack on Starbase Eighteen. Our testimony will mean little without hard evidence to corroborate it. One moment."

Hoto crossed the room to the diagnostic cot she'd been sleeping on. She reached underneath it and pulled out a small container. Using her remaining hand, she pried open the lid and set the container down on the cot. From it, she pulled out a tattered blue piece of cloth. Her Starfleet uniform, Boyce realized. Holding the cloth flat with the heel of her hand, she pulled the Sciences insignia off her tunic.

"What are you doing?" Boyce asked.

Instead of answering, she held the insignia up to her mouth and bit it.

There was a cracking sound, and the insignia popped open.

"Here," Hoto said, holding out the back half of it. A small piece of blue metal.

"What's this?"

"A data card. It should have sufficient storage capacity to copy the required information from the laboratory computer."

"Funny place to keep a data card."

Hoto smiled. "As Mr. Spock is always telling us, it is important to be prepared."

Boyce shook his head. Spock the Vulcan boy scout. He took the card and put it into his medikit.

"I'll see what I can do," he said.

Twelve hours, approximately, was the timeframe they settled on for Hoto to trigger the system overload. When the power failures began, Boyce was to make his way back to the medical wing. The lieutenant would be waiting there for him; they would journey together to the ship's other, operative shuttlebay, on the far side of the vessel. Climb in, and make their escape to Federation—or at least neutral—territory.

It sounded easy. Logical. Straightforward. At least, back in the treatment room.

Standing here in the lab, in front of the LeKarz, two guards watching his every move, Boyce gave it slightly less than a snowball's chance in Vulcan of working.

The doctor turned his attention back to the data screen in front of him. He had been asking himself a lot of 'what if's' these last few hours, hoping to stimulate his own thinking, hoping to send his mind scurrying down avenues that Zandar and her predecessors hadn't tried. Right now, he was considering the reactivity of chemicals within the serum besides gamina. The serum contained many of the same components as the universal-blood-donor packet—albumin analogues, other proteins, trace amounts of magnesium. Boyce had been running a series of simulations on the LeKarz, watching how those substances interacted with each other and gamina. The former series of simulations had been fairly predictable, the latter anything but. The LeKarz was unable to make heads or tails out of gamina's behavior; it kept outputting the same screen. Internal error. Boyce had traced that error back to a conflict between the system's database and the modeled molecule.

The gamina in the machine, in other words, was not behaving the way gamina did in real life. It was behaving like gamina-B, the replicated serum.

It wasn't working.

"Dr. Boyce."

He turned, and Deleen was standing there.

"How is your work progressing?"

"It's not." He lowered his voice so that the guards standing nearby couldn't hear. "I haven't learned much of anything new, to tell you the truth."

She nodded. She didn't seem surprised by the news. "I have," she said.

"What do you mean?"

"I'll show you."

She gestured toward a nearby terminal. Boyce, trying not to glance back at the guards, whose eyes he could feel on him every step of the way, followed her to it. She keyed in a series of commands; data filled the screen. A list of some sort, keyed to a series of numbers.

"These represent a series of recordings made by the sentry, along with associated stardates."

The sentry. Boyce looked across the bay. "Gozen, you mean?"

"Yes, Gozen." She lowered her voice. "I've been thinking about what happened before—in the command center."

Boyce understood instantly what she meant: Liyan's explosion, her temper.

"Go on," he said.

"The tallith . . . she has not been herself these last few days. Weeks, even. The decision to attack Starbase

Eighteen . . ." Deleen shook her head. "It was unchar-
acteristic."

Boyce didn't know what to say to that, so he simply
nodded.

"And then . . . I was in my quarters, looking at the
storage modules, when I remembered these recordings." She gestured toward the screen; the list began
scrolling past. There had to be hundreds of entries. "I
have been viewing them, reviewing them, in light of the
tallith's recent behavior. I want to show some of them
to you now, Doctor."

Deleen keyed in another command; the list stopped
scrolling. She touched the screen, one of the entries.

The terminal display went to black.

And then it filled with the image of an Orion male's
face. The sentry Gozen. He was sitting in the command
chair of what looked like the bridge of a starship.

"Report from Imperial sentry ship Ligara *to the
Emperor K'rgon. The Klingons are in retreat, my Lord.
Details of the battle. Following our engagement in the
Musan system on stardate 211, we pursued the remain-
ing Klingon force across the Denari line—"*

Deleen reached forward and paused the recording.

"Stardate 211." Boyce did the math in his head.
"That's more than two thousand years ago."

"Yes. According to some of the historical material I
found within the storage modules, the sentries were initially posted to all corners of the Empire as commanders

of their own vessels. Subsequently, it seems, the decision was made to . . . isolate them. Here. A later recording."

She touched the screen once more. Gozen appeared again. No longer on the bridge of a starship, though it was hard to tell exactly where he was, as his face was close to the recording lens.

"Stardate 814.454. The Imperial sentry Gozen, sector ten, reporting to the Emperor's Council. The potential threat referred to earlier has been eliminated."

The sentry's features looked different to Boyce in this recording, thicker, fleshier somehow. As if he'd gained a great deal of weight. His eyes were bloodshot. The veins on his neck stood out like black ropes.

Light reflected off the surface behind him, a faceted metal substance that the doctor recognized now.

"He's in the shuttle," Boyce said.

"Yes." The screen went dark. "And one more."

Deleen scrolled down the list and touched the last entry in the series. Gozen appeared again. He looked worse—much, much worse. There were deep, dark circles under his eyes. His face was splotchy, blemished. The veins on his forehead stood out. Those on his neck were like steel cables, pulsing beneath the surface of his skin.

"Stardate 834.3. The Imperial sentry Gozen, from the tenth sector, recording." His voice was husky and drawn. *"Re: previous report, civilization in sector Levy Six has achieved impulse flight. Recommended course*

of action—" The sentry blinked and shook his head. *"Recommended course of action,"* he said again, and twitched. Then he started to cry. *"I cannot do this anymore,"* he said, and looked straight into the recorder lens. *"I cannot."* He blinked, and the screen went dark.

The two of them were silent a moment.

"The gap between the first two recordings is several hundred years," Deleen said. "Between the latter two, only a matter of months."

Boyce nodded. The sentry's condition had deteriorated rapidly; that much was obvious. His mental condition, in particular.

Resisting once more the urge to look over at the guards, Boyce cleared his throat. "You think this is what's happening now?" he asked quietly. "To Liyan?"

"Don't you?" She shook her head. "I don't know what to do, Doctor."

"What happens if the tallith is unable to continue?"

"She must," Deleen said. "There is no alternative."

"There have to be provisions for succession. What happens in case of assassination?"

"The Confederacy has a council. Gorlea, whom you saw in the command center—"

"The older officer."

"He would be in charge. Nominally. But the other clans—the Singhino . . ."

"What about you?"

"Me?" Deleen shook her head. "No. Succession is

not dynastic. Besides which, this is not something I can do. My mother, the tallith, she has held the clans together for seventy-five years, through the force of her personality."

Personality, Boyce thought. That was one word for it, he supposed.

"The serum, Dr. Boyce. You must find a way to replicate it."

"I don't know if I can do that," he said. And he really didn't. Even if focused on that alone set aside Hoto's escape plan and the preparations he was making for it . . . "Those kinds of things take time."

"We must gain time, then. Remove the Singhino as a threat."

"How do you propose we do that?"

"Gurgis," Deleen said. "Couldn't you give him something that would make him more pliant, suggestible?"

"I could," Boyce said. "But the Singhino want to see him, don't they? And any kind of drug I give him, anything that powerful . . ."

"They'll notice. I understand." Deleen was silent a moment. "It is all falling apart, Doctor. Everything we have achieved. All that the tallith has struggled to do, all that she has fought for."

"I'm sorry," he said.

"Yes. So am I. All of this . . ." Deleen gestured at the artifacts in the bay around them. "Will be lost. The Singhino will destroy all of it. Everything we have learned, all the technology we have salvaged from the time of the Second Empire."

The doctor glanced over at the shuttle; the faceted surface reflected his own face back at him. He flashed on what had happened earlier, when he'd walked into the medical wing and seen Hoto. What he'd thought to be Hoto, rather, what had turned out to be her mirror image. The lieutenant, in the looking glass. Missing a left arm rather than a right.

"Doctor? Are you all right?" Deleen asked.

"Yes." He couldn't get the image out of his mind. Hoto, working one-handed. Looking exactly the same but different.

Gamina, he thought.

"Gamina," he said out loud.

"What about gamina?"

He turned to Deleen and smiled. "I have an idea."

TWENTY-SIX

It took him the better part of an hour to detect their presence. It was only by running—and rerunning, not once, not twice, but a half-dozen times—the relevant simulation on the LeKarz and taking nanosecond snapshots of the chemical processes at work that he was, at last, able to find what he was looking for.

"There." Boyce pointed toward the analysis screen. "There they are."

"There what are?" Deleen leaned over his shoulder, squinting at the screen.

"Stereoisomers." he said.

"What?"

"Stereoisomers. Substances that are chemically

identical but are structurally—molecularly—mirror images of each other. A left hand and a right."

"You can tell that from these numbers?"

"The numbers represent the bonding actions that are taking place. You can see they're flipped here."

"So that's why the gamina-B doesn't work? The molecules are backward?"

He smiled. "It's a little more complicated than that. But basically, yes, I think so."

"So if you flip them around . . ."

"That ought to do the trick, yes. I'll set up another simulation."

He got to work. Deleen got him coffee.

Halfway through the cup, the intellectual excitement wore off, and the ambivalence set in. Replicating the immortality serum? Why was he doing this? So Liyan could stay in power? For his own intellectual curiosity? For Deleen?

A lot of questions. Boyce couldn't really answer any of them at this point.

It took him another hour to make the necessary changes in the gamina-B serum (or, rather, its computer-generated counterpart), another hour beyond that to set up the necessary simulation. The same split-screen simulation Zandar had shown him earlier, the original gamina molecule on the left, the new and improved gamina-B on the right.

He keyed in a final set of commands and set the LeKarz to run.

On the left, the gamina molecule began attaching itself to other chemicals in the bloodstream.

On the right, the new Gamina-B molecule began doing the same. At first.

And then, all at once, the molecule started bonding with itself once more, clumping together.

"It's not working," Deleen said.

"No."

Boyce had programmed the simulated molecule based on the bonding proportions of right- and lefthand molecules he had gathered in his data snapshots. He altered those proportions and tried a second simulation.

That didn't work, either.

Nor did the third or the fourth.

He went back to the snapshots and studied the data more carefully. Interesting. The relative proportions of right- and left-hand molecules deviated little from the standard mean he'd been using, but the bonding loci of each appeared to follow no set pattern.

"It's totally random," he said, pushing the chair he'd been sitting in back from the LeKarz. "The arrange-ment of right- and lefthanded molecules."

"What does that mean?"

"Well, for one thing, it means the arrangement's going to be impossible to duplicate." Even for the

LeKarz, to simulate an array of possibilities that complex just wasn't possible. It was only a machine, after all.

He sat up a little straighter.

"What?" Deleen asked.

"Another idea," Boyce said.

"A new simulation?"

"No." He shook his head. "Real life."

He crossed the bay, and from the lab station Zandar had shown him earlier, he obtained a vial of one of the failed gamina-B analogues. He unplugged one of the lab's centrifuges.

"What are you doing?" Deleen asked.

"A small electrical charge," he said. "If I'm right, it ought to randomize the molecular arrangement."

"An electrical charge? That's it?"

"The first step, anyway," Boyce said. "We'll find out for sure."

He moved the vial toward the power-supply leads. They touched. The entire lab went dark.

"I didn't do that," Boyce said.

Emergency lights snapped on. The guards, Boyce saw, had their weapons raised.

"What's happening?" Deleen called out.

"Hang on." That came from one of the scientists, who was crossing the room as he spoke, gazing down at a handheld device about the size of Boyce's tricorder.

"Power fluctuations. The grid is going down all across this portion of the ship."

"How is that possible?" Zandar asked.

"I don't know." The other scientist shook his head. "Looks like some sort of phase cascade reaction."

Boyce's eyes widened. Hoto. He'd completely forgotten. All thoughts of gamina left his head.

He turned to Deleen. "Come with me," he said.

"What?"

"Come with me. Now." He started to pull her toward the entry.

A guard stepped forward, blocking his way.

"You are to continue working."

"That's what I'm trying to do," Boyce said, suddenly seeing a way out. "We have to get to the medical wing."

"The medical wing?"

"Yes. This is gamina. For the tallith." He held up the vial. "I need to use the equipment there. Testing procedures."

The guard and Deleen looked at him skeptically.

"Very well." The guard nodded. "Come with me."

He began walking toward the door. As he approached it, he gestured toward another guard, standing nearby.

The first guard led them through the door. The second followed.

Two of them. Boyce hoped Hoto would be as good as her word.

"The medical wing," Deleen, walking side-by-side with him, whispered under her breath. "Dr. Boyce, what are you doing? Really?"

"The ship is going to be destroyed in a few minutes. I know a way out."

"Destroyed." She frowned. "The Singhino, you mean?"

"No," he said.

Deleen stopped in her tracks. "What do you mean by that?"

Boyce opened his mouth to answer her—what he was about to say, he had no idea—when the guard in front of them, all at once, dropped to one knee and drew his weapon.

"Down," he said, motioning with his hand for them to drop as well. "Get—"

A blue beam of light sizzled through the air and caught the Orion square in the chest.

He grunted once and fell to the floor.

The guard behind them stepped forward, firing as he came. Orange weapons fire, light phasing at a very high energy level. There was a slight curve to the corridor where they were; the orange beam caught the wall at that curve. Metal sizzled and smoked.

In the distance, someone cried out.

The guard reached toward a comm panel on the wall. He didn't make it.

Another blue beam of light shot around that curve, and he crumpled to the floor just as his companion had.

"The Singhino." Deleen looked as if she was about to cry. "They're here."

She raised her hands.

Boyce followed suit.

Captain Pike stepped around the corner.

"Ah." He saw Boyce and lowered his weapon. "There you are."

TWENTY-SEVEN

Y ou're dead," Boyce said. "Aren't you dead?"

"Never felt better. Who's this?" He gestured toward the Orion girl standing beside Boyce.

"This," Boyce repeated, looking a little shell-shocked, "is Deleen."

Pike frowned. Not exactly an informative answer.

"I am the tallith's daughter," the girl said.

Pike raised an eyebrow. "The tallith's daughter?"

"Enough talk," growled Kritos. Spock and Hardin, phasers drawn—a step behind him—emerged from the bend in the corridor. "We do not have time to waste. You have found your doctor, now let us continue."

"You're Kritos," Boyce said. "Captain Kritos."

"And you are Boyce. Come with us."

"Come with you?"

"Yes." Kritos stepped forward and took the doctor's arm. "We must reach the medical wing immediately."

"Captain, what's happening?" Boyce asked. "Why are you here? How—"

"One question at a time." Pike smiled. "Among other things, we're here to rescue you."

"And to obtain proof that the Orions were behind the attack at Starbase Eighteen," Spock said. "That is the case, is it not?"

"It is," Boyce said, with such certainty in his voice that Pike, who had been about to accede to Kritos's wishes and urge the others to move on, hesitated.

"You sound as if you know something about it."

The doctor nodded. "I do. The proof you want—it's back that way." He gestured in the direction he and the girl had just come from.

At that instant, the lights dimmed again. The vessel shook.

"That was no power fluctuation," the captain said, turning to Spock.

"Agreed." His science officer nodded. "It felt like an explosion."

"It was," Boyce said.

"I told you. The ship is under attack," Kritos said.

Pike frowned. If the Klingon was right, if the Orion

ships that they had detected earlier circling *Karkon's Wing,* waiting for an opportunity to dock the cloaked shuttle had moved in for the kill, as it were, *Galileo* was in danger.

"It is the Singhino," the girl said.

"No. It's not," Boyce said. "It's Lieutenant Hoto."

"Lieutenant Hoto?" said Pike. "She's alive?"

"Yes." He hesitated a second, glanced over at the girl, and then plunged on. "She's rigged the ship to self-destruct. To cover our escape."

"What?" Deleen said.

"I'm sorry," Boyce said. "I—"

The girl began to back away.

"Not so fast," Hardin said, drawing her weapon again. "Stay right where you are."

"Lieutenant Hoto. I assume she managed to gain access to the ship's control systems?" Spock asked.

"Yes," Boyce said. "I think so."

The Vulcan nodded. "Impressive."

"All the more reason for us to make haste. To locate Druzen and this vessel before it does explode." Kritos looked down and studied the device he carried in his hand. The locator.

He pointed across the corridor. "This way."

"Wait." Pike put a little steel in his voice; perhaps a little too much. Kritos spun around and glared at him.

"Do not presume to command me, Pike."

"I'm not. Just . . . wait. Please. Hang on a second."

The Klingon grunted.

Pike's mind raced. The mission hadn't changed, but the fact that Hoto had rigged the vessel to explode . . . They had a ticking clock to deal with.

"How long do we have, Doctor?" he asked.

"Not sure," Boyce said. "We were going to rendezvous at the medical wing."

"All right. Slight change in plans, people," Pike said. "We're going to split up."

"I am going to the medical wing," Kritos growled.

"Yes," Pike said. "Yes, you are. Lieutenant Hardin, you'll accompany him. You find Druzen and Lieutenant Hoto—"

"No, sir," Hardin said. "I stay with you."

"I think I can handle myself."

"Sir—"

"I can accompany Captain Kritos," Spock said.

"Yes." Kritos nodded. "The Vulcan will accompany me."

"This isn't a democracy," Pike said. "I want you with me, Spock. To verify that proof Dr. Boyce is going to show us."

"The doctor is coming with me, Pike," Kritos said. "As we agreed. To see to Druzen."

"Druzen," Boyce said. "Wait a minute. Who is Druzen?"

"He is the reason we are here," Kritos said. "These *petaQ* have taken him hostage."

"The Klingon," Boyce said. "In the medical wing."

"You have seen him?" Kritos took a step toward Boyce, moving so quickly that the doctor started. "He is well?"

"I think so. Nothing seriously wrong with him, at any rate."

Kritos bared his teeth in a smile. "Hah! Strong as a *targ*. Did I not tell you, Vulcan!"

He turned toward Spock and, for a second, seemed about to actually clap the Vulcan on the back. Spock, clearly, feared the same thing.

"Yes," Spock said, taking a step back. "I believe you did."

Pike stepped forward. "You'll have to tell us how to find that proof you were talking about, Doctor."

Boyce nodded. "It's back that way. Up a single deck. You have to—"

"Sir, what about her?" Hardin gestured toward the Orion girl. "She can show us, can't she?"

"I will do nothing of the kind." The girl glared at Boyce. "You lied to me. You had no intention of replicating the serum. All you were trying to do—"

"I was trying to save your life," Boyce said.

The girl frowned.

Pike frowned, too. Replicating the serum? The captain had a feeling there was a whole long story that went with that, one he didn't have time to hear at the moment.

"Enough talk." Kritos put a hand on Boyce's shoulder. "Come, Doctor."

"Enough talk is right." Hardin raised her weapon and pointed it right at the Orion girl. "Show us where that proof is, or—"

"No need for that, Lieutenant." Pike stepped between the two of them. He turned to the girl. "We have to have that proof. Or there's going to be a war."

"War." She hesitated. "How? Why?"

Pike began to explain. It didn't take long before Deleen was shaking her head.

"This is not what was supposed to . . . our people should be allies. We have common interests . . ."

Her words reminded him of something, someone. A second later, Pike had it. Noguchi. What the admiral had told him that long-ago morning after the officers' briefing, how it would be good to make common cause with the Orions, to have a stabilizing force in this part of the galaxy, a bulwark between the Federation and the Klingon Empire. That conversation seemed suddenly a million miles—a hundred years—away.

"Allies." Pike shook his head. "You people are responsible for the destruction of an entire starbase. And the death of eighty-seven Federation personnel."

Deleen shook her head again. "That was never what we intended."

"Prove it," Pike said to Deleen. "Take us to that proof. And then we'll talk."

She hesitated a second longer—and then nodded.

"Good." The captain turned to Boyce. "Get to Hoto. Stop the countdown."

The doctor nodded. "We'll try."

"We will do it." Kritos clapped Boyce on the back now. "Come, Doctor."

The two set off at a run.

Boyce's head was still spinning.

Captain Pike, alive. Captain Pike here. With Spock. And Hardin. And Kritos.

The Klingon and he were jogging side-by-side, heading down a corridor that, if Boyce's memory served him correctly, would soon intersect the one leading directly to the medical wing.

"Druzen," Boyce said.

"Yes."

"He was at Starbase Eighteen."

"Yes."

"Why?"

Boyce was panting for breath as he talked. Kritos, a few steps ahead of him, was not.

"It is none of your concern," the Klingon said.

"Kronos. It has something to do with Kronos, doesn't it?"

The Klingon glanced at him out of the corner of his eye. "That is none of your concern, either."

"Has to be," Boyce said. "It's the only thing that makes sense. What was it, Kronos? Some kind of medical program or—"

Kritos, a couple of meters ahead of him now, turned around and glared. "Keep up, human." The Klingon put on a fresh burst of speed and pulled farther ahead of Boyce.

The doctor put his head down, banished all questions of Kronos from his mind. If the Klingon in the medical wing was indeed this Druzen, if he was the reason—or part of the reason, anyway—they were there, then the others—Spock, Hardin, Pike—would probably have the answer to those questions, too.

Pike. Alive. How? Is it possible that Ben is, too? Probably not, Boyce decided. The captain would have said something.

Up ahead, Kritos suddenly came to a stop. The Klingon was holding a small device, about the size and shape of a Federation communicator, which Boyce had assumed to be a weapon, in one hand. He was staring at a little screen on it and shaking his head.

"What's the matter?" Boyce said.

"Something is wrong." Kritos ran his hand over the display; he pressed the side of it with one oversized finger, shook his head, and cursed. "Interference," he said, in a half-questioning kind of way that suggested that he didn't really believe it. "There must be interference."

Boyce leaned closer. "What is that?" he asked.

"Biolocator. A prototype."

"Biolocator?" On the screen, he saw a grid of lines. Directional arrows.

"There is no signal." Kritos looked up and glared at Boyce. "What has happened to the signal?"

Boyce shook his head. "I'm not—"

"Here." The Klingon punched a button on the device. "Last known reading. You see!" He held the device up right next to Boyce's face.

Now, in addition to lines and the arrows, there was a single blinking red dot on the screen. If Boyce was reading the display right, it was coming from the direction of the medical wing.

Biolocator.

"The Klingon in the treatment room," he realized. "This dot—"

"Yes. It is him. Druzen. I insisted on the implant before surrendering him to your research team. I did not trust . . ." The Klingon's voice trembled with emotion; it took Boyce a second to recognize what kind.

Fear.

It suddenly occurred to him what the dot's disappearance might imply.

"Which way, human?" Kritos lowered the device. "To the medical wing?"

Boyce pointed, and they ran.

• • •

It took Spock's conscious mind, preoccupied with talk of the image projector the Orion female was telling Captain Pike about (a device whose capabilities seemed more like magic than technology to him, although those capabilities—far better than the distorting effects of the cloaking device, which having spent the last two days observing at work he was now quite familiar with—would fit with, account for the near-impossible sensor readings he had observed just prior to the apparent deaths of Captain Pike and the landing party), a few seconds to catch up with his unconscious one.

The realization that something was wrong—that something had changed—came only after he had followed Captain Pike and the female as they turned down another corridor.

The realization what that something was came an instant later.

Lieutenant Hardin was not behind him.

"Captain."

Pike and the Orion female, two meters in front of him, stopped immediately.

"Lieutenant Hardin," Spock said.

Pike turned and saw the problem. "Where is she?" he asked.

"Unknown. I will—"

"Check it out. Go." Pike waved him back impatiently.

Spock understood the captain's need for haste. In the approximately four and a half minutes since they had split with Dr. Boyce and Captain Kritos, there had been three explosions powerful enough to disrupt the artificial gravity field of the Orion ship, to force them to stop running and make sure of their balance. The lights aboard the ship had dimmed as well, on two of those three occasions; after the second explosion, they had failed to return to full power.

Whatever Lieutenant Hoto had done—or was in the process of doing—Spock suspected they were running out of time to reverse its effects.

The Vulcan ran quickly, as quietly as he could, back to the point of intersection, where he and the others had turned. He flattened himself against the wall and then peered quickly back the way they had come.

Hardin stood in the middle of the corridor, studying her tricorder.

"Lieutenant?"

She looked up, startled. "Mr. Spock. Sorry, sir." She jogged up to him. "Thought I picked an alert from *Galileo*. An automated signal. Someone trying to break in."

"I detected no such signal."

"No, sir. I was wrong."

Spock nodded. "Indeed. Your concern for the

shuttle's security is admirable. But your primary responsibility, Lieutenant, is the captain's safety. Should you detect a similar alert, please bring it to my attention before acting on the matter."

"Sorry, sir. My apologies."

The ship suddenly shook again.

"Mr. Spock!"

The Vulcan turned.

Captain Pike, the Orion female just behind him, was standing in the corridor a dozen meters away.

"You all right?"

"Yes, sir. We both are."

"Then let's move, please."

Two minutes later, they'd reached their destination, a shuttlebay that had apparently been converted into some sort of laboratory, although the need for the lab's temperature to be maintained at what Spock estimated was the rough equivalent of zero degrees Celsius escaped him.

The chamber's only occupants were a group of Orions dressed in heavyweight lab coats—scientists, Spock presumed. One of them broke off from the others and started walking toward them as they entered.

"What's the meaning of this?" The scientist, a female, was speaking to the girl. "Who are these people? You should know better than to—"

"I'm Christopher Pike. Captain of the *U.S.S. Enterprise.*"

The scientist stopped and stared at him. "You are dead."

"So they tell me." The captain turned toward the girl. "Where's the image projector?"

"There."

She pointed across the shuttlebay. Spock's gaze followed her outstretched arm and came to rest on a small white metal pedestal, on top of which, balanced on a cone of blue light, rested a white, perfectly shaped sphere, perhaps thirty centimeters in diameter.

"What are you doing?" the female scientist asked, again speaking to Deleen.

"None of your concern. Please." Lieutenant Hardin stepped forward, phaser in hand. "Back away."

"Mr. Spock. Could you . . ." Pike gestured toward the sphere—Spock, though, was already heading for it.

As he drew closer, he saw that the sphere was not, as he had first supposed, solid white in color. It was instead made of some sort of transluscent material, largely opaque. He took out his tricorder.

The blue cone of light supporting the sphere was a magnetic field of some kind, acting in some way to nullify the artificial gravity of the ship. It was a far more precisely calibrated gravitational field than that of the vessel, keeping within a deviation of point-zero-one nanowebers, as opposed to the three percent deviation allowed under standard Federation construction specifications. Which were, he suspected, by both convention and necessity, roughly equivalent to those aboard this ship.

As for the sphere itself . . . the tricorder could tell him nothing about it. The object was not only opaque in appearance but opaque to his sensors.

"Fascinating."

"You think it's capable of doing what she says?" Pike asked.

"There is no way to be certain. Clearly, it is an artifact produced by a civilization whose technological capacity in many ways surpasses our own; as for its exact function, however—"

"Spock." The captain seemed annoyed.

"Yes, sir?"

"A simple yes or no is what I'm looking for."

Ah. Brevity. Of course. "Then yes."

"Good. Is it safe to take it off that thing?"

"To remove the sphere? Uncertain."

Pike turned in the direction of the Orion scientists; perhaps one of them . . .

His eyes fell on the female scientist, who was backing toward the door.

"Lieutenant."

Even before he spoke, Hardin had her weapon out. "Stop right there," the security officer said, and motioned the scientist back toward the rest of them.

Curious, Spock thought.

The lieutenant had seemed, for a moment, to be preoccupied with something else.

Boyce was a good twenty meters behind Kritos when they made the final turn toward the medical wing.

The Klingon had his weapon out in front of him; Boyce braced himself for the sound of weapons fire. None came.

A second later, as he made that final turn himself, he saw why.

The Orion guards—there were two of them—lay sprawled out in front of the entrance, each flat on his back. Kritos was kneeling down next to one of them, his hand on the guard's neck.

He looked up at Boyce and got to his feet. "Dead," the Klingon grunted.

Boyce's eyes widened in surprise. *I will handle the guards.* Hoto, apparently, was as good as her word. A little too much so, frankly, for his taste.

He looked around, wondering where she was.

"The door is locked."

"Zeph-zeph-gamma."

"What?"

"Here. I'll do it." Boyce stepped forward; Kritos stepped aside.

Boyce punched in the code and stepped through into the medical wing. Kritos was a step behind.

Lieutenant Hoto stood directly in front of them. She

was holding a weapon in her hand, an Orion energy blaster. That explained the guards.

"You are Captain Kritos."

"Yes, I am Kritos. Which way, Doctor?" The Klingon snapped. "Hurry."

"There," he pointed.

Straight ahead, he had been about to say, but the words died on his lips.

Behind Hoto, Boyce could see the door to the treatment room that housed Druzen was wide open. He could also see the Klingon in it—or part of him, anyway. His arm, hanging limply off the bed.

He looked back at Hoto.

She was looking at him, too. She had not, Boyce realized, lowered her weapon.

There was something wrong here.

Kritos realized it as well. Out of the corner of his eye, Boyce saw the Klingon begin to raise his own weapon.

Hoto fired first. Her blaster was set at full power. It hit Kritos square on, directly in the chest, sent the massive Klingon warrior hurtling backward into the wall.

The speed with which he hit it, the way his body crumpled to the floor after impact . . . He was not getting back up again.

"What the hell—why did you—" The doctor had taken a step forward himself. He stopped.

Hoto had the blaster on him now. "The data card, please, Doctor."

"What?"

"The data card I gave you earlier. I assume you were able to obtain the information we discussed from the Orion laboratory . . ."

"No." He'd forgotten all about it. He felt it in his pocket now, right next to the vial of irradiated gamina-B.

"Unfortunate." Hoto shook her head. "Still, not a tragedy."

"Mind telling me what's going on?" Boyce asked. "Why you just did that?"

"He was a Klingon," Hoto said.

"He was working with us. He saved Captain Pike."

"Klingons cannot be trusted. It is a fact. Besides which . . ." The lieutenant shrugged. "There will be a formal declaration of war shortly. I am merely, you might say, getting a head start on things."

"There's not going to be a war," Boyce said. "When Starfleet Command finds out who was really behind the attack—"

"That proof will not reach Starfleet Command, I'm afraid."

Hoto raised the weapon higher, till it was in her line of sight. Then, keeping an eye on Boyce and her index finger on the trigger, she used her thumb to adjust the controls.

Boyce's heart thudded in his chest. "Going to kill me, too?" he asked.

Hoto shook her head. "No. You saved my life, Doctor. I intend to return the kindness."

"Sweet of you."

"You should remain here, though, upon awakening. Within the medical wing. It is the most solidly constructed portion of the ship. It should retain atmospheric integrity long enough to permit your rescue."

Her finger tightened on the trigger; Boyce opened his mouth to protest, to ask again what she was doing and why, who she really was, who she was really working for . . .

And then he saw the blast.

And then he saw nothing.

TWENTY-EIGHT

T he ship shook again.

Pike, who had the image projector—the white sphere—clasped tightly in both hands, wobbled on his feet for a second.

"You all right, sir?"

That came from Hardin, who now had her back to the shuttlebay wall, presumably so she could keep an eye on everyone in the laboratory. The captain didn't see the need; they were all—humans, Orions, and Vulcans alike—gathered in a circle around one of the data terminals.

"Fine," Pike said. *For the moment,* he might have added. Much longer than that, he didn't know about.

Karkon's Wing seemed to be shaking itself apart.

Where the hell was Boyce? And Kritos? And Hoto?

He turned to the girl, Deleen, standing right behind him.

"The medical wing was how far?"

"Less distance than we had to travel."

Damn. They ought to have checked in by now.

"The system rejects my queries as well." One of the Orion scientists spoke now—the one the others had all gathered around, the one sitting at the data terminal everyone's attention was focused on. "I cannot even look at the code to see what has changed."

Pike looked over at his science officer, who was standing behind the terminal as well, hands clasped behind his back, face impassive. "Spock." Pike gestured toward the terminal. "Can you help, or . . ."

"I intend to," the Vulcan said. "As soon as I can contribute productively."

Pike was about to ask what exactly that meant, when a barely audible electronic chirp sounded nearby. It took him a second to recognize what the sound was and where it was coming from. His tricorder.

"Hold this," he said, handing the sphere to Deleen. Just as he did so, the chirp stopped.

Frowning, Pike opened up his tricorder and looked at the display indicator.

"Problem, sir?" Hardin was looking at him.

"Not sure. *Galileo*'s security alarm went off for a second but then stopped on its own."

"Someone trying to break in?" the lieutenant asked.

"Maybe," Pike said.

"It could have been Kritos and the others returning to the shuttle."

"Then why aren't they answering their communicators?"

"Could be some kind of interference," Hardin suggested. "I could go there myself, secure the sphere, see what's happening."

Pike shook his head. "No. I'm not splitting us up again without knowing more about what's going on."

"Yes, sir," Hardin replied.

"You can't leave," Deleen said. "At least, not until I speak with—see—Dr. Boyce again."

"Boyce?" Pike frowned. "Why?"

The girl hesitated.

The bay, all at once, plunged into complete darkness.

Spock used the darkness to contemplate what he had seen so far of the methods Lieutenant Hoto had used to sabotage the Orion vessel's power grid. A very effective series of planned overloads, which used the artificial-intelligence routines built into the system against themselves.

He had made, he believed, significant progress toward conceptualizing effective countermeasures against those programmed outages. The Vulcan needed now to trace the disruptions back to their beginning, to see the initial malicious piece of code the lieutenant had inserted into the system. A few more minutes' work, he suspected, and he would be ready to assist the Orions in regaining control of their vessel.

If the ship stayed intact that long.

The lights came back on. The terminal in front of him, though, on which he'd been monitoring the Orion scientists' efforts to trace and neutralize the damages Lieutenant Hoto had inflicted on their ship—that stayed dark.

"Connection to the mainframe is gone." The scientist who had been sitting in front of the terminal—a female whose name, Spock gathered, was Zandar—stood. "We need to find a working access point to the mainframe."

"Or the mainframe itself," suggested one of the other scientists.

"The command center." Zandar nodded. "That may be the best course of action."

"Where is the command center?" Spock asked.

"That way." Zandar pointed to the chamber ceiling. "Almost directly above us. Three levels."

"Then what are we waiting for?" the captain said. "Let's go."

Extenuating circumstances.

Pike had dismissed Boyce's earlier comment the instant the doctor had said it. What on earth could possibly excuse what had taken place at Starbase 18? But if even half of what Deleen had been telling him was true, the discoveries that had been made at Zai Romeen, this serum whose secrets the doctor had supposedly unraveled at last . . . There was more to what was happening here, what had been happening aboard this vessel for the last three-quarters of a century, than met the eye.

The port turbolift was out; the starboard one still seemed to be working. They took it to the command center, which was roughly equivalent in size and layout to *Enterprise*'s bridge. The focus of activity was a series of terminals at the front of the room. A half-dozen Orions in military uniform gathered around those terminals, looking simultaneously harried, frantic, and helpless.

Liyan was standing a few paces back from them, the expression on her face much the same.

"Halt!" The voice came from behind him; Pike turned and saw not a guard but an older Orion male, hand weapon drawn and aimed at them.

There were guards stationed at the back of the command center; a split-second later, they had their weapons drawn as well.

By then, Liyan had turned around, and Pike got his first good look at her. He saw now that at least part of what the girl had been telling him was true. The tallith was not well.

She had changed drastically in the few days since Pike had first seen her; she looked pale to his eye and diminished somehow. Not so much shrunken in size as in force and personality . . .

Pheromones.

"Captain Christopher Pike. Should I be surprised to see you alive?" The tallith shook her head. "I suppose not, given your history. You've come to gloat, I assume. To celebrate your survival and my destruction."

"Gloat?" Pike shook his head. "Not at all."

"Talk to him." The girl at his side took a step forward. "Mother—"

"Talk?" Liyan's face twisted up in anger. "Please. Do not be so naïve, daughter. Talk is unnecessary. Actions are what matters, and your actions, Captain Pike, speak for themselves. Your plan has worked. Your spy has destroyed my ship."

"My plan?" Pike shook his head. "You've got it all wrong."

"You lie!" Liyan practically spat out the words; the muscles on her neck stood out like cords against her skin. No. Those weren't muscles. They were her veins, Pike saw.

"Lieutenant Hoto is no spy," he said. "She's just—"

"Sorry to interrupt, sir." The words came from Lieutenant Hardin. "But I've got to correct you on that."

Pike turned around to see Hardin holding her phaser up to the side of Deleen's head.

"Lieutenant." He was utterly flabbergasted. "What are you doing?"

"Well." Hardin's eyes glittered. "I suppose you could say I was seeing to the security of the Federation, Captain."

Pike shook his head. He had no idea what she was talking about. "Put that weapon down, Lieutenant Hardin. Now."

"Can't do that, sir. Lieutenant Hoto might not have been your spy, Captain. But she was mine. Or rather—"

"Starfleet Intelligence." Spock took a step forward. "The feedback circuit Chief Pitcairn detected. That was you."

Hardin nodded. "That's right. The situation seemed to call for it."

"Situation?" It took Pike a second to figure it out. "Black Snow. The cloaking device. Is that what this is about?"

"Klingons get a weapon like that working, Captain, it changes the balance of power. Drastically."

"You're going to steal the shuttle."

Hardin's smile was answer enough.

"You can't do that, Lieutenant," Pike said. "I made Captain Kritos a promise—"

"Captain Kritos doesn't enter into the equation anymore."

Pike didn't need to hear her speak the words to know what she meant.

He felt a slow rage beginning to boil inside him. "Kritos saved my life. I owed him—"

"I'm sorry, sir. Truly I am."

"Dr. Boyce," Spock said. "Have you killed him as well?"

"Dr. Boyce is fine."

"And where is he?"

"Ship's medical wing, I believe."

Hardin's communicator beeped. Using her free hand, she flipped it open. "Ready," she said, keeping her eyes focused straight ahead, the phaser pressed tightly to the back of Deleen's skull.

"Acknowledged," a voice replied.

Pike recognized it at once. So did Spock.

"That is Lieutenant Hoto." The Vulcan's expression came as close to betraying surprise as the captain had ever seen.

Hardin smiled. "Stand by," she said, and closed the communicator.

"She is aboard *Galileo*."

"She is."

"A traitor as well, then," Spock said.

Hardin's expression, for the first time, betrayed something other than calm. It gave Pike a second's worth of satisfaction. "That's debatable," Hardin said.

"I think not," Spock said. "Your actions betray the ideals of the Federation as well as the officers who trusted you."

"Ben Tuval, for one," Pike added.

Hardin glared. "These bastards killed Ben Tuval. Along with eighty-seven other people."

"Stop this, Lieutenant," Pike said. "Here and now. Before it's too late."

The ship, as if on cue, shook again.

"Might already be too late, sir. I do hope you figure out how to stop the ship from blowing up."

"Thanks for your good wishes," Pike said.

Hardin took a step back. "You're welcome. Now," she said, "about those eighty-seven deaths . . ."

Her hand on the phaser tensed. The weapon began to swing around.

In that instant, Pike realized her intent, and he moved, too.

He hurled himself toward Liyan.

The captain heard the sound of weapons fire—the familiar sound of a Starfleet phaser, then the barely audible buzz of an Orion energy blaster, more than one, somewhere nearby, the sound of a turbolift door opening and shutting—

And then he heard a scream. The girl. Deleen.

Pike caught the tallith by the knees and took her to the ground.

Even as she fell, though, Pike knew he was already too late.

TWENTY-NINE

There was a buzzing in his ear. A loud buzzing. Boyce wanted it to go away; all he wanted to do was sleep. Sleep for a hundred years. His head was pounding, like the worst hangover he'd ever had in his life, like the hangovers he used to get back on Argelius, those first few weeks after it became clear that the treatment hadn't gone exactly as planned. That something was wrong with Jaya and the others. Bad blood, bad DNA.

Bad headache.

The buzzing wouldn't go away, though. In fact, it was getting louder. The buzzing, he realized, was some-body's voice.

"Boyce. Doctor. Boyce. Phil. Come on. Where are you? Boyce. We need you . . ."

The voice sounded awfully familiar to him all at once. It sounded like Captain Pike. Of course, that couldn't be; Captain Pike was dead. The Orions. They'd—

The doctor sat up.

He was lying exactly where he'd fallen; so was Kritos. The door to the medical wing was wide open.

It all came rushing back.

"Boyce. Come on, where are you . . ."

Captain Pike's voice was coming from a comm panel set in the corridor wall. Boyce ran to it.

"Boyce. Dr. Boyce. Phil . . ."

"Captain."

"Phil. Good to hear your voice. The command center. You have to get up here right away."

"The command center. Right." He was still a little woozy. He wobbled on his feet for a second.

"Dr. Boyce," the captain snapped. *"You there?"*

"Right here, sir. Captain, I've got to tell you. Lieutenant Hoto—"

"Never mind about Hoto. I know about Hoto. Just get up here. On the double."

"Yes, sir.

The comm went silent.

The command center. That was up, Boyce recalled. Top of the ship. Just like the bridge on *Enterprise*.

The doctor emerged from the turbolift into a scene of absolute madness. Sparking consoles, some of them billowing smoke. A cacophony of voices. A body lying in the middle of the floor.

He realized it was Liyan. The tallith.

Deleen was there, too, holding her mother's head in her lap. She glanced up at Boyce as he entered.

"There they are. That's them."

He heard the captain's voice and turned.

Pike was leaning over the shoulder of one of Liyan's officers, pointing at the display screen.

"There was nothing there a second ago." The officer, a female, shook her head. "Systems failure. There must be a problem with the sensors—"

"There's no problem," Pike said. "That's the cloaking device. They're trying to figure out how it works, make the adjustments so that they stay hidden when they go to warp. Do you have weapons?"

"No." The officer shook her head once more. "We don't even have atmosphere control anymore. The next big hull rupture, and—"

"Doctor." Pike spotted him and straightened up.

Boyce started forward. "Sir, Lieutenant Hoto— she . . ."

"It's not just Hoto. It's Hardin, too. They're working together. Starfleet Intelligence." Boyce barely had time to absorb that bit of news before Pike stepped forward and took his arm. "Come here. We need your help."

He led the doctor down to the lower level of the command center, where Spock and a group of Orions were standing around a console, watching Zandar work.

"That's not it, either." Zandar stared at the screen, frustration obvious in her voice. "Whatever encryption protocol she used—"

"I don't think she used an encryption at all. I think the interface is malfunctioning, too. The code we're seeing here is not the code she entered."

Pike pushed forward, through the group, dragging Boyce with him. "Spock."

The Vulcan—the only person on the bridge who seemed not even the slightest bit perturbed by the calamity unfolding around them—turned.

"Dr. Boyce. Good. Can you please recall exactly what Lieutenant Hoto said to you regarding the manner in which she planned to sabotage this vessel?"

"What she said."

"Yes. Her exact language, if you can recall it."

Boyce thought a moment. "She said the conduits were stressed. She was going to overload them."

"Interesting." Spock, hands clasped behind his back, nodded. "What else?"

"I don't know." How long had it been since he and Hoto had that conversation? How many days, hours, ago?

A sudden wave of exhaustion came over him. He realized it had been a long, long time since he had slept.

"Dr. Boyce?" Spock prompted. "What else?"

"I'm thinking."

The ship shook.

"Explosive decompression on Deck Two, Sector Twelve," a voice announced from somewhere.

"The lab." Boyce turned quickly and saw Deleen—who still sat on the floor, cradling the tallith's body; he had almost forgotten about her entirely—looking up at him, the sadness in her eyes even more pronounced. "Gozen. The hull fragments . . ."

"Boyce!" That was the captain; the doctor turned and saw Spock and Pike standing side-by-side, looking at him expectantly.

"The destruction was going to occur in stages," Boyce said. "The conduits were stressed; she was going to overload them."

"We need to abandon ship. Commander Gorlea." Behind Spock, Zandar stood up, shaking her head. "I can't vouch for hull integrity much more than another few minutes."

"Abandon ship." The gray-haired Orion officer, who had been standing near Deleen, now moved toward the middle of the command center, toward the command chair Liyan had vacated. "That is not a viable option. The number of passengers our shuttles can carry—"

"We can summon the Singhino, sir. Warlord Videl." That came from another of the Orions, a male officer who had been among those crowded around Zandar. "Ask for his assistance."

"Assistance? From the Singhino?" Gorlea shook his head. "I'm not sure many of us would survive that."

"More than would survive the ship exploding into a million pieces," the same officer replied.

"Doctor." Spock again; Boyce now detected a tone of urgency in his voice. "Anything at all you can remember?"

"The power grid. She said something about setting up a reaction in the power grid."

"The power grid," Spock said.

"Yes." Boyce closed his eyes and concentrated, trying to remember the exact phrase she'd used. *Phrase.*

That rang a bell.

"Phase cascade reaction," Boyce said. "That was what she was doing. Setting up a phase cascade reaction. She said the ship's systems were already operating close to overload."

Spock nodded. "Phase cascade reaction. Interesting terminology. Not only does it suggest the self-perpetuating series of malfunctions we are witnessing, but it also is reminiscent of a famous series of power-flow equations which—"

"Spock." The captain pointed toward the now-vacant chair where Zandar had been sitting. "If you know something, or even think you know something, I think now—"

"Yes, sir," the Vulcan said, and took a seat. He flexed his fingers and regarded the console.

Pike regarded him. "Spock . . ."

"A moment, sir."

"I'm not sure that we have a moment."

"Precipitous action on my part would be as bad as none, sir. Possibly worse. The consequences—"

"Human! Captain Pike!" The voice came from the back of the command center, from the female at the console the captain had been leaning over when Boyce first arrived.

The doctor—along with everyone else—turned toward that voice.

"Your shuttlecraft," the female said. "They are powering up for warp."

Pike's heart thudded in his chest.

Galileo, going to warp. Black Snow, in the hands of Starfleet Intelligence.

A week or so ago, he would have thought it a good thing. Now, though . . . he couldn't let it happen.

Kritos had saved his life; Kritos had made it possible for them to get there in *Galileo,* to try to stop a war between the Federation and the Klingon Empire. The one thing he'd asked of Pike in return was to promise that the captain would not try to acquire the secrets of the cloaking device for Starfleet. Pike had sworn he would do all in his power to prevent that from happening.

Maybe Kritos was dead, but that promise still held.

He looked back over at his science officer. "Spock . . ."

The Vulcan looked up at Zandar. "Can you access the ship's power grid for me, please?"

"The power grid?"

"Yes."

"I don't know what good that'll do at this point, but . . ."

He pushed back from the console; she leaned in.

Her fingers flew across the keypad. "There you are."

"Thank you."

Spock leaned forward. He flexed his fingers; he pointed his right index finger. He touched it quickly to the screen and just as quickly drew it back.

"Spock," Pike said. "Whatever you're going to do . . ."

The Vulcan looked up at him. "That is all I can do at the moment, sir."

Pike—trying not to let his disappointment show—nodded. "All right. Then let's—"

The ship shuddered again, a different kind of shudder. A kind of bump, which was accompanied by a low-pitched rumble that hiccoughed once and then smoothed out. The lights came back on, all at once. Full power.

"But I think that should be sufficient," Spock said.

The captain looked around the bridge. Not only were the lights on, but the bridge displays—half of which had been dimmed or flickering a second earlier—had come back to life.

"Nice work," Pike said.

Spock nodded.

"Grid is operational again on Decks One, Two, and part of Three," a voice announced. "We have communications. Atmospheric control—"

"Weapons." Pike turned away from Spock, back toward the main portion of the command center. "Do you have weapons control?"

"We do."

He glared at the viewscreen, which now showed an image of the surrounding space and a small silver dot which the captain could only assume was *Galileo*. In about two seconds, Hoto and Hardin were going to see that *Karkon's Wing* had all systems back online and was fully functional, and the second they did, they were going to go to warp, whether or not the cloaking device was working, which had to be the only reason they hadn't done so yet.

And he couldn't let that happen.

The whole time Spock had been working, Pike had been working as well. Not just figuring out where the weapons console was but getting a rough idea of how to work it. He sat down to that console now, next to the Orion weapons officer, and aligned the targeting matrix.

"What are you doing?"

"Keeping a promise." *I hope*, he added silently, bringing first the starboard and then the port weapons batteries to bear.

He fired. A split-second later, *Galileo* exploded in a burst of sudden blue-white light.

Pike had never seen a Federation craft blow up that way before, with those colors. His guess was that it had something to do with the cloaking device.

He supposed he'd never really know for certain.

Pike sighed and rested his arms on the console. He closed his eyes for a second.

"Captain Pike," Spock said.

Pike looked up to see that the main viewscreen was no longer filled with the image of a starfield but now displayed the face of a single Orion male. An immense Orion male. Head shaved bald, wearing pirate leathers.

"*Karkon's Wing. This is Videl, prime warlord of the Clan Singhino. We note your ship is severely damaged. We will provide assistance.*"

Commander Gorlea—who had at some point, Pike saw, assumed the command chair—straightened in his seat and spoke. "The damage is not as severe as it might seem. You make a generous offer, Videl, but—"

"*You err, Codruta. We made no offer, merely a statement of fact. We will provide assistance.*" The Orion smiled. "*Stand down your weapons, and prepare to be boarded.*"

THIRTY

Boyce had feared disaster. Things turned out to be nowhere near as bad as all that. In fact, the arrival of the Singhino seemed to be, at least initially, a good thing.

They provided assistance, as promised: medical supplies, which came via shuttle through a hull breach near enough to the command center that Boyce was able to watch them unload. The Singhino warlord—Videl, the same one Boyce had spoken to earlier, briefly, at Liyan's insistence—had been huddled in conference with Captain Pike for some time now. Some of the Codruta had been led off the bridge; others remained. Among the latter were Gorlea—the older male—and Deleen, who, although she had finally gotten up off the floor, still hadn't moved very far from the tallith's body.

From what Boyce had overheard, Videl seemed prepared to offer the three of them—the captain, Spock, and himself—safe passage back to *Enterprise*. In return for which, Pike would treat with the Singhino not just as heads of the Trade Confederacy but as innocents with regard to the attack on Starbase 18. All well and good.

Where they were stuck, though, was on the matter of the image projector, the Second Empire technology that had made that attack possible, that pushed the Federation and the Klingon Empire to the brink of war. Videl, who seemed singularly uninterested in the device's capabilities, was nonetheless refusing to allow Captain Pike to take the image projector with him. The captain was being just as firm about having something in hand to show Starfleet Command. The conversation was spirited. Not unfriendly.

At least, until the second that the port turbolift opened, and Gurgis stepped out.

Boyce was among the first to see him; the Orion had not bothered to change or even, the doctor suspected, clean himself after his imprisonment. His face was still bruised, his clothes torn. He had no shoes. He looked altogether terrifying.

"You are here. You are alive." Videl broke off the conversation he'd been having with Captain Pike and stepped toward Gurgis.

"No thanks to you, Warlord." Gurgis's eyes traveled past Videl. "Ah, Captain Pike. I remember you."

"I remember you as well, Gurgis."

"Yes. I am head of Clan Singhino—unless my position has been usurped."

Videl shook his head. "No. You remain clan leader."

"Yet I see you negotiating with the human, Warlord. Who granted you authority to do that?"

"In your absence, someone had to."

The two stared at each other.

Videl's manner, his words . . . they were not exactly what the doctor would have called deferential. Judging from the look on Gurgis's face as well, Boyce suspected the two were not fond of each other.

And then, all at once, that expression changed. Gurgis looked past Videl and smiled. He walked by the others, toward Deleen and the tallith's body.

"Codruta."

"Gurgis."

"Now it is you who live and die at my whim, yes?"

"I'm not afraid," she said, which was a lie.

Even from where he stood, Boyce could see her trembling.

Gurgis could obviously see it, too. His smile grew broader.

Captain Pike stepped forward. "If you're in charge of those ships out there, you and I have a lot to talk about. Starfleet and the Orions have common interests in this sector."

Gurgis nodded. "In a moment." He reached out a hand, and touched Deleen's chin.

"As I promised, my people have come for me. Your mother, though—" He shrugged. "It seems I won't have a chance to honor the remainder of the vow I made to you. Do you remember that vow, girl?"

Deleen pulled backward, trying to shrug off his grip. "Leave me alone," she said.

"Do you remember?" Gurgis asked.

Boyce did. "That's enough," he said, stepping forward.

Gurgis's head whipped around. "The Codruta have fallen, human. I am in charge here." He nodded toward two Singhino soldiers, who stepped forward, weapons drawn.

The command center was suddenly completely silent.

Captain Pike put a hand on his arm; Boyce realized he was shaking, too. "Easy, Doctor."

Gurgis turned back to Deleen. "You will serve a useful political purpose. The new leader of the Codruta, willfully subordinating herself to the Singhino."

"An alliance with the Federation would be even more politically useful, wouldn't it?" Pike asked.

"I don't think the two are mutually exclusive."

Boyce didn't like the insinuating tone in the Orion's voice; he liked even less what that tone implied. But he didn't see that there was anything he could do about it.

Biology as destiny. Maybe Deleen had been right after all.

Gurgis took her by the arm and dragged her to her feet.

Boyce must have reacted unconsciously, taken a step forward without being aware of it. He became aware of Pike's hand, on his arm once more, holding him back, squeezing even tighter. And then he became aware of something else as well.

The gamina in his pocket. The gamina Deleen had wanted him to give to Liyan, to help the tallith out of her quandary. That was no longer possible, of course.

It occurred to him, though, that there might still be a use for the serum after all.

"Hang on a second," he said, and drew the vial out of his pocket.

Deleen saw it, and her eyes widened.

"Gamina," she said.

"That's right." Boyce pulled a hypo from the medikit and turned to face her.

And the past rose around him once more.

Mobile 7. Argelius. Neema and Cadan stood in the doorway of the lab, watching him like hawks. Making sure—Neema in particular—that he explained not just the procedure but its potential side effects. He was doing his best.

Jaya, among the three candidates they'd chosen, was doing her best, too.

Even back then, she was a bit of a scientist.

"Repair the genome?" she asked. "What does that mean, exactly?"

"Think of it this way," Boyce said. "We all—all of us—every living thing in the universe—come with a set of instructions. Things that tell our bodies how to grow and when to stop growing. And that's—"

"The genome," Jaya finished.

"Yes. That's right, Jaya. That's the genome."

"It's a very complicated set of instructions, though." Neema stepped forward. "I want you to be sure you understand that. It's a very complicated set of instructions, and we're not entirely sure that we've got all the pieces of it right yet. So—"

"So why don't we wait?" That was another of the children speaking, a boy named Connall, just about Jaya's age. "Until you're sure you have it right. One hundred percent right."

"You can do that if you want, Connall," Neema said. "That's a perfectly valid choice. You can all do that."

"Wait and see what happens," Jaya said.

"Yes," Neema replied.

"But I'm in the final phase, aren't I, Dr. Boyce?" Jaya asked. "A few weeks, and the Dezzla's will start, won't it?"

"A few weeks. A few months." Boyce shook his head. "Hard to be certain of the exact time frame."

A shadow fell over him then. He knew without turning who it was. Neema. He knew what she wanted to say—rather, what she wanted him to say—as well.

"What I should also tell you, all of you, we're learning more about Dezzla's every day. Odds are, we can help you survive it—what's going to happen to you—without the treatment. Without repairing the genome."

"Survive," Jaya said.

"Yes."

"The way she did?" The girl gestured behind Boyce, toward Cadan.

"I don't know," Boyce said. "There's a lot that's still a mystery to us."

Cadan cleared her throat. "What happened to me, it's not so bad, children. And they have treatments now—more every day."

"I don't want to wait," Jaya said, standing. "I want you to fix me. Now."

Boyce nodded. That was what he wanted, too.

"Wait, human." Gurgis stepped between Boyce and Deleen. He gestured to the hypo. "What is that?"

"The cure."

"Cure?" The Orion frowned. "For what?"

"This." He reached down, took hold of Liyan's arm, and pulled back the sleeve of the gown the tallith had been wearing, exposing both pale green flesh and black, rope-like veins.

"Fascinating," Spock said. "Some sort of circulatory condition."

"It affected her neuro-muscular system as well," Boyce said. "Her behavior. Especially the last few months. You must have noticed."

He was speaking to Gurgis, who frowned now. Boyce doubted the man had noticed anything in Li-yan's thrall, as it were.

"Without it, the same thing will happen to her," the doctor said, gesturing to Deleen.

"Inject her," Gurgis snapped. "Immediately. Then you, Videl, will take the humans to the courier *Hostil*. And from there to the edge of the Borderland."

"Escort duty." Videl snorted. "I will give the task to one of the other commanders."

"I want you to do it yourself," Gurgis snapped.

The two began arguing.

Boyce turned to Deleen. If he had seen any hesitation in her eyes, he would have found an excuse, somehow, to avoid the injection. All he saw, though, was certainty.

"I'm ready," she said.

"Hang on." Captain Pike stepped forward. "You sure about this, doctor?"

Boyce looked at him and realized that somehow, Pike had figured out there was something going on here. More than met the eye. The captain knew him better than he'd thought, Boyce supposed.

Three months of working together would do that.

"I'm sure," he said, and Pike stepped back.

Boyce stepped up next to the girl. If he was right, the gamina would change her. Do to Deleen what it had done to her mother. For a while, at least. It was only one dose. Hopefully, it would be enough for her to save herself, at least, from Gurgis. Possibly it would last long enough to prevent the Trade Confederacy from falling apart completely. Maybe Deleen would be able to preserve a portion of her mother's legacy. Maybe.

Boyce stepped up next to her, and put the hypo to her arm.

"I don't know what's going to happen," he whispered.

"That's all right." She nodded. "No one ever docs."

EPILOGUE

The fleets, Klingon and Federation, were in the process of disbanding. Returning home, back to patrol, back to normalcy. Standing down from battle stations, from the brink of war. Supposedly. Pike wasn't so sure. He wasn't so sure about anything having to do with the Klingons anymore. Kritos he could trust. This K'Zon, from what he'd seen, what he'd heard . . .

Things were going to be different out here now. And not necessarily for the better.

The comm sounded.

"Pike here."

Garrison's face appeared on the little viewscreen. *"I have Excalibur for you, sir. Captain Vlasidovich."*

"Patch him through."

Dmitri's face appeared. He looked over Pike's shoulder and frowned.

"You have rearranged furniture."

"I rearranged?" Pike smiled. "You're the one who moved things around."

"New arrangement was more efficient use of space. Do you not value efficiency?"

"Did Nolan move your things around?"

"He knew better." Dmitri smiled. *"You have good crew. Pitcairn, especially. Tell him to request transfer to my ship."*

"Hah. You'll have to send me two engineers to replace him."

Dmitri nodded. *"I suppose. Which two?"*

"Give me a few years. I'll let you know."

"Hah yourself. Good-bye, Christopher."

"Good-bye, Dmitri."

Pike reached for the keypad to end the transmission.

"Wait. I have almost forgotten. I have message from Michaela for you."

"Michaela." She—and *Hood*—had warped out of orbit earlier that morning, while he was sleeping. Without even saying good-bye. When he woke up, Pike had been, frankly, miffed. "Go ahead."

"Softie."

"That's the message?"

"That is message."

Pike smiled again. "You see her before I do, you tell her to say that to my face."

"I am recalling she did already. In your cabin."

Pike reached for the keypad again. "Good-bye, Dmitri."

"Good-bye, Christopher."

The screen went dark. He stared at it a moment.

Softie. Huh.

He punched up *Hood*'s patrol schedule.

Two months from now, she was scheduled for R&R at Ceros 4. *Enterprise* was going to be in the neighborhood—relatively speaking. It would be a little ahead of schedule, but Dmitri was right. He had a good crew. They deserved a little R&R too.

The door comm sounded.

"Come."

Boyce entered the room. "You wanted to see me?"

"I did. Have a seat, please. Want a drink?"

"No."

Pike shrugged. "Suit yourself."

He reached into the cabinet beneath the table, pulled out the bottle Dmitri had left him, and poured himself a glass.

Boyce looked at the label and whistled.

"Double V. This stuff's hard to get."

"Not necessarily. Depends on whom you know." Dmitri, for example, knew the distillery's owners. Back at the Academy, Dmitri used to get a case to give to the staff at winter break.

The captain took a sip—too big a sip, he realized instantly; he was not a drinker—and promptly was seized by a coughing fit.

Boyce, watching with amusement, waited till he was finished coughing to speak. "Smooth, eh?"

"You bet. You sure you don't want some?"

"I'm fine."

"Okay." Pike took another—much smaller—sip. "Let's talk about it, Phil."

"Talk about what?"

"Whatever. Argelius. Ben Tùval. The Orions." He shrugged. "Jaya, even. You never talk about her. Or Argelius, for that matter."

The doctor was quiet for a second. "There's a reason for that," he said. "I messed up. Everyone thinks I'm such a hero for what happened there, but the truth is . . ." He sighed and shook his head.

"The truth is what?" Pike pressed.

"It's a long story," Boyce said.

The captain waited for the doctor to continue. He waited five seconds and then ten. Boyce shifted position in his chair and opened his mouth. And shook his head.

Pike took another glass out of the cabinet and set it down on the table.

Boyce looked up at him and smiled wryly. "You think that's going to help?"

"Maybe. There are some things a man will tell his bartender that he won't tell his commanding officer."

Boyce looked at him a moment, then nodded. "I guess that's true."

"Of course it is."

Pike poured him a fingerful, then settled back in his chair.

The doctor took a sip and began, at last, to talk.

AUTHOR'S NOTE

Gene and Majel Roddenberry are space dust; DeForest Kelley and James Doohan are gone as well. Harve Bennett has left the stage; Chris Pine is James T. Kirk.

In other words, change is afoot in the *Star Trek* universe, and considering that Gene Roddenberry's original series bible dates back to the early sixties, I think it perhaps high time, and J. J. Abrams's 2009 reimagining of *Trek* not only recharged my twenty-third-century batteries, but freed me of the need to write specifically to one vision of humanity's future.

The Children of Kings is a prequel to that 2009 film; the *Enterprise* as it might have been under Captain Christopher Pike (though I have to admit when I was writing Pike's scenes, I still pictured Jeffrey Hunter, rather than Bruce Greenwood. Old habits, dying hard, I suppose). I've drawn from the original *Trek* pilot, *The Cage,* of course, for some of the characters/characterizations, as well as D. C. Fontana's novel *Vulcan's*

Glory, and Margaret Wander Bonanno's *Burning Dreams.* For the science behind gamina and the bronchial shunt (among other things), I am grateful to Mike Stamm and Ann Carlson. I am grateful to my family, as well, for their six-eyed support while I wrote this book.

And finally, I must thank Margaret Clark, not only for suggesting I combine Captain Pike, the Orions, and Dr. Boyce into a novel, but for her support over the years. It has meant a lot. It still does.

Dave Stern
December 1, 2009